You are the Small Gods,
walking amongst us.

Also by Ben Langdon

The Miranda Contract

This Mutant Life (editor)

This Mutant Life: Bad Company (editor)

THE MIRANDA CONTRACT

CONTRACT

BOOK ONE OF THE SMALL GODS

BEN LANGDON

KALAMITYPRESS

Published by Kalamity Press, Portland Australia

kalamitypress.com

ISBN: 978-0-9875-3084-4

Cover design by Milan Jovanovic of Chameleon Studio.

Interior design by Benjamin Carrancho of Damonza.

To grandpa who was not evil and not mad, but the greatest of role models and the kindest of men.

*To Jack, Eliza and Luca,
my own heroes-in-training.*

PROLOGUE

MELBOURNE, FIVE YEARS BEFORE

DAN FUMBLED WITH his gloves inside the shattered remains of the bookshop. He stretched them off his fingers with a snapping sound, trying not to get the blood on his bare skin. He let them drop to the ground while he rested against the wall of paperbacks. His chest heaved, the tightness threatening to cut off his breathing altogether.

He couldn't shake the ringing in his ears. The explosion had knocked them all to the ground, flattened them like pins in a bowling alley. But it wasn't a game, it wasn't pretend.

There had been so much blood.

Back in the street he could hear the sirens cutting through the ringing sensation in his ears. Police were moving through the devastation, looking for survivors, hunting the killers. And his mask was torn, revealing his face, speckled with crimson blood which was not his own.

Dan Galkin was now a killer. He was twelve years old, but as he looked down at his chest, rising and falling, he saw the torn costume and the deep gash across his belly. And he knew he was dead meat. He forced his eyes shut and wiped his dirty hand across his forehead, pushing back his dark blonde hair.

"Dead meat," he repeated audibly and started to slide down the wall.

When he hit the hardness of the floor it grounded him, somehow making everything more solid, more real. Short bursts of lightning streaked across his vision, and electricity popped from his skin and fizzed into the open air, especially around his wound. The uncontrollable discharge of energy had been happening most of the morning and he could sense it slowing, fading. The power was leaving him. Maybe he was dying, he didn't have a clue, but the numbness was welcome. Masking pain was preferable now.

He didn't know where the others were. He had seen Bree vanish into dust as the shockwave knocked him into the bookshop. The Small Gods had faltered, revealed as the children they were in a suddenly ruthless, adult world. Dan squeezed his eyes harder. The blue lights exploded into white, bringing back the pain. He clutched frantically to return to the numbness, but it was gone.

He replayed the explosion in his mind, the way his father's body seemed to expand like a balloon before it ruptured into the flames which swept so terribly through the public square.

And his father was dead now; he had to be. And if he wasn't, Dan really didn't want to think about the possibility. Gone, even though he'd only just come back into Dan's life. It seemed like such a waste of time, the awkward reunion and now the sudden immolation. It might have been better if his father had never walked through the kitchen door, back into Dan's life. His sheepish grin, crooked glasses and messy beard were memories now, nothing more than road-kill.

Dead meat.

"You thought you could run?" a voice boomed at him through the open window of the shop.

Dan felt pressure against his body, like the air was heating up and ready for a second explosion. He opened his eyes, his breathing shifting further into panic.

Standing with one boot firmly planted in the bookshop's window display was a man clad in gold and white, exuding authority and, more importantly, removing any hope of escaping this hell. The man pulled himself through what was left of the window, transforming it into heated slag as he passed. It was Castus, one of the Celestial Knights. Dark haired, but with the glowing eyes of a sun, Castus wielded the strength to topple buildings, the invulnerability to survive a free-fall to Earth from near orbit, and the obvious rage to crush the body of a scared twelve year old without a second thought.

Castus moved closer, the heat rolling off his body, curling the books scattered on the floor and still on the shelves. Dan could see the man's face change. Rage was there still, pushing against him as a corona of churning heat, but something else as well, something darker and broken. It was like the man had lost something, like he'd lost a part of himself. And now he wanted someone to pay.

"*Tha mou kaneis t atria, dyo…*"

The voice was low. Dan scrambled to his knees and then

up, grabbing for the crumbling books to steady himself as his feet slipped from under him.

"What?"

Castus reached out and grabbed Dan's neck, cutting off his words, the heat burning into his bare skin. The man shoved Dan back up the shelves, ramming his head into each new ledge until he started to kick out at the air, unable to touch the floor. Castus was well over six feet tall, maybe even pushing seven, Dan thought, horrified. His own hands clawed at Castus' grip, strands of pathetic blue lightning running harmlessly down the man's arm.

Dan couldn't breathe. The heat marked his skin, blisters forming around the hold. He managed a cough, but that only made Castus tighten his hand, and lean in closer.

"You will meet your creator," the hero whispered, his olive skin so very close to Dan's clammy cheek. "No escape this time."

But instead of death, a blast of gritty sand suddenly filled the shop, rushing in from outside and then packing together in such a concentrated burst that Dan knew it must have been Bree. He felt the grip around his neck fade. In fact he felt his entire body fade away, pushed back into the shelves and then impossibly through the wall. He became part of the swirling sandstorm, transformed and protected.

Dan clutched for her but his body was gone and he held his breath as the sand blasted its way through shop after shop until the darkness of the interiors was replaced by the brightness of the day outside. His body reformed, piece by piece, and Dan looked out to the glowing ruins of the square. Everything was twisted away from the epi-center of his father's explosion: a tram buckled on its side;

slow-moving people, hobbling and smeared black like beggars; the acrid smells from the fires reaching across to him where he stood with Bree.

"What'd we do?" he asked.

Bree's face was covered with a black scarf, leaving only her eyes visible. She watched him, taking him in, checking to see if he was injured. Dan reflexively touched the gash in his belly again.

"You have to run," she said.

"What?"

Her eyes flickered with annoyance but then softened just as quickly. She looked down the strip of broken shops.

"If you stay, you go to prison, Dan," she said. "It's that simple."

Bree was like Dan, a kid who could do things that ordinary kids couldn't, or shouldn't, do. While Dan could muster up sparks of lightning and command electrical appliances on a good day, Bree could dissolve herself into granules of sand and then reform herself at will. Under the tutelage of Dan's grandfather, Bree learned how to change other things too, like her clothes, furniture, or even other people. She was the best of them all, the teacher's pet, and Dan knew she had just saved his life.

And then she was gone. Like dust.

He stumbled into the square, tossing his mask to the ground as he scanned the area for anyone he knew. There were bodies in places but he didn't stop to look closer. They were obviously shoppers; their torn and burned everyday clothes marked them as bystanders. His friends were wearing costumes, playing the roles they'd been given by his grandfather. They had been promised a fun day out, a chance to strut their powers in public and maybe even become famous. He called them the Small Gods.

His grandfather's words still echoed in his mind, but the promises were losing their innocence as he stumbled through the haze. Sirens seemed to surround him on all sides but he couldn't work out where the police were. His hand against his belly, pressing as hard as he could, Dan made his way towards the tram. The lightning in his body managed to stem the flow of blood and it did feel a bit better, but even Dan knew he'd need a hospital soon.

Behind him, columns of concrete exploded outward. Chunks scattered past him, knocking his legs and skittering ahead of him. He kept running, pushing himself, leaping over the larger chunks and looking ahead for the policemen. He could see a group of them at the end of the square, huddled cautiously near a burning car. There were helicopters in the sky too, but they were all too far away. Behind him, Castus stormed out into the open. The air was still hazy, almost grainy with the after-effects of the explosion. Part of Dan hated to think about the possibility of the air being polluted with the atoms of his exploded father, but it was something he just couldn't keep out of his mind.

A wave of heat slammed into his back as he ran, smashing him to the ground face first and rupturing his belly wound again. He pulled himself forward, reaching out for the twisted metal of a bench, knowing that Castus was capable of unleashing more than a concussive heat wave. Last year, Dan had watched a television report featuring Castus and the other Knights laying waste to an entire fortress somewhere in northern Africa. Now he knew Castus was playing a game. The darkness he'd seen in the hero's face wanted something more than an arrest. Fear plagued Dan's body and he clutched for the sundered bench, not wanting to be found helpless and alone out in the square. His nose was bleeding, gushing out, but he couldn't stop it. He pulled himself along the bench, catching sight of Castus as he stepped closer, glowing so white it hurt to look.

The singing voice emerged from the general ringing in his ears, revealing itself gently at first, even as his heart beat faster and faster. When he did finally recognize it, the humming and the rising and falling tune, his body relaxed. He took a breath. A simple breath. He unclenched his fists and let the song wash over him.

Castus kept walking, closing the gap.

Dan followed the song with his mind, smiling now that he could sense it so close. And there it was, just a little further past the broken bench. He propped himself up and looked away from Castus and towards the source. He saw the ruptured electricity box and instantly felt his awareness shoot off in a million directions as he traced the pathways of electricity – scattering through the scorched high-rises lining the square, further afield into the traffic lights and surveillance systems of the city, and at the outermost points he felt himself drift into the homes of families: nice, normal families who had, as yet, no knowledge of the disaster which had befallen their city.

But this was no time for sightseeing. Dan pulled at the myriad lines of power; he tugged them back into himself, drawing them from their mundane duties so that he could protect himself from the sun god bearing down on him. Traffic lights were extinguished, whole computer networks were shut down, and the electricity burst through the damaged box into the open air, arcing upward like an inverted lightning bolt. Dan called it all into him, never before having dared to play with so much power.

He turned to Castus, so close now.

Instead of the approaching heat, all Dan could feel was a coolness spreading through his body. He looked down at himself, floating a little above the ground, his body blue-white and infused with the power of the city.

He managed a smile.

Nothing hurt anymore. His wounds were swallowed up in the light, blinded out of existence, stitched back together as his entire body moved from a tangible state to something more electric.

He was evolving.

This was what it was all about, he thought. This was what it felt like being a god.

CHAPTER 1

DAN

EVERY TIME THE doors slid back, Dan Galkin looked up expecting to see his mother, but all he got was a wintery blast of June air and the half-surprised look of customers stumbling into the shop. He waited for their orders, smiled in the right places, and took the money. The guys in the back were having all the fun, as usual; listening to music while they slipped burgers into microwaves, cracking jokes and exchanging tales at the deep fryer. And Dan was stuck at the front of shop, exposed to the public and their appetites – the 'smile until you die' job – and because he was late to work, again, he didn't know whether the others had rigged the roster or whether the world just hated him.

And then there was the thing with his mother. She'd called him that morning, all half-construed, panicked sentences and pauses that moved uncomfortably into one-sided small talk. She hadn't spoken to him in three years and Dan hated having to forget all of that to fill the gaps in their phone conversation. He hated her, or he wanted to.

Then she said she would come to the city and see him, and he didn't know whether it was just the easiest thing to say at the time, or whether she did plan to track him down to Birdie's and play the role of attentive mother over a plate of spicy chicken and a coke.

She hadn't wished him a happy birthday, probably hadn't remembered. Seventeen years old wasn't really an important one, he figured. Nothing to phone home about. Apparently.

There was a tapping at the front doors, followed by a gentle shuddering as the new kid tried to jimmy them open. He'd locked himself out of the shop again, flipping the automatic sensors off as he sprayed and cleaned the glass panels on the outside. He'd managed to get himself locked out three times in the past week which wasn't exactly a glowing recommendation. Sure, the criteria for working at Birdie's Chicken and Pizza wasn't too extensive, but the new kid seemed hopeless. Dan wanted to tell him to just walk away, to hang up the little cap, slide back the name badge and go home. It wasn't too late for him. He was barely fifteen, went to the local school, had a future in some other non-fast food industry. But the kid gave him an apologetic shrug from behind the glass and Dan shook his head, secretly channeling the faintest of surges through the air and into the electronic doors which leapt back into life, parting and allowing the kid inside.

Dan wasn't like any other fast food service employee. He was uberhuman, born with a twist to his genetic code giving him the potential to develop strange and seemingly impossible gifts. In his case, Dan discovered in his eleventh year that he could change the channels on his television without using the remote. This ability grew over time so that he could eventually 'hear' the electrical world around him and in most cases he could exert some control over it.

But it wasn't like anyone knew that Dan could tell the appliances what to do, or command the doors to open and close at will. In the past he had been a bit more forthcoming, but it never ended well. People were all very understanding and accepting at first, but eventually the charade crumbled and people realized he was just a freak, albeit a useful freak. Demands were made; little things like coaxing the slot machines or just topping up bank accounts until the next pay day. Friends dropped away when the favors ended.

There were lots of other ubers though, spread across the world doing all sorts of useful things. Websites tracked their deeds, bloggers and social commentators ranked and re-ranked them, and all the while, life sort of went to crap for Dan. He was working at a place that couldn't seem to decide whether it was a pizza shop or a fried and spicy chicken place. He dropped out of school a year before, somewhere between Year 11 and 12, and was semi-squatting in an apartment with people he didn't even really know.

"Thanks, man," the new kid said, panting slightly as he stashed the cleaning stuff in the cupboard and tied on a new apron. "Won't happen again."

Dan nodded. Not convinced.

Out in the back someone laughed at a joke and he could hear the delivery drivers arriving for the afternoon debriefing with the day manager. It was depressing, but Dan wondered whether one day he might make it as a manager. At least there was the possibility of incentive payments in management rather than minimum tips doing deliveries or the base level wage he scored at the counter.

Customers floated in, but Dan ignored them to let the new kid practice his 'smile while slowly dying inside' skills. He made himself look busy by fiddling with the drink machine, hoping the hours would suddenly melt away like the slushed ice pouring out over his hands. Instead, his phone chirped twice, vibrating in his pocket, and calling him away from sorting through the syrup dispenser. He wiped his hands dry on his apron and pulled the phone out, but it wasn't ringing. He flipped it closed again and felt the vibrations still coming from his pocket.

It was his other phone, the small black one. It wasn't the 'happy phone', that was for sure. He looked at the screen and read the caller ID: Owens. The message was simple: Office midnight.

Dan wondered whether he should just delete it.

"Dan?" the new kid nudged him and he quickly slipped the phone back into his pocket, wiping his hands again on his apron. "You've got a … a customer," the new kid said, looking confused.

The woman wasn't a customer. She wore a stretchy black and red striped long sleeve top which almost covered her hands, and a straw hat and shades which almost covered her face. After nodding in a vague way, she turned and found a seat at one of the booths commonly used by school girls to discuss the day's events and complain about their friends and family. Dan wondered whether he could sneak out the back and disappear into the streets, but the new kid blocked his way, the confused smile still playing on his face.

"Man, she's got like…" he said softly, looking down

at his hands with wide eyes. "You think she's here for the Human Tour?"

"What?" Dan pulled his eyes away from the woman.

"Miranda Brody's concert, you know? The Human Tour."

He moved past the kid and walked towards the booth, noticing how she hadn't really changed much in the years he'd been in the city. Her hair was a little drier than usual, and her arms were bony, but he couldn't remember a time when she wasn't thin and brittle. Handle with care, they always used to say.

Dan sat down but kept his hands in his lap.

"I didn't think you were really coming," he said.

She smiled, awkwardly, and looked down at her hands, rubbing each finger, easing the aches. The flecked blue skin was dry, like her wiry hair and chipped nails. When she noticed Dan watching her, she pulled her sleeves even longer and cupped the hands away out of sight. Her body seemed to shrink from the harsh lights, the straw hat giving her some refuge from stares and open-mouthed looks. Over at the counter, the new kid took orders in between glances at the freakish blue-skinned woman.

"I'm your mother," she said in a raspy voice. "Of course I would come."

"Seriously?" Dan said.

She pulled her hands out of sight into her own lap, her shoulders dropping. She turned her head and looked out of the window, which gave Dan a glimpse of her profile. Hawkish nose, old tortoise-shell shades, cracked lips.

"It's been…" she stalled.

"Three years," Dan finished for her.

"Difficult," she said, not looking back. "When your ... father died, I ... well, I didn't cope very well, Danny."

She hadn't coped very well her entire life. At sixteen her skin blistered and peeled, revealing a bluish hue underneath that never washed away no matter how hard she scrubbed, no matter how many lotions she applied. Dan's father, the less than impressive Nico, knocked her up in the first few weeks of courting and then managed to get himself arrested for a half-assed bank robbery. So, no, Theresa Galkin hadn't coped very well at all with life.

"I guess not," Dan said.

"You are doing well," she said softly. He couldn't tell whether it was a question or an opinion. He pulled off his Birdie's cap and tossed it on the table. His mother's head turned back from the window and looked at the cap.

"I'm not dead, I guess," he said.

She swallowed, her neck bird-like as she tried to compose herself.

"It's been difficult," she said again, rehearsing her lines.

A group of school kids took up a second booth near Dan and he heard them chattering about their lives, about music and boys and girls and homework and holidays.

"Your grandfather is back," she said.

Dan watched her lips. They were pressed tightly together, not quite hiding the hate she must have been tasting.

His grandfather had returned. From the dead.

It wasn't that he couldn't believe what she said. People like his grandfather never really took death seriously. Dan just didn't know how he felt about the development. Five years before, his grandfather had been everything to him.

He had been the stand-in father when the real one was locked in prison. He had been the only calm influence the night Dan's body started sucking up all the electricity in the house. He had become the confidant, the teacher. And eventually the betrayer.

"Great," Dan said, grabbing his cap and standing up. "Can't wait for the happy reunion."

He walked back to the counter, blinking hard against the flashes of light in his eyes. Sometimes when he was stressed, the electrical charges his body generated would try to burst out of him, to unleash themselves on the world and cause havoc and destruction. Sometimes his body wanted to become the weapon his grandfather trained him for. But Dan didn't have to do what anyone said anymore. He wasn't a pawn in the old man's game; it had already been played out. And Dan had lost.

"Next?" he asked, a little too fiercely, as he checked into the console next to the new kid.

A couple slipped into line and started to discuss the menu. Dan felt the console humming beneath his fingertips. He followed the couple's discussion, bringing up their orders, revising them, adding all sorts of extras as they casually changed their minds. His fingers didn't move but the orders entered directly from minuscule surges from his mind.

"Take your time," Dan said, forcing a smile. They didn't even hear him.

And suddenly Dan's mother was at the counter again, her bony blue fingers splayed against the shiny white plastic surface. She wasn't tall, but she leaned across so that she was directly in Dan's space. Her eyes were bare now, the shades discarded. The whites were yellowish, bloodshot.

"You have a choice," she hissed. Her breath was stale. How long had she been locked up inside, he wondered; his thoughts leaving the console and harking back to when he lived with her in the beach house. "You don't have to live like me."

She turned on the young couple, whipping her hat off and tossing it away to her right. She leered at them, her frizzy dead hair and her flaky blue face too much to ignore. In a second she swept her head towards the school kids and snarled at them, her dark blue lips pulled back to reveal the jagged yellow teeth. She played the wicked witch, the crazy blue skinned woman, the insane uberhuman freak.

Dan stepped back, away from the whirling confrontation. The people in lines scuttled to each side and his mother swayed a little more before retreating to the sliding doors. She looked back at him, teeth still bared, but there was sadness there in her eyes. She pointed a finger at him.

"You have been chosen," she said. "You can be more… so much more."

And then she was gone, pushing through the automatic doors when they didn't open quickly enough, and out into the street.

"Man," the new kid said. "That is weird shit."

Dan just shrugged.

Customers shook themselves back into line and some of the workers from out the back came into the front wondering what the crazy customer had done. The manager was on a cigarette break, but later she would curse herself for missing the action. Not much exciting ever happened at Birdie's.

CHAPTER 2
MIRANDA

THERE WASN'T ANYTHING actually wrong with the hotel, but Miranda Brody found herself crying her eyes out in the bathroom, with her back against the door and the balls of her palms crushed against her eyes. On the other side of the door her retainers hovered and checked the time, read and returned texts, and generally waited for Miranda to recover from what they assumed were regular pop diva antics.

But it wasn't a tantrum. She wasn't pouting because of hotel management. She hadn't broken up with her high profile boyfriend, or just got out of a five star rehab program. When it came down to it, although Miranda Brody was a teenage pop sensation on both sides of the Pacific and throughout most of Europe, she just wasn't particularly stuck up or demanding.

She didn't even have a boyfriend anymore. Or a drug problem. Or overbearing parents or jealous siblings. Miranda was weirdly sane, almost normal. After coming third in an American music reality show, Miranda had been snatched up and signed by a music company to cash in on her national profile. At first it had been exciting. It had been all her dreams, and more. But now her music wasn't even her music, and when she saw posters of herself in magazines or on billboards she felt like she was looking at someone completely different.

There was a knock on the door, the third in ten minutes, perfectly choreographed in even intervals. It was Evie, probably, and Miranda shifted the palms of her hands from her eyes to her ears, trying to block out the woman's voice.

"I don't need anyone," Miranda said, but it came out too low for the crowd on the other side of the door to hear. She sniffed and blew out her tremulous breath. She did it again, tried to center herself. "Just go away. Go away until Sully gets here."

Without waiting to hear whether Evie and the others understood, Miranda pulled herself together and stood up in the bathroom. She rubbed at her eyes, drying away the wetness there, and then tugged at her dark hair, capturing it into a ponytail. She caught her reflection in the floor-to-ceiling mirrors but forced her attention away. She had seen enough of this other Miranda during the three months of touring, first in the States, then across to Japan and down to...

Jakarta.

Miranda knew she wasn't going to be able to forget about Jakarta. She could smile at the cameras, look serious and then flighty during interviews, but she couldn't get the image of the boy out of her mind. He burnt so brightly, so hot that she felt the flames on her skin, could smell the gasoline blowing off of him. His arms were akimbo, relaxed and dying.

Like a star, the reporters had written.

But Miranda only remembered the face blackening, being pulled away from her by security, the relaxed boy slipping away into nothing, smothered into death.

She breathed out again, twice; like she had been taught.

Jakarta was behind her now. The last leg of her Human Tour was in Melbourne, Australia – somewhere out past those hotel walls. Her ride from the airport had been swift. She hadn't looked up and most of the time her eyes were closed behind her large shades. She didn't know these people who met her, who smiled at her, touched her, wanted to make her so happy. Her regular crew were still in Jakarta, except for Evie and a couple of the dancers. It had all been so rushed, like an evacuation.

And Sully was still back in Indonesia, cleaning up her mess, as usual. He was her constant throughout the Tour. The backup singers, the dancers, the audio and light crew were all replaceable, and had been changed several times through the last three months, but Sully was her rock. He was her family when she was on the road, and probably most importantly, he was her friend.

He was the only one who made her feel safe.

Normally.

But now she was in Australia and alone amongst the industry vultures. She was nineteen, of course, and an adult who could handle the pressures, but she didn't want to handle them alone. She'd been doing the music thing for four years, but the past two had been insane with her face recognized across most of the Western world.

There was another knock on the door. Miranda looked at her phone next to the basin. Three minutes had passed, another scheduled reminder that she was needed somewhere.

She ran the taps and splashed cool water on her face, reaching for the hand towel as she walked to the door. She opened it with another practiced exhale and looked out into one of her rooms. Evie was standing there with her skinny arms crossed. Behind her were two hotel workers fussing about near the bed, but they didn't look up. For a second Miranda thought of her mom and felt like she was going to cry again.

"You look awful," Evie said.

"Thanks," Miranda said, sniffing. "Is Sully here?"

The backup singer shook her head, and then thrust a pamphlet into Miranda's hands. It was a press release for the record company's welcome party. Apart from the venue and the Australian flag tucked up in the corner, there wasn't anything especially different about it.

"It looks fine," she said and handed it back to Evie, but Evie shook her head.

"Read it," she snapped.

Miranda looked at the sheet again, her eyes glazing over as she read about sales figures, reviews and the tendency for these parties to 'absolutely rock!' She shrugged and handed the pamphlet back again.

"I don't get it."

"You are hopeless," Evie said and snatched the sheet, stepping back into the room and turning around twice, letting her short dress lift slightly. The girl was energized. Miranda shot a glance around the room as the hotel workers left, wondering how much coffee or energy drinks Evie had downed since they had arrived. The place looked spotless.

Evie had been singing with Miranda for a month, picked up in Seattle just before the trip to Japan. At first Miranda found her annoying. She was too loud for such a slender person: big pouty mouth, short styled blonde hair and a turned up nose. It wasn't her original nose.

"New freaks," Evie said. "It says we get new freaks."

Miranda wasn't following. It wasn't unusual for Evie to carry on one-sided conversations, but Miranda took back the pamphlet and read it again, trying to work out what Evie was so excited about. At the bottom of the release, beyond the drone of statistics and promises, there was a paragraph on new 'freaks' being on display for the final concert. It was the first Miranda had heard of it.

"I didn't authorize this," she said.

Evie just grinned. "New freaks," she said again.

Freak Chic was one of Miranda's top selling songs and The Human Tour was basically built around the song's success. It was all about embracing the weird and she showcased ubers as dancers in her shows. Her company had hired eight of them over the course of the tour, although she didn't really know them apart from choreography and the actual performances. Evie, on the other hand, made it her business to get to know them intimately.

"Do you think we'll get a koala one?" Evie asked.

"I have no idea."

She wondered what happened to the other freaks and whether they were still back in Jakarta. Maybe they were angry with her. Maybe they blamed her for the boy's death. Maybe they were just tired of being looked at and exploited.

There hadn't been many protestors in Jakarta, at least. The moral outrage against the concert might have stopped in the States. Her manager had told her not to worry about it, to forget about the radicals and the haters, but Miranda had seen the anger in the eyes of the protestors, placards damning her and her treatment of the ubers. It was just another spin in the whirlwind of her music career.

Miranda wanted to get off.

"You've got to go," Miranda said to Evie.

"I know!"

"No, seriously, you have to go now. Leave my room. Go see Melbourne and buy things. I need to be by myself for a while."

Evie shook her head, disgusted.

"You are not going to miss this party," she said. "I will seriously hunt you down and kill you if you dare miss this party."

Miranda looked at the press release for the last time and then back at Evie. There was something compelling about the girl, and she smiled and nodded.

"I'll be there."

And then she bundled Evie out of the room and locked the door.

She was in Melbourne for four nights. One concert, one record company party and a half dozen interviews. Moving to the balcony she parted the curtains and looked out into the afternoon. It was like any other city she'd been to. There was steel and glass and people far below criss-crossing the streets.

There were no protestors, no shaking signs and shouts of rage. It was quiet. She looked back to the door, to possibilities.

Back home, in Riverside, her family were asleep.

She needed to get out of the hotel.

CHAPTER 3

DAN

DAN PULLED OFF his helmet after kicking his bike stand into place on the curb. He looked across to the hotel and adjusted his pizza satchel. The street was packed with teenagers, milling around, and he saw a lot of bored older people sitting in cars up and down the street. Parents, he figured. Outside the double doors of the hotel, he checked the address again. It was one of the expensive ones. He pushed through to the lobby, ignored the frown at reception, and reeled off his customer name and room number while looking at the ceiling. He was waved through to the elevator and sighed as the lobby disappeared from view.

Dan wasn't having a good night. Even without his mother's performance at work, the afternoon and now evening wasn't turning out well either. No tips, lots of attitude, a bit of indiscriminate nudity and two 'no answers' which meant cold pizza and no pay.

The elevator stopped and a long stretch of rooms extended in both directions, equally beige. He checked the number, heaved his satchel straps up to his shoulder again and walked out. It was strange that no one was walking around. When he found the number he knocked twice and checked his phone. He was within the time limit. No chance of the customer declaring the pizza free on this one.

The door was pulled open by a girl wearing glasses, and she squinted at him with her head tilted. Behind her, Dan saw the room was dark apart from a couple of free-standing lamps. A peal of laughter came from within, but the girl with the glasses guarded the entrance, pulling the door back.

"Are you the pizza guy?" she asked.

Dan looked at the two pizza boxes in his hand and then back at the girl without saying anything. She looked closer at his chest, at the logo for Birdie's, and eventually pulled her neck back and seemed satisfied. He reeled off the order, announced the price and then had to wait while she slipped back inside the room and started collecting the money from her friends.

When she reappeared the girl was flanked by a taller blonde girl with long hanging earrings. Dan figured they were both in their early-teens and considering the hotel wasn't the cheapest in town he wondered how they'd managed to scrounge the money together for a room when they seemed so hard-pressed coming up with the money for their pepperoni and supreme pizzas.

"So you're having a party?" Dan asked.

"Totally," the new girl said. "I'm Donna and this's Asi. What's your name?"

"No we're not, not really," the dark-haired girl said, making angry eyes at Donna. "Just a few friends."

"Oh yeah, right," the blonde corrected herself. "It's not a party."

"But you've got supervision, right?" Dan asked.

"Totally," Donna said, nodding vigorously. "Asi's sister, is like, supervising us, yeah."

"She's eighteen," said the girl with glasses, pushing them back up her nose, looking impressed.

Dan smiled and craned his neck a little as they took the pizza boxes. He could see another couple of girls with their faces up against the window looking out into the main street. And then there was a mess of arms and legs and bodies wrestling on the bed. Dan grinned and pulled back his head.

"Your sister's got a friend," he said.

"That's Andy."

"No kidding," Dan said. "Are you girls spies or something?"

They both giggled and the blonde one nodded in a general way.

"You sure look the part," he said.

"We're waiting for Miranda," Donna said.

"Miranda Brody," Asi added, and then they both seemed overcome with something.

"The singer?" Dan asked.

"She's staying across the road."

He'd been hearing the name all day. Miranda Brody was an American celebrity and Dan figured that meant she spent her life gracing covers of magazines, entering mild controversies, and living it up without a care in the world. She was the singer-type celebrity which meant she probably had a manufactured, inoffensive and marketable sound.

Dan hadn't really heard her music, at least he didn't think he had, but he figured he knew the type.

"She's on the sixteenth floor."

"And she's only here for one concert."

"Do you want to come in?"

Dan smiled at the girls and stepped back. Apart from the pop music which was now playing inside the room, the oblivious older sister getting it on with her boyfriend, the girls were barely pubescent and he had enough problems without stepping inside and possibly having his hair braided while they all chatted about Miranda Brody.

"Ah, look, I've got to get back to my deliveries," he said, shouldering his satchel again. "But good luck with the celebrity watch. I hope you get to see her. And don't get your sticky fingers all over the windows. This place is really serious about that stuff."

He left them with the pizza and pop star, moving quickly to the elevator. Inside he allowed himself to scramble the music with his mind, reducing the repetitive sounds to static and then silence. He closed his eyes and felt the elevator moving slowly down to street level again. He tried not to think about his grandfather.

When Dan stepped out into the night he noticed two things had changed: the street was now thick with photographers, lights and film crews, and his bike was blocked in by the double-parked media. The electrical spikes from phones, satellite hook-ups and excess lights were almost as irritating as the bursts of camera flash. It had taken less than ten minutes to deliver the pizza but now his entire night would be compromised. Birdie's rules were clear – if the pizza arrived late, it was always the delivery at fault, never the customer.

He only had one more delivery, and then he could go home and try to forget everything. He could forget that his grandfather was back, and he could forget about all the grandfather-related skeletons in his closet. He could forget he even had a closet.

Dan pushed his way through the gawkers at the back of the mob, squeezing past teenagers and in between couples. At his bike he realized that getting it started and then back on to the road was going to be impossible. It didn't have enough grunt to intimidate the crowds into parting and even if it did he doubted his boss would appreciate the adverse publicity it'd bring.

The crowd shifted and seemed to move as one organism. Its many heads turned together, suddenly catching sight of the celebrity. Dan couldn't resist looking as well, and saw a cluster of black suited men and women pushing their way through the outer rings of fans. Dan caught glimpses of a girl in their protective circle and he could tell she wasn't comfortable with the attention. Her head was down and her hands were up to her face trying to block out the calls and screams. She wore shades and a baseball cap but Dan recognized her from the posters being thrust in the air by loyal fans all around him.

The flashes of cameras lit up her face behind the impressive wall of retainers and each time the cameras surged forward Miranda seemed to shrink back. The group were finding it difficult navigating the mob as well and for all their bulk and determination they didn't seem capable of knocking down the fans, especially with all the cameras present.

A reporter hitched herself up onto the van next to Dan's bike and with a hand from her assistant, managed to scuttle up to the roof. In less than thirty seconds she preened herself and stood with the hotel masterfully presented behind her. A cameraman was shooting film from across the street, clear of the chaos. Dan could tell that her microphone was transmitting live. Its signal sung into the night joining the chorus of other feeds from the dozen or so reporters at the scene.

At the entrance to the hotel another small group of Miranda Brody's people waited, but the gulf between the two groups seemed to be getting larger.

Dan looked at his watch.

Then he looked back up at the hotel across the street. The girls were probably pressing their little faces against the glass screaming their little hearts out. Everywhere he looked he saw the same thing: ecstatic screams, red faces, open mouths, posters of the pop star.

But the one they were all screaming for looked more like a scared little girl than a media magnet. It didn't seem fair. The situation was ridiculous and without even the hint of a police presence it wasn't going to improve. And that meant Dan's final delivery would be delayed.

He closed his eyes, rubbing at them to clear the image of his shaggy, wide-eyed and bearded grandfather. He was getting a headache. Two loud-mouthed girls shoved him as they made their way to the front of the crowd. His bike teetered a little and other people started to move around it leaving Dan with a vision of chipped paint or a toppled bike.

Blue lightning streaked across his eyes as he opened them. Sometimes he hated the city.

More fans jostled around him, their screams pushing against him like a physical force. The pack surged forward and then back a little when it hit the ring of security. Dan felt himself getting pulled along. His bike was just out of reach.

He felt the electricity just under his skin now.

A part of him wanted to taser the whole bunch and leave them convulsing in the night. He looked around for another option but all he found was more tear-streaked hysteria.

It seemed inevitable.

His fingers twitched.

With another look at his besieged bike, Dan made the decision to save the girl. He clenched his fist and let the idea of stunning the crowd fall away.

He had other options.

The reporter on top of the van held her hair in place as she spoke to the unseen audience. He concentrated on the signals buzzing around her and isolated the woman's mobile phone, accessing its number and contacts list. It was quite extensive and included a number of other industry reporters, many of whom were probably prowling through the crowds trying to get closer to the pinned celebrity.

Dan pulled out his own phone and mentally composed a text. Using his control over the electrical world he dragged the database of numbers from the reporter's phone and brought it across to his own. The message was then sent to dozens of other numbers, some of them close by. Dan allowed himself to track them at least in the short term, but soon the signals were buzzing in all directions like a swarm of invisible wasps. It was a nice development.

He watched with satisfaction as the woman on the van reflexively touched her pocket. She had taken a break from directly talking to the camera and pulled out her phone. She looked at it closer and then across to the pack of Miranda's security. Dan smiled as he saw the reporter's face change from one of blank surprise to a more cunning flash of excitement.

The mobile network suddenly surged again as the texts continued flying back and forth through the invisible web of people and their phones. With a little effort Dan managed to heighten the urgency, duplicating messages around him and thrusting them in different directions, spinning them into oblivion.

The message was the same though.

And the people started to receive it and immediately reacted. The woman on the van slid down to the pavement right next to Dan. Her skirt rode up her thigh and she tried to pull it down as she raced across to her partner on the other side of the road. He was already gunning the car's accelerator.

Other people started hurrying down towards the north end of the street like lemmings and behind them the parked vehicles hummed into action. More lights streaked across in all directions as cars pulled illegal u-turns and nearly ran down the scuttling fans and other gawking people.

Miranda Brody's group remained pinned against the window of the hotel. They had received the message as well and Dan could see at least two of them puzzling over their phones.

"All in a day's work," Dan smirked and climbed on to his bike, kicking the stand back and rolling it to the roadside.

He slipped his helmet on and turned the key. The street was already emptying and he had a clear passage to the south end of the street, just as he had planned.

A man grabbed his arm as he began to move off, surprising Dan. He struggled to free himself but the man held on. It was one of Brody's people, all dark shades and expensive suits.

"Did you do that?" the man asked. He pulled off his shades and looked directly at Dan, eyeball to eyeball. "Did you just do what I think you did?"

Dan shook his arm again, pulling himself free.

"Man, I didn't do anything," Dan said. "This is all your mess."

He kick started his bike and roared up the street, but the man's eyes stayed on his back. Dan couldn't resist a glance in his side mirror. Behind him he caught the convergence of Brody's two groups of people as they ushered their star inside the hotel. Some of them were looking towards him but he didn't care about them anymore.

He had his bike and a clear path to the last job.

The message he sent was already erased from his phone and the people who flocked to the other entrance of the hotel would later be wondering who sent them the text. Young celebrities were well known for media stunts so when they heard that a decoy was drawing their attention at the front of the hotel while the real Miranda was only just arriving at the back, there wasn't anything to question.

CHAPTER 4

THE MAD RUSSIAN

T HE SKIES WERE always steel grey in the old country, reflecting the hard land beneath, and the constant of death all around. In his youth, so distant now and entwined with the mists of invention and re-invention, he would often watch the skies for signs. The old women nodded at him, knowing but not knowing, and the men walked around him, eyes averted. He was never young, though, and no one knew his story or his blood. He was simply there one day, walking through the village, eyes to the skittering clouds which seemed to glow with far-away lightning. No one asked where he came from. There were rumors, frequent crossings of chests and pursed lips, but no questions.

They named him after the Hebrew woman at the edge of the village who took him in, and then they tried to forget about him and the storm of that day which threatened but never really broke.

In his office overlooking Collins Street, thousands of miles and many decades later, Galkin watched as a new storm brewed in the distance. So much had changed since those early days, but more recently, storms like the one outside brought him back to those older times. He still watched the skies for signs, but decided long ago to make his own way in the world instead of waiting. Looking back at his reflection in the window he realized just how far his strategy had spread from one hemisphere to the next, from one generation to the next. Losing five years had made everything that much clearer. The pattern was becoming unmistakable. And it gave him some pleasure.

Even at the end of his life he could see the potential of the world, the possibility of his legacy.

"Contact has been made?" he asked without turning back to the room. His breath frosted on the glass.

The boy behind him was slouching on a sofa, boots crossed at his ankles. It irritated Galkin but the boy was worth overlooking a few insolent indiscretions. Sohail had been with him for nearly ten years, raised on the fringe of Melbourne with a purpose in mind, a part to play. As Halo, the boy had been one of Galkin's Small Gods, bringers of chaos, the generation of broken hope. The memories brought a faint smile to his face, creased as it was.

"Danny met his mum this afternoon," Halo said, flipping through a magazine. "Had a chat over some chicken."

"How is he?" Galkin asked softly, the breath clouding the glass again.

Halo dropped the magazine and shrugged. The mirror reflection of the boy played with Galkin's mind and for a second he thought he caught glimpses of his own son and then his grandson. The movement was so natural, so unguarded. Galkin turned around.

It was not Halo's style to be so casual.

"You play with me, Sohail? You withhold from me? From me?"

Halo straightened up quickly, stood up and clasped his hands behind his back, at attention like the little soldier he was. Galkin held his stare for a few more seconds, the temptation to reprimand further, tantalizingly close, prickling his skin, ready to strike.

"Dan's fine, he's good."

Behind Galkin, the skies darkened. Halo noticed: it was clear in his eyes.

"He knows you're back in town," Halo continued. "Theresa told him you were back, looking for him. She did what she was told."

Galkin nodded once. The ploy to send the mother was a risk, but to announce his own return in person, to just appear before the boy, was unthinkable. The mother's fractured state of mind, her cocktail of guilt and remorse and anger had its purpose. She had always been easily manipulated, although not altogether trustworthy. It was a gamble, of course, but a necessary one in the fine act of setting up his grandson for the next move. Perhaps, the final move.

"You worry me some of these times, Sohail," Galkin said. "We will not fail."

Halo relaxed slightly, hands shifting from his back to the pockets of his jacket. Galkin could sense it in the subtle shift of adrenalin, the softening of the edges. He blinked and saw the boy as a collection of electrical impulses, connected, heightened and then receding. The fine network was right there in front of him, so precious and so vulnerable.

Just a prick here or a scramble there. Such little

alterations and the boy could be a twitching mess on the floor. Maimed, broken, dead: it was all possible.

"Danya…" he sighed, dismissing Halo with his hand. The storm spread across the city, turning the late afternoon into night. Up and down the street, and even across the city, lights were flickering on, fighting back the darkness. But Galkin knew that sometimes the darkness just had to come out. There could be no stopping what needed to happen; the pain would be fleeting in the grand scheme of things, the transformation worth every tear, every bruise on his grandson's body.

He ran his fingers across the glass, tracing the line of his own face. Danya was seventeen now, almost a man, but cut off from his father and grandfather. Aimless, wandering. Galkin frowned at himself, taking the wordless blame for his son's failure, his unearned hubris. The signs were there early, in childhood; the irrational responses, the urgency, the desperation to be seen and heard and, worse, the need to be listened to. No child demanded more from its parents. Galkin could still hear the cries, the high-pitched wail of his son which seemed to carry itself through infancy and into childhood. But it didn't stop there; rather, it seemed to intensify, to career its way through adolescence and then into adulthood.

Many times he wished death upon his son, his own blood; but there were lines you could not cross.

The son ultimately perished in the flames of his own creation and Galkin noted some kind of poetry in that. He could not articulate it, of course, and had no real desire to do so; but there was no doubt that dying in such an irreversible, public manner seemed to reflect the nature of his son.

He sighed, and then pushed himself through the window; his fingers pressing into the suddenly malleable surface, peeling it back so he could step out and onto the impossibly narrow ledge outside. The night air was charged with the coming storm and as Galkin breathed out he thought he could feel the city's undulating energy enter him.

When his whole body passed through the window, it closed up behind him, perfect again – remade. It was a simple matter for him to spread the molecules, tease them apart to let him through. People often forgot that the Mad Russian was more than a simple parlor magician.

There was real power in his blood.

In fact, there was real power in all of his blood. His attention turned to the west, down into the metropolis where his grandson slaved away at a pathetic job, serving pathetic humans their pathetic and fleeting desires. It suddenly appeared prophetic the way Danya was lost to him in such a bleak, colorless world. And now, five years later he would bring his boy back into his rightful position.

"Pain will transform you, bring you back to me."

Inside the office, Halo edged towards the door. The boy was familiar with Galkin's power, but such unnatural actions like walking through walls, still managed to capture an audience, even a streetwise one. Galkin let him go without a word or even a glance. Halo was, after all, simply a mouse scurrying back to the streets. He was a good boy, really. Useful, resourceful, perhaps even a little like Galkin himself. But in the end he was not blood.

And therefore he was ultimately expendable.

CHAPTER 5
DAN

B ACK AT HIS apartment, nestled in between a Chinese restaurant and a Skin and Beauty salon, Dan kicked off his trainers and folded himself into the sofa, swinging his legs across the arm rest to the chair beside him. From that angle he could clearly see the television as well as stretch himself out fully to unlock the kinks he'd collected on his pizza delivery run.

Outside he heard the police and ambulance sirens. A helicopter swept low over the city and a car alarm was droning down in the basement car park across the street. But Dan was home, and out of what was turning into an impressive rain storm. His shoes were off, his phones were on silent, and he could breathe slowly again.

He shared the second-storey place with Brian and Noah, both of them in their twenties and earning decent salaries. Dan had met them through Brian's little brother, at a time when they were desperate to replace a recently absconded flatmate. Dan was still in high school but he was juggling enough part time jobs to pay thirds in the rent. And he was the only serious option in a series of unsuitable applicants.

Less than a year later and even Dan was beginning to sense that having a teenager in the apartment was cramping their style. Brian was now on what he referred to as a fast track to management in human resources, and Noah had conjured up a premature mid-life crisis at twenty-four and discovered that he was an actor, even though his qualifications were in accounting. In fact it was Noah's inability to match Brian's income that allowed Dan to stay on for as long as he had, and even though he hated to admit it, Dan was only too aware of the situation.

The apartment itself was what real estate agents called a generous two bedroom townhouse. It was close to the train station, but not too close. It was within walking distance of the essentials but with three men living in a two bedroom place, Dan was relegated to the study nook – a minor setback he didn't mind being burdened with given the alternative was going back into foster care or, worse, back to live with his mother. The nook was wide enough to accommodate his fold-out sofa bed and there was a ledge with enough room for his belongings.

Originally, Dan had only expected to stay for his final exams. Foster care hadn't worked out, and the nook provided him with a place to feel safe, to cram for the tests and to ground himself in a seriously unwieldy time.

As he lay on the shared sofa looking towards the television he realized that, although he was comfortable enough, the screen was blank. He closed his eyes and rubbed at his forehead trying to decide where the others had misplaced the remote control.

Normally he'd just command the television to turn on, sending out an invisible pulse from his mind which would force a connection and bring up the images. He could sense it laying dormant in the corner of the room almost like it was asleep, gently snoring. But there were house rules in the apartment, rules which had been hastily discussed and implemented between Brian and Noah a number of weeks before. There had been an incident, or perhaps a series of incidents, involving the fusing of wires and a small house fire. It wasn't particularly Dan's fault. It was an old building and the landlord was more interested in harvesting rent money than in maintaining the integrity of the place. And that meant that the landlord hadn't kept the wiring in good working order. And that, in turn, meant that when Dan absently played with the electrical networks he unintentionally overloaded the antiquated system. And that, of course, led to the small fire in the wall.

To Dan it was ancient history, but he knew Noah was still upset about it. So, as Dan lay watching the blank television screen, he resisted the temptation to simply activate the set with his mind. Instead, he turned his attention to the remote and he tracked the batteries and signal to the ledge above the gas heater. The remote was an equal distance away from him as the television.

It was as if Noah had done it deliberately.

"You're home early," Brian said from the doorway leading to the kitchen.

Dan arched his neck to look around and acknowledge his flatmate. He immediately severed the link he'd established with the remote control and sat up looking at Brian as if he'd just been caught out. Brian looked equally as uncomfortable as Dan.

"What's up?" Dan asked.

"We've got to talk," Brian said, as if from a script. Dan could imagine the two of them arguing over who would talk to the 'kid'. Brian must have scored the short straw, or else Noah had thrown one of his theatrical fits. Either way it was clear that Brian found himself in a difficult and unwanted conversation with Dan.

"What's the matter?"

"We can't really have you here anymore," Brian said. "The place isn't big enough."

Dan hadn't expected an eviction, or at least, not that night. He'd been working hard since the morning and all he wanted to do was curl up and switch off his brain, to close his eyes and sleep. Brian, on the other hand, wasn't about to let him rest. He stood in the doorway, not coming closer. Dan wanted to run.

"So, you don't really fit in here anymore, Dan. School's finished," Brian said. His hands were stuffed in his pockets and he affected a disinterested stance, eyes watching the space just above and to the left of Dan's head. Dan wondered if he spoke like this with his clients.

"I don't take up much space," Dan said, discreetly pulling his legs off the chair and trying to look innocuous.

"Yeah, but it's space, you know. It's not about how much you take up as it's that you do take it up. The space, I mean."

"Right."

"And Noah's girl's getting serious, sending out the signals, you know? And let's be honest…" Brian finally met Dan's gaze, as if the word 'honest' required a certain degree of connectedness. It was only a brief moment and then Brian rolled his eyes and looked to the ceiling.

"Yeah."

"Ever since you and Stacey and the party…"

Brian waved the details away with his hand, eye contact well and truly gone. It was as if he was waving away the details they both thought they knew while neither one really had any idea at all. There was some confusion over whether Noah and Stacey were still seeing each other, some escalating flirtation and then a morning that followed which featured an explosive Noah and an awkwardness that just never seemed to dissipate.

"Noah's been weird about it," Dan suggested.

"We're all a little weird about it, Dan," Brian said.

"No, Noah's gone and … and gone weird about it. But he's weird about a lot of things lately, as if you haven't noticed. Like the newspaper, the crappy newspaper every morning, folded just right. And how he has to be the first to use the coffee plunger, as if we've all got leprosy or something, and don't start on about the bloody cups."

Dan stood up and a pulse of angry energy rippled through the lounge room, making the lights shimmer slightly and setting the clocks on the DVD player back to a flashing default. He pulled back on the wave, hoping Brian hadn't noticed, but Brian hadn't really paid attention to anything apart from the ceiling features.

"It's our name on the lease," he said.

And that was when Dan realized the truth. In classic shared accommodation style there were the official occupants and then there were the sub-letting, sub-human occupants who slept on a pull-out bed in the study nook.

"Are you going to give me notice?" Dan asked.

Brian waved his hand again and Dan wanted to yell at

him to stop playing the hand waving act. Instead he stood there and watched Brian walk back into the kitchen.

"This is notice, Galkin," Brian said.

Dan felt his fists clench and he raised them up so he could see the whites of his knuckles. Just below the surface he knew that he was capable of letting loose, that if he wanted to, he could turn the apartment into a swirling maelstrom of lightning and destruction.

He could hear his grandfather's voice. The coaxing, reassuring commands.

He shot a glance at the kitchen and heard Brian preparing something. He looked back at his fists and unclenched them, freeing his fingers and watching them separate slowly.

Dan didn't follow his grandfather anymore.

He wasn't a brainless kid.

The room was suddenly too hot and too crowded, even though Dan was the only one left. Brian's continued presence was felt, but the noises coming from the kitchen provided nothing but a dismissive reminder that he wasn't wanted anymore.

His sofa was still in its place, wedged into the nook which looked smaller than it ever had before. There was no way he would sleep in it again, no way he could pull it out and crawl inside the covers. It had always been an inconvenience, jutting out into the lounge area, but now the whole idea of it was suddenly and irreversibly gone. Like dust.

CHAPTER 6
THE SMALL GODS

DUST.

It was everywhere, covering every surface in the dimly lit basement. The old man was standing in the middle of the room with his eyes looking up at the ceiling, his wild grey hair standing up in tufts like he'd only just woken up. And that newly awake look was in his eyes too, with flashes of light reflected from the torches they'd brought down with them.

"He looks crazy," Bree said softly, shifting the weight of her backpack from one slender shoulder to the next. Dan shrugged. He'd seen crazy before.

His grandfather had brought the four of them on a hiking trip to the Grampians, far to the west of the state. Dan was used to being alone with his grandfather, but he wasn't accustomed to the presence of other kids, especially the ones his grandfather had assembled.

Bree was three years older than him, and at fifteen she seemed to have left childhood behind and looked at the world with knowing eyes. Dan thought maybe he was a little in love with her. The other two were older still. Halo was the eldest at sixteen and brimming with anger; while the quiet, wide-eyed Lily was somewhere in between. They'd never met before, although Dan knew that Lily was family in a way, being sort of cousins despite her being Chinese and him being Russian.

"Is this a bomb shelter?" Halo asked, arms crossed as he stood at the top of the stairs leading down into the basement. Lily, Bree and Dan had wandered down with the old man but Halo hadn't left the filtered sunlight coming in the windows from upstairs. Dan looked up and noticed the way the light formed around his head, casting his features into darkness but brightening the edges.

"Of a sort, yes," the old man said. "A shelter for bombs."

He coughed a little and waved away motes of dust. After a few more waves of his hands, the lights in the basement suddenly burst into life, flickering a little before burning at full intensity. Dan felt the wave of energy coming from his grandfather and it washed over him like a warm breeze, tingling his skin.

"And then there was light," Bree muttered as she dropped her bag to the floor. "Are you coming down or are you just going to hover up there?"

Halo leaned against the door, keeping it open, but said nothing. He hadn't spoken at all on the trip from Melbourne.

"This isn't my idea of a holiday either, you know?" Bree continued, although she didn't look up at him, instead concentrating on the benches and cabinets set up in neat rows like a museum. "My guardians didn't give me a choice."

"None had choice," the man said. "This is no holiday. Each of you is here for training."

Dan sat on a high stool at a bench and leaned his head

on folded arms. He watched Lily reach out to touch a glass cylinder containing a skeleton of some small, slender creature. All around them were remnants of strange collections. Lily's fingers stopped before they touched the surface but Dan could see the glass frost suddenly, blossoming outward from where the girl's fingers hesitated. Their eyes met and she quickly dropped her hands, thrusting them into her jeans, and turned away to look listlessly at more dust.

"What kind of training?" Halo asked, stepping down two of the steps. Dan lifted his head and watched the Pakistani kid come closer. His head was shaven and he wore a tank top which accentuated the hardness of his toned body. Dan felt like a minnow next to Halo.

"For our powers obviously," Bree jumped in, suddenly surrounded by a mistral whirlwind of dust. She weaved her hand, index finger extended, around her body and the dust trailed after it. In the light of the basement it looked spectacular. With her captivated audience following the dust trail, Bree wiggled her finger a final time and the dust concentrated in on itself until it formed a dark solid ball, the size of a marble. She opened her palm under the dust ball and it dropped innocently into her hand.

The man clapped his hands three times, clearly proud of the moment.

"You are gods," he said with a wide open smile. He pressed the hair back down on his head and nodded to himself. "You are the small gods, walking amongst us."

"We're not gods," Halo said. "We're monsters."

The man took in a breath at the words, as if he recalled them from an earlier time. He looked up at Halo and his face was reflective of the boy's pain. Dan turned away, resting his cheek on his arms which lay on the bench. He could see a console to his left, small red lights lit up in a row. There was a hum from within the machine and he absently played with the circuitry, channeling energy one way and then the next, testing its limits and formulating new paths, new possibilities. The console was a monitoring device and Dan felt the remote cameras and sensors which lay out beyond the cabin, all focused on maintaining the secrecy of this hidden place.

"You are gods," the man repeated louder, having walked up to meet Halo on the stairs. He took the boy's hand, unclenched the fist and held it within his own. "You see this?" he asked, gently shaking the combined hands. "This is promise to you, Sohail Pirzada."

Dan took a second look at them. His grandfather was below the boy, almost in a supplicating pose. A part of him wanted to be where Halo stood, to be the center of his grandfather's attention.

"A promise," the man repeated. "You will be god."

Later that night, after they pitched their tents in the open quadrangle between the cabin and what was supposed to be a boat or trailer shed, the four campers sat around a campfire. Dan's grandfather was in the basement, supposedly re-establishing its glory days, whatever that meant.

Halo brightened up during the day, filled with the confidence that one day he would be able to crush all those who had ever opposed him. He flashed his charismatic smile at the girls and told them about his family, about their escape from persecution, their arrival in Australia followed by their meteoric rise to fortune. He was a self-described golden child and they all believed him.

Especially Bree.

"But what about your gifts?" Bree asked him. "What can you do?"

He leaned in close to her, tucking a strand of black hair behind her ear. She kept his gaze but made no other effort to play his game. Dan felt his heart sink.

"I'm golden," he said. "And I can read your mind."

She looked away then, smiling a little self-consciously.

"You're a liar," she said.

"I can talk to machines," Dan said, desperate to change the topic, desperate to fill the awkward gap that opened up between him and Bree. "Sometimes."

"Sometimes?" Halo mocked.

Dan nodded.

"And what do machines have to say?" Halo asked.

"Leave him," Bree said. She leaned back on her arms and cocked her head up towards the stars. "That's a great gift," she said. Dan closed his eyes and smiled, letting the words hang in the air.

"Yeah, well, let's see how great it is tomorrow in training," Halo said.

"Yeah," Dan said, hopeful.

CHAPTER 7

DAN

MELBOURNE, PRESENT DAY

"THIS HAS TO be illegal, doesn't it?" Dan asked as he leaned against the railing and looked down to the street. There was a breeze behind him and it was picking up, blowing his hair forward across his face. "I mean, are you actually serious about me spying on your boyfriend?"

Alsana Owens stood next to him on top of the seven storey car park, but she didn't hold on to the railing. Instead, her hands were stuffed deep into the pockets of her black duffel coat. Her hair was held down by a beret and her face was severe with piercing green, deadly eyes.

It was close to midnight. All of the normal people of the city were either partying or sleeping. The satchel at his feet contained a bunch of clothes and stuff he'd grabbed from the apartment. It felt pathetic against his leg. He looked at Alsana, at her gaunt profile in the moonlight, and then back across the street. Neither of them was normal, he figured. Probably hadn't been normal for a very long time.

Alsana was his handler, a government appointed official

with a tenuous link to the Uberhuman Affairs Office. After being arrested as a twelve year old supervillain and bundled through the courts and juvenile justice system, Dan had been nominated to be up-cycled. It was a program for underage ubers who managed to get on the wrong side of the law, usually for petty crimes. But in Dan's case, things were a little more complicated. Dan had been involved in a massacre. People had died. And then there was the issue of his family.

His grandfather was the Mad Russian, an international psychopath with enough atrocities in his name to rank him up with the worst of the 20th Century supervillains, like Doctor Death or the Armageddon Krew. He was able to bring the forces of law and order to their knees in his time. But his time was, of course, firmly in the Cold War-era, well before Dan was even born. Since disappearing five years ago without a trace, the Mad Russian was generally written off as killed or otherwise indisposed. But now Dan heard his grandfather was back in town, not dead at all. He wondered what Alsana would make of that. Not that he'd ever volunteer that information. He wasn't stupid.

And after being apprehended, tried in a juvenile court and finally up-cycled, Dan was working for the greater good on a regular basis. Redemption had no payment, but Alsana often laughed that it was good for his soul.

He wasn't the only one, of course. The beauty of the up-cycled program was that a handful of uberhuman juvenile delinquents moved through the courts every year and those who were convicted were slapped with the program. In some cases, especially up north in Sydney, ubers with useful and impressive powers were trained to work in government-funded teams of law enforcers. It was a case of giving back to the community. In Melbourne, things were more low-key. Alsana had only three or four ubers on her books at any one time, and deployed them as she saw fit. The program was deliberately vague when it came to the duration of service. Dan had been a part of it since he was thirteen. There were others who had been in longer. In the end it seemed to depend on how useful an uber was. If they were more of a pest than an asset then they were generally let go after a few months. And so, Dan tried his best to irritate without getting into worse trouble.

"This is a training exercise," Alsana said, keeping her eyes on the land cruiser below them. Dan blew into his hands to keep them warm.

"We've never had training before."

Her eyes shifted to him and he shrugged. It wasn't as if he was ever going to disagree with Alsana for more than a few jousts anyway, so Dan dropped his protests and focused his senses down below where a man in his fifties was talking on his cell phone while negotiating a tight exit from a parallel park.

The man was a married solicitor who had been doing the dirty with Alsana for about six months. Dan was gently appalled by the whole prospect, but also amused to finally find a chink in his handler's armor. She'd always been so efficiently inhuman. It was nice to find out her life was just as messed up as his.

"Phone line is clear. It's his wife."

Dan could hear the conversation inside his head, electrical impulses that were intercepted and decoded. The man was distraught, his voice punctuated with sobs and pauses.

Dan found his pleas a little boring, but the gist of the conversation was one of admission and repentance.

"He told her about the affair," Dan said. "Promised that it didn't mean anything. I think I saw this episode already."

"What did he say, *exactly*?" Alsana turned around and looked away, back towards the stairwell. Her posture was stiff. Dan knew it was dangerous for him to be too frank, even though he was desperate for some payback. Alsana never treated him with anything close to kindness.

She was a horrible person.

But she wasn't his enemy.

Dan closed his eyes, going for a theatrical stance in case she watched him. He lifted his left hand, fingers splayed, as if he was reading the broadcast. The truth was he received it instantly and translated it just as quickly.

"He's saying that it wasn't love," Dan said.

"His words."

"Right," Dan said, awkwardness flooding through him. "I don't love her, never did. I'd never hurt you."

Alsana clucked her tongue.

"What else?" she asked.

"The wife is crying, saying she feels cheated."

"Words, Galkin, words."

"Right. It's not that easy, you know? I'm not a voice recorder."

"That's exactly what you are," Alsana said. "A device."

Dan remembered how much he hated her, but he still couldn't translate all of the hurtful details.

"I'll never forgive you. You're a … well, she's not happy. But then he kind of grabs for her attention with something about their kids."

Alsana walked off towards the exit, strong, deliberate steps.

"There's a lot of swearing," Dan called after her. She was hurting, but it was her own fault. What did she actually expect, Dan wondered, as if her little affair was going to end differently. He gave a last glance down to the car and followed her.

Back in the office, Dan cranked up the heating with his mind and took a seat opposite Alsana's cluttered desk. There were always piles of reports on the desk and he wondered how much of the up-cycled program was kept on hard copy. Of course, he'd sneaked a look at the computer files hundreds of times, but she always seemed to have the mountains of files on her desk. His eyes darted to the small fan she had next to a reading light. Dan bit his lip and resisted the urge to turn it on and send the papers spiraling through the room. She didn't look at him as he crossed his feet in front of him and stifled a yawn. She shuffled some of the papers into her top drawer and put on her reading glasses which made her look older. It also made her a little more approachable and he felt a rising guilt in his stomach, like he maybe did owe her something after all these years.

"Do you want me to blow up his car?" Dan asked.

"What?" she snapped, eyes narrowed for a moment before she ignored his comment and booted up her laptop. "Forget it."

"I could…"

She stopped him with a sharp, severe intake of breath which rushed up her nostrils, flaring them slightly. It was business. Whatever happened on the rooftop was over. Dan wondered why the guy had parked out the front of the office and how convenient it was, but then realized he probably came to see Alsana. Maybe for the last time.

"Do you have a job for me?" he asked, instead of thinking more about Alsana's messed-up life.

Her eyes moved back to the laptop for a moment before she turned it around for him to see. A photograph of Miranda Brody smiled out at him. Dan wondered why the girl kept popping up into his world all of a sudden. The screen's image was from a promotional concert poster. Miranda's headshot was flanked by six monsters, which looked like prosthetic and makeup until he read the words, and realized the heads belonged to ubers.

"The Human Tour?" he asked. "Isn't that kind of insulting?"

"To you, perhaps. You'll be working for Miranda Brody's management team," Alsana said, as if she were reading from a particularly dull pamphlet. Her eyes were locked on to him over her dipped reading glasses and Dan knew she was waiting for his usual arguments.

Despite his best efforts Dan was still obliged to work for her, and while it usually entailed surveillance work or decryptions using his powers, Alsana wasn't too particular about what she got him to do. For four years he was required to sign in every fortnight, attend seminars on responsibility and civic duty, convince the counselors that he wasn't lapsing into criminal tendencies, and do whatever it was that Alsana Owens deemed necessary for his rehabilitation.

He had been a teenage super-villain for two weeks. And no one was going to let him forget about it.

"So what would I actually do?" Dan asked.

"You tag along," Alsana said. "There's been some little

problems in the States and something in Indonesia, so we've been asked to send you in."

"Security?"

She sniffed and shook her head.

"If it was a security issue, they'd send in a professional. No, this Brody girl has a thing for freaks. Her management has agreed to let you in as surveillance. Turns out you've already met their security detail tonight. They seem to like your look, they're interested in your powers, but don't want anything more than a visually appealing footnote, okay? No heroics."

She laughed and swung her chair around so she could stand up.

"I told them not to worry about that," Alsana continued. "Danny's not the heroic type."

Dan remained silent. He knew it would be a few more minutes before Alsana would allow him to leave, so he purposefully looked at the window. It was dark outside, clouds smothering the stars and moon.

"You've got a meet and greet tomorrow night," she said, moving around behind him as she cut laps in her office. "They've requested you dress in black, nothing too flashy, nothing too off the rack."

Dan set his jaw and bided his time.

"Then you'll be given details on the concert. Aren't you the luckiest little uber-crim in the world?"

"Can I go now?" Dan asked. "It's past my bedtime."

"You can thank me," she said instead. "Anytime now. I mean, people would think you'd prefer the alternative than to be this little princess's play thing."

Alsana never offered alternatives. They were phantoms,

like fringe benefits or the concept of a personal life in her eyes. But Dan also knew she required penance and she liked to talk her way into clever conversation.

"What alternative?"

"Prison, wearing those orange jumpsuits and scrubbing the floors of the shower block. A part of me would love to see you there, Danny, of course I would, but prison isn't actually a very nice place."

She smiled and Dan felt like walking out. He knew how the conversation would play out, but he didn't go anywhere. If he did anything stupid, she would reprimand him, write up an incident report, and he'd have to go back through the counseling course. So, instead, he sat and waited.

"But you know that anyway, don't you?" she said. He knew what he was supposed to say, to do. He was supposed to get angry, maybe fry some circuits. "Do you even remember daddy's face?"

"Not so much," Dan said and stood up, avoiding her cruel face. There were bright flashes at the corner of his eyes, threatening to bring up memories from the plaza five years before. But he wasn't going to let her play him so easily. He picked up his satchel and slung it over his shoulder as he turned to the door. Alsana made it back to her desk and she leaned on it, studying him. Dan figured a full lap of the office was enough of a lecture. He reached for the handle.

"Disappointing."

"Get used to it," he said "So the meet and greet is at six? I'll be there."

"You'll need this," Alsana said.

He turned back, reluctantly, and looked at a silver wrist band on her desk. The Human Tour was clearly visible and his mind could detect subtle electricity within the silver band. He recognized it as a security tag. State of the art but still just a way to label a person.

"Thanks," he said, took it in a quick swipe, and headed for the door again.

He could feel Alsana's eyes on his back as he left but she made no more sound. Outside the office he walked past the security camera which fed directly into Alsana's office, and then jogged down the front steps, eyes closed as the cold air greeted him.

Stupid.

It was pointless to aggravate Alsana, and Dan knew it.

As he walked down the street he wondered how Miranda's people found out about him. He remembered the security guy outside the hotel, but it still seemed a stretch for them to put everything together, especially in the one night.

But it was late and Dan just needed to find a place to crash. Even though he hated the idea of it, he found himself on the route to his work. Each step seemed like another reminder at how pathetic he had become.

"Can I crash here tonight?"

Dan had his hoody pulled up against the rain, but the light from inside Birdie's back room sliced across his face and made him blink. The woman who opened the door didn't look surprised to see him. Her mouth was loose around a sad looking cigarette, and her painted-on eyebrows were frozen-serious. She rubbed her hands dry on an apron and let the door open wider for Dan before heading back to cleaning the grills and fry-pits, cigarette ash dispersed in her wake. Tabitha lived above the shop and knew the owner, Marco, from some trip to Europe. She'd managed to score a cash-only job cleaning his place when she rocked up in Melbourne a few years before. She wasn't an especially nice person, but she generally let others ruin their own lives and got on about the business of ruining her own. Since Dan started working at Birdie's he'd heard about the procession of dead-beat boyfriends and late-night hospital visits. Some stories were back-room myth, some were true. Tonight, though, he just wanted to sleep it all away and work out his problems in the morning. Besides, Dan had all the unpleasant personalities he could handle with Alsana.

Marco had a small office in the back of the shop, and while he only ever visited in the weeks before the end of financial year, or when there was someone to hire or fire; the office was kept spotless. This was because of the electronic key lock on the door rather than through any sense of loyalty from the employees.

Dan dropped his satchel on the floor and leaned against one of the benches Tabitha had already cleaned. He looked around and figured she had another twenty minutes to go, and because he didn't want her to see him break into the office, he decided to watch her instead.

Her hair was tied up on either side of her face in thick piggy tails, but she wasn't a young woman and wore it that way for practical purposes rather than vanity. In fact, apart from the eyebrows, Tabitha seemed to be devoid of any kind of self-love. She worked without talking, rubbing at the benches with a cloth after a spray of disinfectant, all the while chewing on the end of her cigarette. Dan would have opted for headphones and music to get him through the shift, but Tabitha didn't even hum or do the little shuffle-dance he'd seen some of the girls do at closing time. She just worked her way through.

"Have you got another one of those?" he asked as she moved past him to grab the stringy broom which hung behind the back door. She looked at him and took it down, banging it twice on the side of the bench to dislodge any dust.

Dan pointed.

"Another cigarette?" he asked.

She leaned the broom against the bench and pulled out the stub from her mouth, crushing it into the bench top. Her eyes were on him, and Dan felt like pulling the hoody back up and just waiting for her to go. Instead, she walked towards him and pulled out a crumpled packet of smokes.

"These are mine," she said. "You want to kill yourself; you buy your own, okay?"

"Just asking," Dan said.

"Just telling. Now get your ass out of the kitchen so I can finish up. And if you come here again after tonight, I'm gonna tell Marco."

Dan shook his head and smiled at her.

"Figures."

"You think you have problems?" she asked, stepping back into his space. "You're a kid, you have no idea what life can throw at you. Sure, you're whining because your mummy came in and embarrassed you today, showed everyone that you're a freak."

Dan felt his fists clench over the bench top. She

shouldn't have known about that, he'd made sure the cameras were wiped and none of the other staff would dare talk to Tabitha. He'd even paid the new kid twenty dollars to keep his mouth shut.

The kitchen lights flickered.

"Suck up your pride, Dan," Tabitha said. "Apologize to whoever you ticked off and go back to your little suburban life, okay? Blue skin or not, you've still got a mum and I bet you still have your prissy friends. Don't think you've got it tough."

She picked up the broom again and started to shove it hard across the floor, sweeping thick lines along the linoleum. Dan grabbed his bag and slipped out of the kitchen. He pressed his hand against the office keypad, scrambled the signals and pushed into the small room.

It smelled of rice.

But it was dark and secure and Tabitha would be going away up to her apartment and out of his life. And in the morning, Dan had a feeling he'd play it all over again, only this time he wouldn't have anywhere else to be kicked out of.

CHAPTER 8
MIRANDA

THE THICK HOTEL curtains held back the day as Miranda woke suddenly, the smell of fuel in the room, a shriek clutched at the very edge of her consciousness. She had been dreaming of Jakarta again.

The boy had died. Her legal team briefed her late the night before, but it still didn't feel real, or else she wanted it to feel *more* real, like it actually mattered. Her manager declared the whole situation unfortunate but not anything to worry about – legally. Miranda wanted to know how things got so messed up, how it didn't seem to really matter if someone died. But having the boy up on her stage, smiling like they shared some secret and then burning himself to death; Miranda wanted it to mean something.

Anything.

She got dressed and sprayed deodorant around the room. The vanilla scent masked her dreams and reminded her of the early days when she and her sister played at being rock stars in cheap hotel rooms, while her mother cleaned. Miranda looked at the large suite around her and felt the absence of her family deeper. Even the music had changed now she was famous. Her fingers ached for her guitar. She missed the feeling of the nylon strings, the sensation of strumming, the connection between her hands and her voice. It was gone now, outsourced to the faceless band. All she had left was her voice, and even that had been transformed.

Made better.

She picked up her tablet and ran her fingers across its surface. She flicked the screens of her schedule, her eyes taking in media appointments, choreography and then the Big Event in the evening where she would be singing and smiling and hopefully making the record companies and distributors very happy.

She tossed the tablet on the bed and walked to the window, pulling it across as she stepped from one end to the other, letting in the light which looked somehow different to the California sun she knew so well. It was brighter here, or perhaps whiter. She looked down at the street and saw a number of people walking past. There were no large crowds like the night before, no screaming fans or probing journalists. She smiled. Perhaps it would be a better day.

There was a knock on the door and she turned as it opened. The man only barely fit through the door, his head nearly scraping the top. He wore a dark suit which looked brand new, and barely concealed his enormous wrestler's physique. He bowed his head slightly and stepped in, closing the door behind him.

"Sully," Miranda said with more relief than she expected. She ran to him and leapt, wrapping her arms around his neck and burying her face in his shirt. He smelled of jasmine.

"How are you, little one?" he asked softly, holding her

up like a father would. He gently kissed her head and then she reluctantly slid out of his embrace and shrugged her shoulders.

"I don't know," she admitted. "Better than the boy in Jakarta."

Sully frowned. And then he touched her arm, no words necessary. She quickly showed him the suite and walked to the balcony. Sully nodded his approval at the view and then stroked his black beard, looking closely at Miranda.

"This riot last night, it has made you a little melancholy," he said, like he had assessed her as they walked through the suite. "Too much pressure cannot be good for one so young."

It was his usual speech. She turned away from him and looked down at the street again, the breeze blowing her hair back.

"You were younger than me when you started your career," she said. "You've told me enough times, and I know you don't really think I'm too young, or too naïve."

"Perhaps."

"No," she said, turning on him with a smile. "Not perhaps. You know this is nothing to me."

Miranda stopped as she realized the words which had come out. Sully raised his eyebrows. He seemed amused.

"I mean it doesn't bother me, no stress. Those kids last night just wanted to get close, to see me in the flesh instead of on websites or whatever. It's part of the job. There wasn't any protest, no hatred. I wasn't in any danger, not really."

"And what about the boy?"

Miranda had a flash of the burning boy again. She clenched her jaw and pushed the image away, replacing it deliberately with memories of Box Springs Mountain, its reddish hue reminding her of childhood summers, with just Miranda and her dad.

"The pizza boy?" Sully added.

"Who?"

"The boy last night, the one who came to your rescue," Sully said, enjoying himself. His short dark beard only barely hid the grin.

Miranda hadn't actually seen the pizza boy; she'd been surprised by the weight of the crowd, especially since she only planned to go for a short stroll to clear her head. But her security detail showed her CCTV footage of the boy from the hotel cameras: a scrawny blonde kid in a striped blue and white shirt.

"What about him?"

"He is entourage," Sully said. He was making fun of her. "Three local uberhumans for the final show. This young man is on security detail with me; the others are dancers, I believe."

"Hang on," Miranda said. "Back up a bit. That pizza kid is my bodyguard?"

"No, Miranda. I, as always, will be your bodyguard. The boy will assist us. He has very interesting abilities."

Miranda shook her head.

"What? He can flip a pizza?"

Sully shrugged.

"That I do not know, but he has an affinity with electrical devices, quite useful for us. Last night he diffused the crowds and allowed you your privacy. For that, I think, you should … how do you say it? Cut him some slack?"

"You're a comedian," she said.

"At one time, perhaps," Sully said. "But today I am simply

your Sully. And as your Sully, may I turn your attention away from boys for the moment and to more peaceful, dare I suggest, relaxing pursuits. We have organized two excursions out from the city, for your pleasure. The first is to visit with those koala bears you were interested in."

"I was only half serious," she said.

"Then you will be at least half very happy. And that is an improvement from what I see here this morning. The second excursion will be tonight after the party. You will be flying to an island. Very exotic, some friends of yours from Hollywood are having their own private party. Very private. You will be able to relax."

"Maybe," she said. She didn't really have many friends, let alone ones she could relax with. And the ones from Hollywood were hardly going to give her a break. Mostly they were keeping her close so they could exploit her if she made it big. She knew the friendships would only last as long as her music career maintained its top ten status. After that she would be sent packing, back to Riverside.

"That sounds great, actually," she mumbled.

Sully nodded and checked his silver watch. It was a habit and Miranda knew he hardly ever noted what the time actually was. He gave the room a second glance from the balcony, and then bowed his head to her, smiling widely.

"We will see these koala bears after breakfast," he said. "Until then, I have to untangle some of that red tape these government people like to spin whenever a celebrity comes to their shores."

"What's wrong?"

"Nothing," he said, waving his hand. "It's just a matter of clearing the use of uberhumans on the tour. They have agencies here to monitor ubers, interestingly they have an employment agency also. Australians!"

Sully's laugh echoed through the suite as he waved goodbye again and left, leaving Miranda out on the balcony enjoying the morning sunshine. The idea of going to an animal sanctuary suddenly sounded good. Australian animals surely wouldn't be impressed by her.

As he inserted his room card into the slot, Sully could sense someone was already inside. He wasn't psychic, but he was right; so when the door clicked and he pushed it open, Sully gave the man in the pinstripe suit a casual glance before ignoring him.

"Good morning, Mister Sully," the man said. He spoke with an English accent: private education, born into money.

Sully took off his jacket and hung it carefully. His back and shoulder muscles flexed in the man's direction. Sully was not about to be intimidated.

"My name is Curtis," the man continued. Sully caught a smirk on the man's face in the narrow mirror. "I'm here on business, from Mister Klein."

Thurston Klein was Miranda's manager, as well as the one who signed Sully's cheques each month. A self-serving entertainment expert, Klein managed to position Miranda at the right places at the right times, and even Sully admitted there was some form of art in that.

"I have never heard of you, Mister Curtis," Sully said. "You bring bad news."

"Terribly sad, what happened in Indonesia," Curtis said.

"A boy like that; in front of all those cameras, those adoring fans."

Sully remembered the concert, remembered the boy and his five seconds of fame. But it wasn't the boy's face which kept him awake at night. It wasn't the tragedy of his death. It was the effect it had on Miranda which troubled him so much more. She was nineteen, a child, really; even if she would never admit it. And Sully could still see the horror on her face, the shock, the brutal awakening, as the boy smiled his way into death to please her.

Sully said nothing. His fingers loosened the shirt from around his neck before carefully undoing the top three buttons. It was good to be able to breathe again, he thought.

"Unfortunately this whole mess in Indonesia won't be fixed with apologies and sad faces, Mister Sully. The girl needs to shake it off, laugh at the whole thing, take it in her god-damned stride."

Miranda would never laugh it off. And that was why Sully worked for her, to protect the integrity, the beauty which held court in her mind and body.

"Do you have a message from Mister Klein, perhaps?" Sully asked.

Curtis opened his palm and gestured to the table, deeper within the room. Sully's eyes tracked the movement and took in a sophisticated laptop and projector. Sometimes Klein would negotiate terms via the internet, or hold conferences across continents. Personally, Sully preferred the face to face negotiations, but perhaps Klein was reluctant because of Sully's physical presence. He didn't blame the man, of course.

Curtis shifted to the laptop, tapped the keyboard twice

and a beam of light spread from the projector to the blank wall over Sully's bed. Klein's bald head appeared a little too large on the flat wall, the perspective a little off, transforming him into something not quite human.

"Salaam," Sully said.

"Is it morning over there?" Klein asked. "Did I wake you, Suleyman?"

"It is not inconvenient. And you have, as always, my full attention, Mister Klein."

"I've sent Curtis to assist with these latest developments," Klein said. "Miranda needs to use this or she's finished. I can't work miracles, Suleyman, no matter how hard I try."

Sully shrugged.

"Miracles are not our vocation, Mister Klein."

"This is make or break," the manager said. "If she has a breakdown, good. If she goes a little crazy, even better. But we can't have her moping around when every damned teenager on the planet is looking to her right now."

"We all react to these things differently," Sully said.

"No kidding. I'm saying, and I'm saying it very clearly to you, right now Sully. If she doesn't react, and react in the way we need her to, then I'm cutting her off. She can go and sing country and western for all I care. We need razzle, here. We need drama, movement, insanity if we can muster it."

Curtis moved to stand a little to Sully's side. In his hand was a briefcase, silver and sleek. Sully hadn't seen it before.

"Perhaps we should give her more time," Sully suggested. "The rest of the tour has been quite successful."

"Successful?" Klein shouted, his face turning a little red despite being plastered across the hotel wall. "You aren't here, Suleyman. Here, in the heart of things, she is a complete disaster. A complete farce, from Seattle to bloody Indonesia. Her girl-next-door game doesn't wash with the fans anymore. They want extreme."

Klein wiped his mouth with the back of his hand as he realized he was losing his composure.

"Perhaps I should continue?" asked Curtis. His clipped voice was in stark contrast to Klein's rant. The manager nodded his head and reached for a glass of water, off-screen. "We have a solution," Curtis continued. "It will require a little game of cat-and-mouse, but ultimately harmless to all concerned."

Sully wondered what kind of cat-and-mouse game was ever harmless. He had known a number of mice in his time and none of them had ever reminisced happily about being the subject of a game.

Curtis handed him the suitcase. It was lightweight, with a chain and cuff dangling from the handle.

"Inside this briefcase is our young lady's salvation."

"Possible," Klein added, leaning forward on the screen, his face filling the wall again. "Possible salvation. I'm not even one hundred per cent certain she has a chance anymore."

"Go on, Mister Curtis," Sully said, testing the strength of the chain and its overall design.

"The financial people want publicity, which translates into sales and profits, of course. The Human Tour has been somewhat lackluster in that department up until now. There was hope that with the buzz surrounding that poor boy's death on stage, but… well, things didn't turn out as planned."

Sully's eyes narrowed, but Curtis was unimpressed.

"Our people in Los Angeles and London have begun

work on a new angle for our dear Miranda, but it requires a little prop at this end of the operation."

Curtis smiled and moved his hand to caress the air above the briefcase.

"What's inside?" Sully asked.

"Air and magic," Curtis said. "The magic of innuendo, the sorcery of scandal. Our people will generate a story and you will simply be required to carry this briefcase in your entourage."

"You don't need to know anything more about it," Klein said.

"There is one other thing," Curtis said.

"There always is," Sully said.

"Quite. There is a boy, an Australian boy; and our people require that he be a part of this attempt at salvation. Kind of a balance, perhaps, bringing in this new, living boy to replace the burnt-out one from the last concert."

Sully ignored the crass comments and turned to Klein.

"What boy?"

"All in good time," Curtis continued. "It's all set up, Mister Sully. You just need to do your job and we shall do ours."

"And if you don't do it, Suleyman," Klein said. "We've always understood each other. If you don't do this, then we part company."

"Of course," Sully said, and bowed slightly to the screen. "There is always, in your line of business, Mister Klein, a point when the snake can no longer take the risk of basking in the glory and profit of a fading sun."

Klein sat back, his lips turning into a smile as he shook his head.

"It has been a pleasure, Suleyman. A real pleasure."

And then the connection was cut and Sully found himself alone with the Englishman. Curtis closed the laptop and began to pack it into a larger briefcase.

"Is it a bomb, then?" Sully asked. But it was Curtis's turn to ignore the comments in the room. He clicked the case shut and straightened himself, turning at last to Sully who stood between him and the door.

"A bomb to kill the boy?" Sully asked again, louder.

"I simply cannot answer, Mister Sully," Curtis said, slowly. Sully noticed the man's eyes were hard. His voice was pleasant enough, but there was nothing pleasant about what lay behind Curtis's eyes. "The boy will be the only one who can unlock the case, when it is time."

"How? Who is this boy?"

"Your little delivery boy, Mister Sully. I know you've already been prepped on his addition to the entourage, and now you know why."

"You overestimate my knowledge, Mister Curtis."

"Quite possibly, and yet, there is something about you which does not add up. You aren't exactly hired muscle, are you, Mister Sully? No, and when the boy comes to meet Miss Miranda at the airport in the morning, it is then that you will ask him to open the case. If you don't do this, then we move to Plan B."

"How many will be hurt, do you think?"

Curtis smiled.

"What if I took her away from all of this?" Sully said, possibly more to himself than to Curtis. "What if she didn't want this life you have made for her anymore?"

"Well, I suppose we shall just have to wait and see."

Miranda had been at the rehearsal for twenty minutes before she got to step up to the stage. Her retainers were elsewhere, preparations underway, so she walked to the performance space by herself.

The last time up in front of the crowds was still fresh in her mind, but she didn't feel the anxiety or fear as she walked out under the bright lights. The seats were empty. A few maintenance people moved about the rows and she saw a small crowd of security reviewing exits, but there were no fans there.

Just her on the stage.

The arena could hold 15,000 fans, apparently, and from overhearing Christie on his phone earlier, she had already sold over 12,000. It wasn't the biggest concert she'd played, and there was disappointment in Christie's voice. Somehow 12,000 wasn't good enough. She turned her attention back to the stage spreading out around her. She walked up the steps to a platform which would lift her higher still on the night.

This was the entry point. She would come in from the roof, the platform like an elevator from the heavens.

One of the dancers was there at the top, stretching one leg like a ballerina up above her head. She had bright pink skin and ornate blue tattoos up and down her arms. As Miranda came closer, the girl smiled at her and more tattoos emerged on her face, the ink welling up from within her to make the intricate swirls of blue.

"I'm Kyla," the girl said, switching her legs.

"Miranda." She felt foolish for saying that and sunk her

hands deeper into the pockets of her jacket. "Have you performed here before?"

The girl shook her head.

"First time," she said. "I've been here for the tennis though. Roof was open. Beautiful day."

Miranda looked to the roof which was sealed. Her team had transformed the stadium into a concert hall, but she knew it would be easy enough to change back. Everything about this business moved quickly.

Kyla slid slowly to the floor in a perfectly controlled split. Miranda could tell the girl was a trained dancer. She was surrounded by professionals even if she felt like a phony the whole time.

"When did you... I mean, when did you know you were uber?" Miranda asked.

"I was born like this," Kyla said. "Pink skin, you know, but the ink came later. I can't do anything useful or anything."

"It's beautiful."

"It's freakish, come on," Kyla said and laughed. Miranda laughed too and then waved goodbye, leaving Kyla to her warm-ups. Todd Christie appeared at the bottom of the steps, his face sweating under the lights. He gestured to her and she stepped down, her hands still in her pockets.

"The pyrotechnics will be housed here," he said, waving to a raised section either side of a runway. "And along here. Insurance was a nightmare, but we've got the flare guns for the girls."

Miranda hadn't wanted the fire routine, but management had insisted. Said it was a tribute to Jakarta. Christie passed her a stylized ray-gun and she hefted it in her hands, testing its weight. She hadn't ever handled a real gun, but it felt lighter than it should have.

"Do I get to shoot one?" she asked, striking a slow-motion pose, aiming the gun at the invisible crowd.

"God no," Christie said, taking it away from her. "Can you imagine the costs if you got hurt? Leave it to the rest of us, princess."

Miranda frowned as he stashed the gun along with the others in the box. Everything about the Australian show was beginning to look like her swan song. Christie hardly met her eyes, probably knowing she was finished.

The party that night was a last chance to hold on to her career. Sully knew it, although he wouldn't admit it. Christie certainly knew it too. The Human Tour was coming to a close, and Miranda wasn't sure what she would be doing after the final act.

A part of her wanted to slip back into obscurity.

She could ride her bikes in the mountains, kick up mud and camp for a week with her dad. She could fold everything back where it came from and go back to Riverside.

Miranda shifted her eyes back to the seating as posters unfurled along columns at each of the levels. Her frozen-smile face stared back at her from the promotional photo-graphs: so confident, her stars aligned.

CHAPTER 9

DAN

DAN FOUND IT difficult to take his eyes off the electric billboard advertising The Human Tour. It featured a carousel of images meant to capture the freakishness of ubers with extreme close-ups of fangs and feathered appendages, flaming hair and cracking fireworks. He stood outside in the rain for a long time. If he went inside he was selling out. If he left the assignment he was inviting trouble Alsana-style.

The billboard glowed above him, wiping the images away with large letters spelling out Miranda's name. The crowds behind him exploded into cheers and shouts. The two suited gatekeepers at the door looked at him with impassive faces. Most of the guests had already arrived.

"Are you in or out?" asked one of the men in suits.

"I think I'm in," Dan said and stepped forward, raising his hand so the security band was visible. The man scanned it and nodded him through.

There was no sign of Brody at the party, but everyone was talking about her. Some of the guests were wearing prosthetic *freak chic*. One woman stood with impressive iridescent wings spread out behind her, while two men played at being conjoined twins. Dan ignored them but wondered briefly how his grandfather would feel about regular people pretending to be ubers. Waiters moved in and around the crowds with thin glasses of champagne, and expensive food plated up on silver trays. The drinks seemed more decorated than the sparse black décor around them and the music system was state of the art. Dan recognized a handful of the guests from television but most were just regular people in party clothes.

"Are you lost?" a girl asked him. "Or just wearing a puppy dog face?"

She was skinny and had a pixie face with sparkling almond-shaped eyes and a turned up nose. Her hair was short and sculpted and her body was sheathed in a dark green dress. She carried a slender glass of champagne and studied him with a deliberate glint in her eye.

"This is just my normal face, I'm afraid."

"Hardly normal."

Dan blushed and wondered how things had slipped from being an unobtrusive observer to being the one studied. The girl handed him the glass and he took it with a smile of thanks. She lifted her arm and without even looking at the waiter moving past her, managed to scoop another two glasses from the tray.

"Drink up," she said, taking a sip from her fresh glass.

Dan finished her first one and then exchanged it for the next, the girl passing the empty glass to another waiter.

"Smooth," he said.

"You're the sparky aren't you?" she asked. Her free hand fingered his jacket, bringing them closer together. He was taller than her, perhaps by half a head, but she managed to control his movement, guiding him along and into the party.

"I'm Dan," he said

"Evie."

She finished her glass and then reached out to take Dan's, draining it and freeing their hands as another waiter passed. She glanced towards the dance floor. Miranda's music was still playing and professional dancers were appointed in strategic positions amongst the rest of the party-goers. One of the dancers whipped her prehensile hair in circles, the dreadlocked threads moving like spider legs in the air. Another dancer had pink skin tattooed with blue hieroglyphs. Dan felt himself drawn towards the dancers. He took a breath of Evie's perfume, caught up in her like he hadn't been for a long time, and then he let her pull him along. With each step he felt more distant from everything. The techno-treatment favored a strong beat and as he and Evie moved into the first wave of people, Dan began to lose himself in it. The lights pulsed – visually as well as electronically – and he felt the energy all around him.

Miranda Brody arrived in between orchestrated song changes and the sudden focus away from the dance floor gave Dan a chance to retreat from the intensity of the room. His senses were heightened, his body overcharged and ready to explode. At other times when he felt like he'd absorbed too much power from the world around him, Dan had been anxious and tried to shut down his whole body, but the party had given him a different take on things. Everything was exploding around him – music, lights, party people, and Evie. Everything was let loose, free. He couldn't remember a time recently when he'd felt so unencumbered by the crap that seemed to follow him through his life. It didn't seem to matter that he had no friends, that he'd just been kicked out of his house.

He accepted another drink from a waiter and as he closed his fingers around the slender glass he saw the blue flashes of electricity just under his skin. Dan smiled, biting his lip, feeling it coursing through his body, feeling it numbing his tongue.

"A celebration beyond expectation," a deep voice rumbled near Dan's ear and as he turned around he saw the bearded head of Miranda Brody's bodyguard: the strongest, most muscle-bound man Dan had ever seen in real life. Sully had his arms crossed and was wearing a turban matching his dark purple tie and an expensive looking black suit. Dan glanced down at his own t-shirt and jacket. He couldn't help it.

Sully took the glass out of Dan's hand and passed it off to another one of Miranda's people who was standing behind him. The man's dark eyes pinned Dan in place and he felt a little withered, the energy dancing under his skin all across his body suddenly thinned.

"Come," Sully commanded and led Dan by the arm to a booth along one of the walls. Dan looked around for Evie but she had melted into the crowds that were pushing to the center of the space, presumably towards Miranda.

Dan slid into the booth and crossed his own arms, mimicking the large Middle Eastern man opposite. Sully didn't seem to notice. Instead, the bodyguard placed a case onto the table. It looked like it was stainless steel. Dan saw the blurred reflection of the world around him in its shiny surface.

"This is a briefcase," Sully said slowly. Dan nodded, trying not to grin. It didn't seem like the big man smiled much at all, and Dan didn't want to be the one who looked like a fool. As Alsana was clear to point out, this was a professional job.

"It sure looks like a briefcase."

"This is an important briefcase," Sully continued. "It will become your responsibility for the next 48 hours."

"Is it full of cash?"

"It is not full of cash."

"Drugs?"

Sully's eyes narrowed and Dan shrugged and looked down at the case.

It was silver and sleek, and he noticed there was a computer code latch instead of a lock on the top. He could hear the soft hum of the circuitry as he ran his fingertips over the surface, his genetic code calling out to the electronic one. Even with his attention on Sully, Dan was absently working out the algorithms, reading them like a familiar tune.

"Your assignment is to carry this case with you when you collect Miss Brody tomorrow morning from the airport. Do not attempt to lose it."

"The airport," Dan said, nodding while still trying to unlock the case with his mind.

"She will be arriving on an early flight from an undisclosed location," Sully continued. "You will not be late. And you will bring this case with you."

"I thought she was here."

"She is here, presently," Sully said.

"But not all night?"

"Miss Brody will be required elsewhere after this engagement. You, however, shall not."

"Be required?"

"No, not until the morning. Do not lose it."

"So what's in it, really?" Dan asked, although he was more interested in why Sully thought he might try to lose it rather than crack it open. He'd already established it wasn't money.

"Important documents," Sully said finally.

"Why don't you carry them?"

Sully was intimidating, Dan didn't mind admitting that to himself, but there was also something noble about him. He looked at a person when he spoke to them and he thought before he responded.

"Carry this at all times," Sully said again. He turned the case towards Dan and then reached out, gripped Dan's wrist and snapped the chain to his security bracelet. The clicking sound cut through the music somehow.

"Isn't that a bit over the top?" Dan asked, testing the length of the thin chain.

"In this business it is not about realities but more about perceptions of realities."

"Are you sure you're a bodyguard?"

Sully raised his eyebrows and said nothing. Dan looked closer at the band and the chain. He gave it another tug. His vision blurred a little and he stretched his shoulders. The music crushed in on him, his hearing and sight numbed for a second.

"You're the boss, I guess," Dan said. "So I keep this on, make it look important and pick up your girl tomorrow at the airport?"

"You would think it was a simple task, wouldn't you?" Sully asked, probably more to himself than to Dan. "There is no key-code."

"Uh-huh."

"You will be the only one who can open it," Sully said. "With your gifts, you will be able to access the ever-changing sequence of numbers when we require it to become not locked."

Dan could feel the whir of the changing code. Even while speaking with Sully, his mind was tracking the changes, calibrating the sequence and then chasing it to the next series of numbers.

"Couldn't I get this tomorrow?"

"It is better if you get it tonight, now. As I mentioned already, Miss Brody has another engagement later this evening and we will not be seeing you again until the airport."

Dan shrugged. There was something irritating about the band around his wrist. The metal wasn't like the briefcase and it had tightened. Really tight. His skin itched already.

A waiter arrived and offered them more drinks. Sully ignored the man entirely. Dan picked up a glass but then returned it quickly under Sully's unrelenting stare. Dan figured the sooner he left the large man, the sooner he could sneak another drink and try to shake off what was probably the start of a headache.

"It's a little tight," Dan said.

Sully looked over Dan's shoulder at some change in the party.

The crowd beyond the booth shifted suddenly, people moving backward as another group made its way across the room. Standing close to seven feet tall, Sully had no trouble seeing the group coming, but Dan had to settle for watching the shifting edges of the crowd.

Three corporates emerged, flanked by more colorful young people, all impeccably groomed. One of them must have been Miranda Brody, Dan thought. Following just behind the young people came a slick documentary film crew with headsets, miniature cameras and attitude. And then he saw her. She wore a white t-shirt and a tartan skirt with her bare midriff showing. While everyone seemed enthralled by her, Miranda didn't seem to notice. It was a totally different girl from the night before when she had been harried by her fans. This Miranda was in full control. The cameraman weaved ahead of her but she didn't give the impression she cared.

It was clear Sully didn't like the crew though. He folded his arms across his impressive chest. Dan could read body language. He worked in retail, after all.

"Is this the freak boy?" one of the men asked.

"Yes, Mister Christie," another said, nodding.

Dan felt amused rather than insulted. It might have been the champagne from earlier. Mister Christie had a shiny face and thin, slicked back hair. Dan didn't like him at all.

"Is he all set for the assignment?" Christie asked.

Sully nodded.

"It's alright, Mister Christie. Let's enjoy the night," Miranda said.

While most of the posse glanced in his direction only

Miranda looked directly at him. She kept her gaze on him as the other people began chatting around Sully who had left the booth and now stood silently in their midst. Dan stumbled to his feet, not wanting to be at any more of a disadvantage in this sea suddenly full of sharks.

"So I guess you hate my music," she said as he stood.

Her lips moved deliberately, slowly. She knew he saw her watching him. She was used to being the focus of everyone's attention.

Her dark hair was styled in wavy ringlets that danced on her shoulders.

"It hurts my ears," Dan said, pointing at the side of his head.

They looked at each other like cats while the people, 'her people', stood and waited for the conversation to unfold. Dan knew it wasn't a real conversation and so did Miranda. It was choreographed posturing, but after a few days of mundane routine he felt like an excursion into the surreal world of celebrity. His only other alternative would be to crawl back to his apartment and watch television.

Then he remembered he didn't have an apartment anymore.

He grinned at her, pushing away the thought and the growing headache. Perhaps the best outcome would be for him to be fired. He figured shooting off his mouth might be the best way forward, even if it meant Alsana's wrath and a month of anger management classes.

"You're not going to last a day in my world, *pizza boy*," she said, turning away slightly, but without completely withdrawing her impressive profile. Dan had to admit that she was beautiful. Blow your mind beautiful. Normally he wouldn't have the chance to insult girls like her.

"No kidding."

Miranda looked like she didn't want to be there either, but with images of her all around and her music piping through the walls, she was a required presence. Her eyes were still shielded behind shades, but he thought she was sizing him up – the classic head to shoes assessment. It made him uncomfortable and reminded him that he wasn't a part of this manufactured and polished world. Still, he wasn't too ashamed of his look. After spending half an hour getting his hair just right and slipping the jacket Alsana bought for him over his Gyroscope t-shirt, he figured he looked pretty good. He told himself that the t-shirt was his attempt to juxtapose real music with whatever it was Miranda did.

"Watch yourself," she said softly. Dan read the lips more than he heard the words. No matter how he acted to her face, he couldn't help but be impressed with her beauty, her curved mouth and glimpses of teeth, seemingly intent on cutting him down. He felt a little intimidated by it, kind of like facing a Venus Fly Trap. Part of him wanted to jump in and be devoured. Instead, he flipped his thumb behind him, gesturing to the cameraman who was hovering nearby.

"Seriously," he said. "And here I am without my very own film crew."

She frowned at him. He could see the disappointment there, something he'd become used to in his seventeen years of dealing with people. The cameraman whirred at Dan's side, capturing Dan's profile and Miranda's full celebrity luminosity beyond.

He felt trapped. The young people at the edges were

smirking into their glasses, sharing words through cupped hands. Sully remained serious but he was out of reach. Dan slipped around the cameras and made his way towards the front door, dismissing himself from the strange girl. He'd done what Alsana wanted – he'd met with the client and received his specific instructions. He'd even let them chain him to a designer briefcase full of nothing. He didn't want to spend any more time in the company of celebrities. Sure, he'd thought it would distract him from his boring, suddenly-homeless life, but they weren't half as interesting as they pretended to be. Even the quiet, watchful, hateful Miranda Brody. The party was okay but he'd gone through the hoops, now it was his time.

Behind him the crew filmed his retreat, while cutting back to Miranda's classically unimpressed profile. Her people picked up their chatter, the waiters continued to navigate through with refreshments, and soon Dan Galkin was forgotten.

He edged his way around the dance floor, the music calling him one way while the need to get out pulled him the other. His head hurt: the lightshow strobing to the beats, piercing; the edges of his vision blurred with pin pricks of light.

Suddenly Evie, sparkling eyes of mischief, took his hand in the dark as one song morphed into the next. Dan felt the press of her fingers around his and took in a breath. She was unexpected, a surprise which sent his skin tingling. His head calmed as he focused on the hand. She moved herself around him, close, slipping between Dan and the door, one slender hand encircling his, while the other reached out and under his jacket.

Their faces were close and he studied her more than before, the press of her body against his. Behind him the protective circle of Miranda Brody's documentary crew had forgotten him, but their words and glances were still stinging even though he told himself he didn't care what they thought.

"Let's get out of here, sparky."

CHAPTER 10
THE MAD RUSSIAN

THE TIME WAS close. He could sense it building outside, the storms whipping up in the west, pushed towards them by pressure systems out in the southern oceans. The Russian drew together his most trusted associates, from across the globe and across time, it seemed. None of them were as strong or as young as they had been. Looking around the room, sealed beneath the trembling sounds of Chinatown in the center of Melbourne, the four of them had seen better days.

Grandfather Time stood in a corner, as straight and tall as a grandfather clock, dressed in a tuxedo and top hat. Even though he remained mostly insulated from the physical ravages of time, the old man seemed less animated. Beside him, at one end of a divan, Grim cradled a glass of scotch. He was fat now, his scraggly beard a forest joining with the hair which burst from the neck of his open shirt. It was shot through with grey and white, like a winter coat. In contrast, Pearl retained her elegance, although she seemed to have shrunk further into herself over the years. Her cheekbones were more pronounced, her eyes little black beads in the creases of her face. Against the Russian's wishes, Pearl had brought her nephew, and he stood loyally at the rear of her too-large chair. Luke Ma was barely twenty, a strong young man, with watchful eyes and a thin mouth. He knew the boy well enough and had almost brought him into the exclusive fold of the Small Gods. Instead he had settled on the boy's cousin, Lily. Looking at him now, Galkin wondered whether he should have persisted with the boy. Behind those thin lips were multiple rows of jagged, deadly teeth. Pearl's nephew was no ordinary chaperone.

They had been waiting for twenty minutes. At first they were polite and enquired about each other's family. Grim complained about his decaying lungs, his fitful sleeping and the terrible state of national politics. Pearl relayed news of her sister's death and the birth of a new grandchild – neither one making much of an impact in her expression.

The Russian lost interest. And so did the others. Their glances turned to the room itself, their eyes trailing across the impressive bookshelves and the dark but subtly lit room. It was only when the door opened and the last of their number arrived that the energy returned. The Russian felt his chest expand as he stood from his own chair and walked quickly across the room to meet his dear, old friend.

Seraphima wore a young body to the meeting, sheathed in a black dress and impossible heels. He hadn't seen her in a very long time, but the Russian recognized her *glas myortvy*, the deadness in her eyes. She watched him approach, a smile curving across her lips.

"Sima," he said, taking one of her hands in his and kissing it lightly. "To have come all this way honors me," he continued in Russian.

"You don't seem so mad to me, *mal'chik*," she said in English. "I had come to witness your demise, but it seems you are not nearly as gone to the dogs as I was led to believe."

She smiled across at Grim. The Russian followed her gaze, straightened himself up, and then folded his hands behind his back. He wasn't sure how much she played with him, toying with their shared history, teasing him with her very mixed up chronology.

"Yes, this time concerns my family. Each of you earned my love, my trust, and now payment is due."

"Straight to business, then," Sima said.

Grim shuffled from the divan and clumsily kissed Sima's hand after she moved from the Russian. She tilted her chin at Grandfather Time and Pearl, but completely ignored Luke who stood behind his aunt. With hands on her hips she surveyed the group and from her expression it was clear she was amused by what she saw. The Russian understood her perspective. Seraphima was able to shed her skin at will, always living her life physically as a young woman if she chose to do so. The Russian, also, was accustomed to looking at the world in long drawn-out canvasses of time. When he was a younger man, the world was a very different place.

"You have been gone a long time, old friend," Sima said as she sat on the divan next to Grim. "Some of us thought you were finally dead."

"You make me blush," the Russian said.

"Where have you been?" Grim asked, coughing at the end of his words and scrambling to regain control of his lungs.

"Other places," the Russian said, waving his hand to dismiss the talk. "No need for this in our current discussion.

Returned I have, and need for you to assist me with my … matters of succession."

"But it has been five years," Grim said, refusing to give up the conversation. "You were gone. No trace of you."

"I am here now, good friend," the Russian said. "Come, come…"

He gestured to the door, but Grim coughed again and waved his hand. Pearl's lips twitched.

"We searched the world," Pearl said softly. "From above and from below, from the sides too. You were not here, Galkin. We wish to know where it was you went."

"Some things will be revealed tonight," he said. "And others shall remain my business, Pearl. Grant me this audience, dear lady, and I can promise you that you will not be so worried about my absence. Other things I have planned for us. Come, come…"

He led them out of the library and into a corridor, lined with metal and nothing like the comfortable and warm room they had left. It was a shielded passage, well beyond detection and strong enough to withstand uberhuman assaults. It led further down into the earth and as they passed through a thick vault-like gate Galkin felt like the old times had, at least partially, returned.

"A safe room?" Grandfather Time noted as he bent his balding head to enter. When he straightened his body he returned his top hat to its rightful place and looked with rheumy eyes around the state of the art room. Surveillance was the name of the game, Galkin knew, and from the secret room he was able to monitor everything and everyone.

"Is that my house?" Grim asked, squinting at one screen.

"I would keep you all safe," Galkin said.

Grim itched at his beard but said nothing more.

"And is that your charming grandson, Russian?" Sima asked.

She was always the one to bring them back into focus, to cut through the human ties, the useless prattle. Galkin allowed himself to enjoy simply watching her, her dark eyes, giving away nothing but the hint of humor.

Behind her enigmatic face was a grainy picture of a hotel room. A boy was sleeping face down, his leg hanging off the side of the bed, his hair tussled and unruly.

"Da," he said.

"And this is the successor?" Sima continued, eyebrows arched. "You would have us assist you in crowning this boy the next Mad Russian? Surely you jest, old man. He is nothing but a *shchenok*."

Galkin pressed a finger to his lips, a smile breaking around each side. Sima held his gaze while the others in the room waited silently. He could tell they were all doubtful, that in his absence they had forgotten just what kind of power it was that he wielded.

"He is blood of my blood," he said softly, nodding. "After many years apart we come together again now. And you here tonight, my friends, my people. I ask you to play your part."

"You know we will, Galkin," Grim said. "We all have debts."

"Ah, the locksmith speaks, and without the attendant cough," Sima said, moving away from the main monitor. "I see your handiwork has already entered the picture."

Grim blushed but it was difficult to tell because of his

ruddy complexion. As a tinkerer there was no equal in his time, but with the advances of technology and the millions of pathways innovation had taken in the past decade, it would only be a matter of time before Grim and his skills were rendered redundant.

"Grim has crafted a device," Galkin said, pleased.

"A leash, perhaps?" Sima added. "Something to control the child until coronation? Yes, I recognize the wolf's handiwork there on the screen. But how, dear, old friend, did you deliver it to him?"

"There is a man," Grim said.

"Always, there is a man," she teased.

"And a well placed man," Pearl added, although her sunken eyes remained on the screen rather than the people in the room. "An Englishman on your payroll, Isangrim, and one beyond even my influence."

Grim shrugged but wouldn't face Pearl or her nephew.

"I thought your inheritance had all gone to the bottle, old friend," Sima said.

"I have done as you requested," Grim said to Galkin, bowing his head.

"Even though you doubted me?" Galkin asked. "No matter, you have shown your hand, Grim. And it pleases me."

Galkin reached towards the screen and touched it gently. A flicker of static heralded a change in picture, the hotel room replaced instantly with an image of the Melbourne skyline.

"And Pearl has given me eyes across the city," Galkin said, smiling. "Electronic eyes, and the living ones."

"The seed is sown within the girl's entourage," Pearl

said, and for a second she allowed her arrogance to filter through her usually impassive face.

"But what of the heroes?" Galkin asked the roof, hands spreading in question. "What of the Celestial Knights?" He turned back to the group with a look of mock horror on his face.

"Distracted," Grandfather Time said, ignoring Galkin's melodramatic pose. "And the local derivatives scattered to the winds, at least in a temporary capacity. Certainly long enough for this move you hope to make. But tell me, Russian. Why the American girl?"

Miranda Brody's face appeared on the central screen and the Russian smiled, impressed with his own ability to manipulate the images through the smallest thought. Silent video clips of her concerts flashed across other screens, but the central one remained static, her young face half-smiling for the camera. She was a little older than Danya, but a good match, he thought.

"Why this girl?" he echoed the question. "This girl is the big thing, my friend, the sensation. All the world has eyes for her and soon for my grandson. Once this thing is done, once he has come back to me, there will be no return to … to the flipping burgers, to the shame he brings me. The world will watch and the world will be fearful."

"It makes no difference to me," Sima said. "You could have your boy kill a politician or a business CEO, it doesn't matter. You'll get him back, one way or another."

She touched his shoulder and he smiled at her, bowing his head in gratitude.

"Which leaves us with but one more element," Galkin said, turning to look back at the others. "No protection, no hope of escape, but there needs to be the match. Fire to bring about change."

Sima smiled.

"And that's where I come in, isn't it?" she asked. "After all this time, all you needed was an assassin. A part of me is insulted."

"Never," Galkin mocked.

"It's possible. Although you do know me better than most. I'll do this thing for you, for all the times we've had together in the past. But there must be a line."

Galkin nodded. There was always a line but most of the time no one acknowledged it. The storm outside, threatening but not breaking: it was the warning that things would never be the same again.

An age was coming to pass.

"After tomorrow, you will not hear from me again," Sima said. "None of you."

She looked at Grim, his head down, cheeks twitching. Pearl was shadowed by old age and death too. It was so clear to them all.

"Our time has passed," she continued. "There is a new world here and if you won't embrace it you will be crushed by it."

"We have not been blind Seraphima," Pearl said. "Contingency plans have been put in place, for years."

"And yet the old man has been gone *for years*. Perhaps he missed the memo."

"It matters not," Galkin said. "You each have empires to run or ruin, and I have my grandson. For that I thank you, but now you leave."

He stood in the center of the room, flanked by the

constant hum of monitors surveying the city above him. Pearl and her nephew left first, without farewell; followed by the shambling Grim. Grandfather Time simply vanished, disappearing in between the blinks of an eye.

Sima alone remained.

"You have pretty speech," Galkin said, half in question.

"A warning, perhaps."

"Go on," he said.

She closed the door to the secret room, cutting herself off from those who left before. Galkin could 'see' her in ripples of electricity. She always burned brighter than regular humans, perhaps due to her symbiotic nature, her essence held in place with borrowed skins.

"It is about the wolf."

"Ah," Galkin said, and there was sadness there.

CHAPTER 11

MIRANDA

THE ISLAND RESORT was awash with light, pushing out towards the ocean which shimmered and then fell to black. Waves rolled up the white beach as Miranda stepped off the boat. Her bare toes sank into the cool sand and she marveled at the warm water around her ankles.

"Just a few friends?" she asked Sully, as he stepped down beside her. Ahead of them, Miranda saw about twenty people. There was a pool and a white-walled hotel surrounded by trees and soft-white spotlights.

"You are entitled to some time away from the fans," Sully said. He lifted her luggage from the boat and allowed her to walk ahead. A part of her was worried about who she would meet on the beach. Her real friends had been shunted to the side over the past year or so, and all she had now were these people.

It didn't take long for the paradise to shift.

"Good to see you, luv."

Robbie Rogers looked gorgeous and drunk. He had KL with him, the faux-rapper he'd been partying with in Miami while dating Miranda in Los Angeles. She returned his smile but didn't let him close enough for the kiss.

"Thanks for the flowers," Miranda said.

Robbie looked confused. He had no idea what she was talking about, no idea that a bunch of flowers had arrived after the Jakarta concert, a bunch with his name on it. It must have been her manager's idea, or maybe Robbie's manager.

Miranda had been swept from the stage by security. She remembered being physically lifted away, the burning boy dropping out of reach, and all she could see were lights from the roof and the swirl of colors and smells.

And then in her room all she had was silence.

She sat there for an hour, at least, while the world outside her door plunged into chaos. She called her father and cried into the phone, no words coming from her, just the rack of sobs.

Sully was suddenly there.

And then the plane.

A night evacuation.

Evie sat across from her with the flowers as they flew into Australia. She read the card from Robbie in her lilting voice, her wide eyes watching Miranda the whole time, like she was going to burst into flames as well.

And maybe she was.

She felt a pressure inside her. It stopped her from talking, from thinking, from even moving. But the pressure wasn't just from Jakarta, from the falling, dying boy. It had begun with the competition, with becoming a national identity. Her body wasn't hers anymore. She had been remade, over and over, even in the first few weeks.

Miranda Brody was out of control.

The protests had struck her hard. People shouting hatred. Freak Chic was a hit, but it was also a striking match. Uberhumans had been a part of the world for decades, but no one ever really confronted them – they were a part of the world, but also apart from it.

Miranda's music exploited the freaks, and she knew it. It was all part of the image Thurston Klein and the others had constructed for her. The undulating tentacle girls and the muscled cat men strutting their bodies across the stage while the girl-next-door sang about all the fun that could be had in this new world.

Light music. Empty lyrics.

She hated it.

But that was celebrity, and Miranda wanted to sing to thousands of people. She wanted their eyes on her, their screams for her. It was her stupid dream and she had made it real. Even Robbie Rogers was part of the dream: a member of a British boy band, equally manufactured and equally beautiful.

When Evie left for a moment, Miranda found herself looking at the flowers, the whites and pinks, and she reached across for the card. She remembered how much she'd loved being with Robbie. She remembered how much it had felt like everything fitted together.

And she cried at his words.

Miranda moved through the guests quickly, kissing cheeks and smiling widely at the stories from back home in the States. The gossip, intrigue and industry news washed over her. At last, Sully touched her arm and led her to the hotel. She looked back at Robbie one last time before the doors closed, but then she re-focused herself.

"This isn't fun," she said, frowning.

"Was that Mister Rogers?" Sully asked.

"Yeah, not fun, Sully."

They walked to the second level and Sully led her to a balcony overlooking the beach. She couldn't see anything out there except the stars above, but the rolling waves soothed her.

"Can we go home?" she asked.

"Soon," he said. "But you must be ready, Miss Brody. The dangers are not left back in Indonesia, they circle even now."

"More protests?"

"Perhaps."

"You think it might be worse?" she asked.

Sully drew in a deep breath.

"I have changed the times for your plane tomorrow, just as a precaution. I do not trust Mister Christie at this moment. He is reckless with your safety."

"He's just an industry man."

"He wants to capitalize on you, and that puts you in danger."

Miranda turned around and leaned against the balustrade. She looked up at Sully and frowned. He rubbed at his beard.

"There is more," he said slowly. "I do not know what

plans are afoot, but something terrible will happen and I will not allow you to be involved."

"What are you talking about?"

He turned away but she grabbed his arm and held him there. She'd never seen him so tense, not even after the Jakarta concert.

"Sully, you can't just tell me my life is in danger and walk away. What is it?"

"I promised your father that I would keep you safe on this tour, and Suleyman never breaks his word."

"Have you talked with the police?"

"No," he said. "This danger comes from within. At the end of this tour we shall speak with your manager and renegotiate a balance. This is no life for one such as you."

She let his arm go and he walked away. Down below, the party continued, but Miranda didn't know those people. She was a musician, yes, but she wasn't a celebrity.

Things would change.

The real Miranda would come back. Somehow.

CHAPTER 12
DAN

I T WAS THE smell of coffee that finally woke him, and he followed it upwards from the fading dream like a swimmer kicking for the surface of the sea. The dream he was leaving behind tasted of the sea, too; of salt and sunshine. And he was leaving someone behind down there in the dream, someone he needed to talk to, someone he didn't want to leave behind, not again.

But the coffee's aroma infiltrated his senses and snared his dream self, wrenching it upward, shattering the feelings of abandonment and regret into myriad shards that blinked in the light from the lopsided venetian blinds.

Dan sat up and jammed the balls of his hands into his eyes to clear away whatever it was he had been dreaming. There was a weight on his left wrist and he realized he was attached to a briefcase. He shifted in the bed and looked at the girl perched on a chair beside him, her legs crossed and her hands cradling a plastic cup. He didn't know where he was, or who she was, or why there was a briefcase attached to his wrist. He shifted again and realized he was naked, and out of all the revelations that last one unsettled him the most.

"Where're ma clothes?" he mumbled, turning away from the girl and sliding out to put his feet down on the floor. It wasn't his floor. "And what time is it?"

He breathed in as the girl sucked at her cup, and he felt for the little electrical pulses around the room: the wiring in the walls, the appliances connected to the larger grid, even the wireless internet system that usually provided a constant hum inside his head. But everything was quiet. The system was down. And he had a thumping headache.

"You went off," the girl said, sounding more amused than anything. "Had to get coffee from across the highway."

Dan looked for his clothes. His black t-shirt was bunched at his wrist, twisted off as much as the briefcase would allow.

"Was a crazy night," she said. He caught a glimpse of elfin eyes, sparkling under short tussled hair. "You're a keeper, sparky. In case you were concerned."

She kept smiling at him from behind the cup, long tanned legs crossed, but Dan ignored her and pushed his senses further, spreading his awareness beyond the hotel room and its disabled systems. He could sense the electricity flowing in the wider world, but his room, and several others either side of him, had been fried.

"Clothes?" he asked for the second time, pulling the shirt over his head, but she stood up and walked into the small bathroom. She was ignoring him, returning the favor, so to speak. He found the rest of his clothes near the door, kicked to one side. The night before was coming back to him, although details were still swimming in the dull thud of a hangover. He was supposed to be body guarding Miranda Brody, or probably just the briefcase. He remembered the briefcase was important. He grabbed his watch and knew he was going to be late. It wasn't a surprise.

The girl closed the door between them, which he decided was a fair enough version of goodbye, so he hustled his clothes, slipped them on, and left, leaving the door slightly ajar.

He couldn't find his bike in the hotel's car park and still had trouble getting clear details from the night before. The sense of urgency was building though, and he redialed Alsana Owens for the third time as he waited for a taxi. Her phone was engaged one moment, then rang out the next. Normally he would have traced the phone through the network, but something had happened in the hotel room and his electrical senses were all over the place. He could pick up the local grid with clarity, but the further he pushed it, the cloudier things got. And the more his head hurt.

He checked the time again just as the taxi arrived. He'd only just make it to the airport in time, and hopefully the man they called Sully wouldn't be there. Dan couldn't imagine being cool enough to weather that stare again, especially considering how seedy he already felt.

Thirty minutes later he'd navigated his way to the Melbourne International Airport. As he strode through the airport, he cast his mind back to the previous night, when he partied hard and perhaps had a few too many of everything, although he still didn't remember the girl from the hotel. Even now, as he shouldered his way up the escalator, he couldn't quite reconstruct her face in his mind. She'd been mostly blonde, he figured; perhaps in her early twenties, with green almond-shaped eyes, a tinkling laugh. He shook his head, trying to clear it. She was older than him and she knew what she was doing. Dan figured he knew it too, although he would have liked to have more details. The night itself was a complete write-off, except for the dream which nagged at him even there in the airport.

He knew from experience that his dreams had the potential to set him off, that even while asleep he could effortlessly wipe out electrical systems and sometimes even start fires. The morning's blackout was nothing compared to the damage he'd wrought as a teenager in the early days when he was just getting to know himself and his powers.

Powers.

He laughed as he looked up at the information board all lit up in orange. The numbers of the planes flitted around and a crowd followed its progress like the faithful on Sunday morning, always looking for guidance, always ready for disappointment. A fluttering groan spread through the group as a flight to Brisbane was delayed by thirty minutes. Dan was tempted to play havoc with the board, to plug another 10,000 volts into the system. He smiled but didn't stop to see how far he'd be willing to go. He was late, and it wasn't the first time.

Stepping off the last escalator he looked up and down the concourse, his briefcase secured to his wrist with its almost-discreet steel chain. The bloody thing wouldn't stop rattling, even when he'd looped it around his wrist twice. The airport was crowded with red-faced locals desperate to flee north for the winter. They shuffled along the trave-lator walkways in herds of four or five, mostly adults with their offspring; or huffed their way past him in his t-shirt and jeans, occasionally bumping into him as he stood and waited. None of them wore smiles, he realized, and they were beginning to irritate him. It was the smell of tourists which was most annoying, of course: the mixture of sweat and fickle dreams for a better, indistinct life which was always 'somewhere else'. Dan knew he was a bit cynical but it wasn't really his fault.

He remembered his grandfather was back and sup-pressed a groan. The problems in his life seemed to be lin-ing up in a neat row.

He sniffed and twisted his head to take in the entire space. There were no signs of obvious fan hysteria and no clogged crowds of teenagers anywhere. No film crew. He was standing in the right place, at the end of the concourse with the dozen or so arrival lounges spreading ahead of him, and the flight from Cairns was just sitting out there on the tarmac, solid and unmoving. He wasn't that late, surely. The announcer seemed bored, and with a quick, yet some-what redundant, look at his watch he realized that Miranda Brody was not on the flight. Inside his head, Dan calculated the penalties he would accrue from Alsana and it wouldn't matter that it wasn't his fault. It never did.

Dan flipped open his phone and dialed Miranda's tour manager, Todd Christie, watching the Cairns flight flick away out of existence on the board above his head. The phone line was engaged and with only a slight knitting of his brow, Dan flipped the phone closed and looked down at the briefcase.

"Looks like it's just you and me for a while," he said, and gave his wrist a little jangle. Then he turned away from the lounges and walked to the escalator again, stepping back on and enjoying the ride down. A day without celebrity sounded good. He thought he could smell coffee, but the bright sign of a franchise diminished his hopes. They may have the scents right, but it was all just hype. Still, he figured, given the circumstances and the fact that he was at least half an hour away from the center of Melbourne, the expensive cup of beans and water would have to be his companion – at least until he was dragged back into Miranda's world. The celebrity's van and driver were waiting out the front of the airport, a reminder of his duties that Dan was happy to put off for a few more minutes.

A screech of tyres from the elevated car park drew most people's attention, and there were murmurs of interest from tourists and homecomers alike. It was just another annoying distraction to Dan though, and he pushed his way past a woman with a stroller, heading towards Miranda Brody's empty van, the driver looking bored behind his shades. At least the van was still there, Dan thought. He didn't have to get another taxi.

His foot got caught on the woman's stroller wheel and he yanked it free, annoyed. He didn't mean to be rough with the woman, but she was gawking towards the car park and talking in a careening way that immediately declared the end of the civilized world. He was sick of people like that, so he reclaimed his foot and then guided her a little out of his way, a little shove. She swiveled her elbows around and caught him in the ribs. Then she let loose on him, slandering his mother, criticizing his hair, insulting his manhood. Her eyes were wild, her mouth a fidgeting thing that concealed crooked little teeth. For a moment he just stared at her in disbelief, but then he pushed forward again.

"Shut – up," he said in two distinct sounds, and stepped through the throng of her family, almost feeling sorry for them to be stuck with such a monster. "I don't have time for it."

The screech continued out in the car park, an idiot turning donuts and shredding his tyres. Dan pulled out his phone again and tried to contact Alsana. With the superstar missing, he really didn't want her to find out from someone else, and he needed to head off any criticism that might be coming his way. He winced at the engaged signal.

The first gunshot went unnoticed.

Most of the people on the side of the taxi and bus ranks were still entertained by the hoon driver, but when the second and third shots rang out some of them began to switch their priorities. A scream pierced the air, a young kid's scream, and it seemed to grow from one person to the next, quickly blurring into a rush of people moving away from where Dan stood.

Being a little preoccupied, Dan didn't immediately notice the change in pack behavior, but the fourth shot connected with the bus shelter right behind him, shattering the glass and his reverie.

He dropped down, his hands flat on the concrete, ready

to bolt. The phone had gone, forgotten already. In front of him the black van that was supposed to transport Miranda had bullet holes in it. They must have passed right through from the driver's side. Dan half-leapt towards the van and crouched down again, pressing his body to the ground so that he could look underneath. Beside him, a man in a courier's uniform sheltered with his hands covering his head, holding it as if it was about to explode.

Looking under the van, Dan saw the road and a pathway leading into one of the big hotels which sat directly at the exit gates. He couldn't see any shooter.

A part of him began calculating the bullets' trajectory. The one that nearly collected him came from the van. It must have shot right through both sides and then into the bus shelter. That meant the shooter was roughly at ground level.

Another shot rang out.

The man next to him started to sob and shake at the same time, breathing through his mouth, blubbering. Dan turned a little and sat up next to him. The man's eyes were shut tight, his hands still clutching at his head.

"Dude, it's okay," Dan said softly.

The man shook his head violently.

"Seriously, you're not going to die." Dan gave him a quick rub on the shoulder. "It's going to be okay." He smiled quickly and then shuffled past him to the other end of the van hoping to get a better look at the area. His senses automatically tightened on the surrounding electrical networks despite the growing pain in his head. He had to press his fingers to his temples to really get a good lock on the invisible world around him. He could trace the grid under the road, connecting the airport and the hotel and all the other facilities in the area.

It was amazing what a little adrenalin could do.

From the end of the van he could see the entrance to the hotel. A woman lay on the crossing, her body wrapped around a small child as she tried to move herself out of danger. There was a horrible dark patch on her shoulder and her arm was hanging unnaturally.

The kid would have been about three, Dan thought. He could see its fingers digging into the mother's useless arm, clinging to her and burying its head into her chest. A frail thing, in danger but unable to do anything except hide its face and wish it all away. Dan looked briefly back to the courier. The man was still shaking but his eyes were now open, giant black eyes, terrified.

"Stay here," Dan said. "Don't lose it, okay?"

As Dan lifted himself back to his feet, ready to slip around the edge and into danger, the courier squawked. It was such an unusual sound that Dan hesitated, a small smile playing on his lips.

"What?"

"Y-you can't go out there," the man said.

Dan looked around the edge of the van. The woman had given up trying to move.

"I think I can," Dan said.

"But... but you're not bulletproof."

Dan wasn't really sure that was true, but he gave the man a reassuring smile.

"Neither's she."

It was eerily quiet on the road. Dan walked into the open, his eyes scanning the revolving hotel doors and the designer shrubbery either side. He imagined he'd see a man in black, or a shadow, or something; but all he saw was the woman and her child.

There were vague emergency sounds coming from somewhere but Dan's normal senses were distant now, replaced with the awareness of the electrical world. The buses and taxis lining the streets were an assortment of alarms and automatic transmissions, MP3s and GPS. He pressed the sense down, laying it flat so that he could focus on the woman.

He took another step, and then two more, gaining confidence.

Dan never saw the shooter. The bullet hit him high and he found himself flung backward, his whole body lifting off the ground for a moment. When he collided with the road he was looking upward, at the grey sky.

The clouds skittered across like the world was stuck on fast-forward.

He hadn't realized the winds had picked up.

And his body seemed to be on fire. All at once.

Another shot rang out. Something to his left exploded into strange grey dust.

The woman. She was still there. Just out of reach.

Dan rolled over and planted his face into the hard road, his nose pressing against the asphalt. He knew he had to move.

His hands pushed himself up and he lifted his body. Sparks of lightning flickered across his vision and he could feel it coursing through his veins, hot and angry. He'd been itching to release the stored charge, even tempted to play havoc with the departures board, but now the energy was invigorating him, allowing him to move even though any other person who had been shot would have stayed crumpled and prone on the road.

As he rolled into a crouch, Dan looked to the hotel doors again. With the adrenalin pumping and the electricity so close to the surface, he managed to catch glimpses of the security cameras' vision. Sketchy black and white images were lifted from the hotel's surveillance devices and replayed inside Dan's head.

A figure stood inside the empty lobby, the lights dimmed so that it couldn't be easily seen from outside.

But it was enough.

Dan focused the power inside him. The flickering images danced in his mind and as the figure lifted its arm, Dan fed the electrical beast that was hiding inside the hotel. He fed it a banquet.

The lobby's lights flared beyond their natural capacity. The doors stopped revolving, distorting the shooter's view. The bank of computers along the reception desk exploded and the lobby was showered in sparks and shards of glass and silicon. In the chaos, Dan sensed an unusual energy, powerful but not connected to the hotel's systems.

He shuffled across to the woman, still keeping low. Mysteries could wait.

She looked up at him, her face smudged with tears and gravel. The kid seemed to be asleep, not moving; breathing but in shock. He tried to smile at her, but it wasn't done yet. He looked to the lobby and knew he could talk with her, console her, later. If he wasn't dead.

When he crossed onto the red carpet outside the hotel, Dan blasted the revolving doors, cutting loose with his stored energy. They flew backward so well that Dan grinned, enjoying himself even though he had already been shot once and probably had a few more bullets to take that morning. He crossed the threshold and the lights dimmed again allowing him to draw back the remaining electricity. Wisps of blue and white snaked out from the walls and the floor, merging with his body, charging his unique cells.

The shooter stood in the center of the empty room, a pistol clearly visible, held out to the side. It was a man. Dark, shoulder-length hair, expensive but damaged sunglasses and a coat, burnt at the edges.

Dan wasn't much better. He was bleeding and a bit ripped. He noticed the growing red patch on his t-shirt. It was the one he'd bought at the Gyroscope concert, one of his favorites. Dan sensed something else, a distraction. His eyes darted to the side, dismissing the shooter for a second as he honed in on the strange energy. It seemed familiar, like a pattern, but it was obscured, somewhere behind him near the entrance.

The shooter cocked the pistol. Dan turned back and watched as he raised the gun.

And shot himself.

In the middle of the lobby.

Dead.

Dan stumbled backward, stunned, his eyes dancing with lights and disbelief. Behind him the sirens came into sharper focus, but they were still too far away. The shooter fell to the carpet.

The pattern suddenly began to unfold itself. Dan's eyes stayed on the dead man, but his mind was thrust back to another time and place. His grandfather's face loomed in his mind, the Mad Russian and his veiled tutorials on explosives and terror.

Dan recognized the pattern clearly then. It was there in the deceptive signal, the muted pulse, the engineered madness.

But it was too late. Again.

And the hidden cache of explosives detonated.

CHAPTER 13
MIRANDA

S HE HAD SEEN the effects of explosions on the television news, but seeing the collapsed hotel right in her personal space made Miranda hesitate. She stood in front of Sully, the sun somewhere behind him, hidden from her by his enormous frame.

She had been furious.

She had been storming over to find the pizza boy freak and demand to know why people were trying to kill her, why snipers had taken shots – real shots – at her car.

But now she just stood there, her trainers mere inches from the rubble. Her people managed to get her close enough but now she didn't know what to do. An entire building lay demolished in front of her, like children's blocks smashed to dust and jagged remnants.

While Miranda didn't know what to do, Sully did. His hand was on her shoulder, he'd had it there for a long time – probably since they'd been attacked in the car. A bomb blast on the side of the road followed by a hail of something metal which skittered off the windows and bodywork of their car. Bullets. Lots of them, from both sides of the road.

It all seemed so intense and lethal at the time, but looking at the hotel site shunted her own experience into perspective. And the pizza boy was under there.

Sully squeezed her shoulder gently and then stepped forward, his boots resting on the blocks of cement or wall, testing the resistance. He moved upward, two, then three steps. Behind them, the police muttered into radios and waited for construction trucks to arrive. Miranda blocked out their noise and focused on Sully. He crouched down, placing his palm against the almost-flat surface. And then he jack-hammered his other hand: up, then down, so fast that it was a blur.

She stumbled back, her hands lifting to shield her eyes from the dust as Sully smashed his fists into the rock. A police woman waved her hands at Sully, looking panicked. Two more officers moved towards Miranda.

Sully plunged both his hands into the surface, right up to the biceps on each arm. His back arched, impossible muscles pushed against the fibers of his suit. He didn't look like an ordinary man anymore, and as he lurched upward, bringing a huge chunk of concrete with him, up over his head, Miranda remembered the way he had first been introduced to her: Suleyman the Great.

"Oh my god," the police woman said, and stepped back, holding Miranda's sleeve, guiding her away as well. "That's impossible."

Sully moved back down the slope of rubble and placed the solid section he carried down by the side of the road. He lay it down neatly and then took off his jacket, tossing it to the side, already forgotten. His face was only a little flushed, and he moved smoothly back up to where he had begun excavation and reached down for more collapsed walls to pile down at the roadside.

After a half hour of digging, Sully's body was covered in sweat and concrete dust, but he never paused, never tired. Down in the crater he carved out of the debris, Sully pressed his bare fingers into a thick sheet of metal, spreading the surface enough to gain purchase. He tore the metal apart like unwrapping a present, bending it back in jagged strips. Miranda was in the car, hidden behind the tinted windows and out of the dusty disaster zone. While the driver listened to the radio in the front seat, Miranda looked out on the silent scene, watching Sully toss the layers of metal out of his hole to crash around him. The rest of the site was untouched. She didn't know how he knew where to dig, or why he focused on that particular place. There was a lot about the big man she didn't know.

And then he pulled out the boy.

She could tell it was him because he was still wearing the same clothes he had been wearing the night before, and there was a thin shiny chain hanging from his wrist, sparkling in the sunlight. It had been attached to a suitcase but there was no sign of it now, and Miranda didn't really care. Sully supported the boy, almost carrying him down to the edge of the rubble. Both faces were covered in grey dust. The boy's shirt was ripped and there were red marks there, raked across his skin.

For the first time she didn't feel like hating him. Because of her, she realized, this boy nearly died. He was lucky, she knew, but not because of anything she'd done. The boy in Jakarta had been younger, fourteen perhaps, and he hadn't been able to survive his brush with Miranda Brody's celebrity.

She opened the door and slid out before the driver could say anything in protest. Sully saw her coming but he didn't reprimand her. He crouched down with the boy and let the paramedics come close. Miranda slid in beside Sully, his arm holding her against his reassuring body.

The boy's face was bruised already. There was a cut across his eyebrow and his torso was bleeding too. He winced as the paramedics removed his shirt and began stabilizing him, but no matter what they did, he remained as alert as he could after being buried under a hotel.

"You have our thanks," Sully said, touching the boy's knee.

Miranda had no idea what he meant. She wondered how getting himself blown up could be of any use to her. But her anger quickly fled. Sully was worried about the boy. It wasn't anything to do with her this time.

"Are you…" she asked, but her voice vanished.

He looked at her. Green eyes, somehow still bright, surrounded by the grey dust. He squinted a little, probably in pain, and then lifted his hand to touch his shoulder. It was bruised with a dark red mark there, a dark disk.

"Got shot," he mumbled to her, his lips swollen with the effort.

Miranda nodded. She couldn't see any entry wound, just the bruise. She wondered whether it bounced off him.

"Got buried."

He smiled then, and the paramedics helped him to his feet. An Indian woman wearing a skirt and jacket stood just to the side, flanked by two police officers. She looked furious.

"Is he going to live?" the woman asked.

The boy's smile widened and he turned his head painfully to look at her.

"Alsana, you made it…" he mumbled.

"All his vitals are fine," a paramedic said. "Blood loss was a concern but it seems to have stabilized itself."

"Yes," Alsana said. "Well, Danny here is a most interesting boy. If that's all, we need him to come to the police station. Parole violation," she said, looking at Miranda.

"What?" Miranda asked. "How did he break parole?"

"Hotel fell on me," the boy said. "That'll do it."

"We'll have him back to you if he is viable, Miss Brody," Alsana said. "In the meantime we need to make sure this isn't all his fault."

"Seriously? This boy gets blown up and you think it's his fault?"

"Miss, you really don't know anything about this boy. He is dangerous, even if he doesn't look it." Alsana made sure she didn't actually touch Dan as he moved with the police towards the waiting patrol car.

Miranda stood with Sully and watched. Part of her wanted to scream at the woman, but part of her wondered how much of what she alluded to was true. As Dan reached the car, one of the officers opened the front passenger door for him.

He looked over the car's roof towards Miranda, the smile still on his beaten face.

"This is great," he called out. "I've never been in the front seat before." And then he was gone.

CHAPTER 14

DAN

B EING TRAPPED UNDER a collapsed hotel wasn't as bad as he thought. Sure it was dark and there was a dusty, shattered cement kind of smell, but he managed to avoid being crushed to death in the explosion so he had to admit that was a bonus. As everything had fallen around him, tiles, mortar, the entire front section of the hotel; he instinctively pushed out with what was left of his stored energy and formed a magnetized shell around himself. It had worked, just like his grandfather taught him many years before. The explosives were his grandfather's too, and Dan wondered whether the celebration of the Mad Russian's return was supposed to serve as a warning to Dan, or an invitation for a reunion. The whole thing was choreographed, he could tell that, including the suicidal shooter; but Dan didn't know what he was expected to do about it.

And now he was at the police station. It was always the same one. He sat waiting for the show to begin, having already spent half an hour with Alsana arguing about insurance and indemnities. She'd received a phone call mid-sentence and decided to take it outside the interview room. And she hadn't come back. The whole time he was with her he kept looking at the ceiling, expecting his grandfather to rip it open and snatch him into the air. His thoughts wandered and then doubled back, skirting around the growing thump of a headache. Everything around him was a blur, and the chain attached to his wrist had carved a red line around his wrist which itched and stung at the same time. Since arriving at the station Dan hadn't been able to properly focus on anything electrical. There was still a buzz around him, but it was out of kilter, like an afterglow rather than the real thing.

Dan sat alone in the interview room, his eyes half-closed as he watched through the glass at the uniforms rushing about in the wake of the airport hotel bombing. His head still throbbed but it was getting better. He rubbed at the cold metal bracelet around his wrist, discharging minute shocks of electricity into it, hoping to unlock the code but knowing it was unlikely. In the hours since he'd woken in the unfamiliar hotel he'd tried to get rid of it but all he'd managed with his bursts of electricity was to magnetize the thing.

He didn't see the funny side when the bracelet snapped hard against the metal table. He pulled it across the surface and dislodged the magnetic connection just as the door opened and the familiar figure of Detective Schwarz stepped in. He stopped just inside the room to give Dan a disapproving look. His eyes moved from the bandage on Dan's head, slowly down to the torn shirt and black burn marks.

Dan smiled at him.

Schwarz took a seat opposite, placing his cup of coffee on the table and grunting in greeting. With his hands free, the policeman smoothed down his moustache and sighed. Behind him came a young woman in uniform, with dark hair and a clipboard bursting with files held to her chest. He knew that clipboard: it had his name on it.

"This is Ryan," Schwarz said.

The uniform was obviously new. She didn't look at Dan, and the way she was focusing on the report meant she'd been briefed on his juvenile criminal history. Dan knew the 'up-cycleds' were an office joke. He had four years' experience.

Schwarz shifted in his seat and folded his large arms across his crinkled shirt. Dan was ready for the usual introductions.

"Still having trouble keeping your pants on?" Schwarz said.

Dan shrugged.

"Killed anyone lately?"

"No," Dan said, looking at the table, fingers splayed in front of him. "It's been a slow week."

"Are you trying to be funny?"

"People say I'm not funny."

"You're not funny."

"That's what they say."

Schwarz reached for his cup and smiled through his moustache. It was the same routine.

"You're going to get yourself killed," he said, and it wasn't one of the practiced lines. Dan shrugged. Schwarz was probably right.

Ryan took the cue from her partner and retrieved a document folder from her files. Dan saw the distinctive red and blue logo of the up-cycled program and said nothing as the paperwork was slid across to him. Schwarz handed him a pen.

"You'll need to sign at the crosses," Ryan said but Dan

already knew. The forms were familiar to him. They covered statutory declarations on good behavior, a questionnaire about all activities since the previous form, poorly written threats dressed up as codes of conduct, and finally a waiver for any injury he may incur as being a part of the up-cycled program. Dan finished the last signature with a flourish and sat back.

"There's word that your grandfather is back in town," Schwarz said slowly. Ryan reached across and collected the final sheet of signatures and declarations. "Now, I know you're too smart to get mixed up with him again, but you've got to look out for yourself."

"He's probably gone by now anyway," Dan said.

"There's a reason they call him *Mad*, Danny. You can't predict his behavior, any more than we can."

"He's been gone for years. If he's back then he'll want to get his hands on his war machines and hook up with his Cold War buddies," Dan said.

Schwarz nodded and Dan couldn't help but shake his head and smile in disbelief.

"You think he's going to care about me?"

"I think you're right about his first priorities," Schwarz said. "And Danny, my boy, you are his primary war machine, whether you like it or not."

Dan didn't like it. Ryan clearly didn't like it either, and she gathered up her files and muttered some excuse for leaving. As the door closed Schwarz scratched his moustache and sighed. He reached forward, clicked off the recorder and sighed again. Dan hadn't said a thing. He hadn't even looked Schwarz in the eye.

"I don't say this to make you angry," he said softly. "I say it because I care about you."

"I know," Dan said. "Everyone cares about me."

"This thing is off, you know?" the policeman said. "You don't have to drip the sarcasm anymore. Danny, the Celestial Knights are off-planet. If your grandfather makes a grab for you then we've only got conventional defenses, the good men and women of the force. If he finds out that his enemies are out of the picture then he'll get bold, he'll get reckless."

The Celestial Knights had always opposed Dan's grandfather and other uberpowered megalomaniacs. They were the best of the best and apart from the occasional on-the-job death to prevent the destruction of a planet or an entire dimension, they were pretty much unstoppable.

Dan had personal experience of that. He rubbed his wrist where the metal bracelet still held firm. The dullness in his mind and the familiar energy signature from the hotel at the airport seemed to coalesce.

"He won't be a problem."

Dan's phone vibrated in his pocket. He pulled it out and frowned at the large crack across the screen. He wondered whether he could claim it on insurance but since the phone still worked he couldn't be bothered.

"Important call?" Schwarz asked.

"It's not the Mad Russian, if that's what you mean," Dan said, sliding the phone across to Schwarz. The older man squinted his eyes as he tried to read the text. Then his eyes widened and he smiled, sliding the phone back to Dan.

"That's some girl," he said.

"She probably just wants to yell at me for wrecking her day," Dan shrugged.

"Still, she was worried about you at the site, and her man managed to pull you out of there faster than we could have managed."

"Yeah, I guess she's a little bit awesome."

Schwarz laughed and stood up. He held his hand out to Dan and helped him up, giving him a firm, close handshake at the door. They'd known each other for years and suddenly Dan felt like just hugging the man, not letting go.

"Look after yourself, Danny."

And in the end that's what he had to do.

The text message practically ordered Dan to meet Miranda at another hotel, although not her own one, he noticed. It was near Birdie's and since he'd left his stuff in the boss's office, he agreed to meet her, although he didn't really have a choice.

As he walked through the city he pushed out with his powers, trying to manipulate the world one little energy spike at a time. Changing the traffic lights was easy but pushing his mind into more subtle systems like the telephone networks was beyond him. Whenever he tried there was a grey fog, a dullness that pushed against him, and now he knew it was coming from the bracelet.

Ever since the hotel explosion he hadn't been able to *hear* the world around him. He had been locked out of surveillance, phone and internet networks. The subtlety was gone. And it was somehow connected to his grandfather.

Dan slammed the bracelet into a pole as he stepped up onto the footpath, swinging wide and bringing it in hard and fast. There was a clanging sound and he felt the jarring shudder up his arm, but the bracelet itself was unchanged, no dent, no marks at all.

Nothing changed.

But it did start to rain.

The entourage relaxed into the lobby, folding itself on strategically placed sofas and against pillars of marble. Dan's eyes took in their positions from over the top of the newspaper, but he didn't move from his chair, and tried to look as unimpressed as possible. He counted eight of them, boys and girls, but all wearing designer clothes and attitude. The camera crew was absent.

Miranda Brody sauntered towards him with her hips jutting out like she did on stage. Dan turned the page.

"You nearly got me killed," Brody said. Her arms were on those hips, the red carpet pose.

"I was going to say the same thing," Dan said, folding the paper. He was over-acting, but at the same time he knew she deserved some return-fire attitude for abandoning him. And since Alsana was now missing again, having stormed out at the station, Miranda was the only target. "But I didn't see you come in."

She narrowed her eyes into deadly slits.

"You – nearly – got – me – killed," she said again, slowly, like he was one of her lackeys.

"You're the mega-star," he said. "You're the target."

"I know about your grandfather."

Dan was shocked. He ran his fingers back over his

forehead, pressing his head a little where he had been bleeding. He felt sick.

Miranda sat down opposite him. She reached out a hand, nearly touching his knee, but then she pulled back.

"It wasn't me," Dan said, lifting his arm so that the chain which had been attached to the briefcase was visible. "I think it was this."

Her gaze briefly fell across the broken chain but Dan could tell she didn't know why it was important either. Her people kept their distance.

"What are you talking about?" she said softly.

"It's doing something to me. Making me a bit off, you know."

She shook her head. He managed a smile.

"It's messing with my powers." There was that word again: powers. Dan took a breath and sat up, calming himself while knowing that Miranda was probably right. Everyone knew the Mad Russian was involved, and everyone knew that Dan was always going to be a loose end to be tied up, one way or another.

"So why does he want to kill you?" Miranda asked. "Your grandfather."

Dan shrugged.

"You have no idea?" she asked, still keeping her voice low.

He met her eyes and she didn't look away. God, she was gorgeous.

"I don't know," he said. "But you were attacked too. Someone wants you hurt, or worse."

It was Miranda's turn to shrug and she crossed her legs.

"We're the odd couple, aren't we?" she asked. "Still, we

can't just sit around and wait for the next building to fall on your head."

She stood up and called to her people. They moved towards the exit, but she stopped before she disappeared.

"You're fired, by the way. It's too dangerous for us to be together."

Dan sank back into his chair.

"You're not kidding."

"Don't worry, Dan. I'll be gone soon and you won't have to worry about me anymore."

CHAPTER 15
THE MAD RUSSIAN

THE DARK CLOUDS released the rain in a torrent, reducing visibility and plunging the city into a premature evening. The Russian sat, quite dry and comfortable, in a leather chair below the bustle of the city. His legs were crossed and he held a glass of white wine delicately in his left hand as he watched the street on a video monitor. The room itself was mostly dark, highlighted in the corners with subdued reddish light from hooded lamps. Sima had only just left him and he could still smell her perfume. He swished his glass again slowly, and took a sip. On the screen, he watched as his grandson stumbled out of a hotel looking right and then left.

The Russian smiled. Danya stepped right into the street and was drenched within seconds but he didn't seem to care about his clothes or his own comfort. There was a desperation in his movements, the jutting chin, his eyes trying to look above the skittering crowds as the people made to escape the deluge.

"You looking for someone, Danya?" he chuckled.

There were other cameras, other vantage points, and as

the boy ran down towards the traffic lights the screen flickered and was replaced with a closer view. Pearl's contacts in Chinatown had been meticulous with the surveillance. The Russian made a mental note to thank her and her shark-toothed nephew.

The boy ran across the road, not waiting for the lights to change. He weaved between a taxi and a cyclist before stepping up on to the curb and grabbing past a group of black coated men.

Miranda Brody was there, like a poisonous flower; surrounded by pretty little things hiding from the rain.

"It is like from a film, yes?" the Russian said, taking another sip of the wine. He heard Halo enter, felt the shift in the energy fields which were getting stronger and stronger every day. Sometimes the Russian felt as if he could stab out his own eyes and still see better than the humans around him. Heat flushed through his neck and cheeks as he thought about plucking out his own eyes, the intensity of the feeling making him pause and turn his attention away from his grandson and the reunion with the celebrity girl.

He closed his eyes, took a measured breath; and pushed aside the violence which swirled in his mind. Halo, ever the quiet observer, remained standing just inside the room.

"You wish to be there," the Russian said softly, eyes still closed.

"I know my place," Halo replied. "Timing will be everything."

The Russian nodded, smiling.

"You learn lessons well, Halo. A true son. And very unlike the boy on our screens, yes?"

Both men looked back to see Dan and Miranda arguing

in the rain in front of a fast food place. The girl's retainers were shielding her with black umbrellas, but her hands were wild, flying in all directions, her teeth flashing white.

"My grandson has perhaps met his match."

On the street, Luke Ma watched the unfolding drama through dark shades. He counted six members of Miranda Brody's entourage including two security guards and four assistants. The guards were local. They looked bored by the celebrity's yelling. Their fists were clenched, waiting for even half a reason to intervene, but the girl wouldn't let up. Luke knew the type of security gorillas he was dealing with here, and he thought Dan did as well but the fool kept getting in the girl's face.

The one side of the street was empty apart from his targets, and the traffic dropped off to a slow crawl through the sheets of rain and water covering the road. On the other side, though, there were still groups of shoppers, using the shadow of the skyscrapers to shield themselves from the rain.

Luke looked up from the shoppers towards where his cousin waited. Lily stood with her legs apart, balancing on the awning overhanging a camera store. Her black coat whipped behind her in the wind and Luke realized the storm was coming earlier than expected. A part of him knew the Mad Russian was involved in the build up of energy. There was a madness out there, swirling above them, ready to explode.

But Luke could manage an explosion.

Melbourne was overdue for some action anyway, and Luke was more than willing to be the catalyst. He touched his earpiece and flexed his jaw, the cracking sound clearly audible through his piece.

"Follow my lead," he said. Lily didn't respond, but then again, she hardly spoke at all anymore.

He stepped out onto the street, casually throwing off his coat and letting it flap around on the wet road behind him. He stood there with his arms out to each side, the hard black armor strapped to his torso and forearms glistening in the rain. He cracked his neck twice, once to each side, and then stared down an approaching car.

Normally he would operate in the shadows, use his strength and training to do his aunt's work without most of the world ever knowing about it. But the latest orders were explicit. The Mad Russian wanted to leave an impression on Melbourne. Personally, Luke thought the idea was short sighted; that any exposure now would only hurt their clandestine activities later, but his aunt was not open to discussion. Whatever hold the Russian had on her, it was solid.

And so Luke and Lily were sent out to bring about destruction, chaos and perhaps even a little death. His aunt called them her two little dragons.

The car's tyres screeched and skidded to the right, but the water across the road didn't allow for much traction and it slid towards Luke who waited with open arms. He could see the woman's terrified eyes as she wrestled with the steering wheel. It was a family car. A child's capsule was strapped in the back but there was only the woman inside.

As it slammed into Luke he forced his fingers deep into its door and the force of the impact pushed him back nearly twenty feet before his own boots gathered enough traction to stop the momentum.

He didn't wait to let the woman scramble out. He didn't wait to hear the crowds or even glance towards Dan. Instead, he swung the sedan around behind him, turning like a discus thrower, his fingers gripping the metal and easily lifting the car off the ground. He swung it around three times before letting it go. It sailed up a little before crashing to the street, denting the bonnet before flipping end over end towards Dan and the celebrity group.

Luke grabbed a second car, even as the first was still flipping. It had been driving towards Dan anyway, so Luke only had to swing it around once before sending it careening after the first one.

It was beautiful.

He stood and wiped his hand across his face, the smell of petrol and wet hair in the air and he smiled.

The first car exploded and Luke stepped back in surprise, unsure whether that had been the plan or not, but marveling at his handiwork anyway. The sudden flare of orange highlighted the grey streets, and in the flickering afterglow Luke was impressed to see that he'd hit Dan and the group head-on. A perfect shot.

"Behind you, cousin," Lily called softly through the earpiece.

At the same time, the road trembled, like an earthquake. Luke turned around, smiling through his three sets of jagged shark teeth.

A bearded man crouched in the middle of the road like he'd just landed. The surface was pock-marked and where the man's large hands rested, Luke saw the road had shattered. The man stood up. He was wearing a black turban and suit, and as he unfolded himself to his full height, Luke could tell he was a very tall man.

"This is good," he whispered to his cousin. "Watch me tear this guy up."

"Who is this man?" the Mad Russian demanded, standing up from his chair, forgetting the wine and turning to face Halo who still stood by the door. "Who is this man who falls from the sky?"

Halo was watching the screens too, but he didn't know much more than the Russian. There wasn't any known superhero matching the man's description and he thought it was too much of a coincidence for a new hero to suddenly surface in the middle of his game. The Russian had only made his move for Dan after being certain any real opposition was out of the country.

"Looks like a Muslim," Halo said.

"'Looks like a Muslim'?" the Russian mimicked. "'Looks like a Muslim'?"

"A Sikh?" Halo faltered.

"You paid to know these things, stupid boy. Find out."

"But…"

"No but. You go get this man. I put end to this now. Go."

The Russian's eyes flashed with white light as he swung his head around the room, from the screens to the desk and then to Halo at the door.

Halo nodded quickly and slipped out of the room, a

smile creeping across his face as he heard the sound of shattered glass behind him.

Luke hunched over the lip of the storefront, his gloved fingers thrust deeply into the corrugated iron, holding his place steady. The interrupted shoppers scattered across the street, clutching at their shopping and their children, cries and shouts reaching up to him as he slowly opened his mouth to reveal his triple set of razor teeth.

"Nice punch," he said, spitting blood to the side, as he looked down at the giant man who was pushing his way through the wreckage of the two cars across the street. "Think I might chew your arm off now."

The car wreckage merged with the front of the fast food place, all twisted metal and collapsed mortar. Luke dropped to the street again, his ribs a little sore from where the man had struck him, but nothing too serious.

"You won't find anyone but little pieces, man," Luke called out. "Who are you anyhow?"

The man straightened up from his search and turned around, his hands holding the second car's rear door. Luke noticed some movement around the wreckage. The fast food place had people in it too, silhouettes shifting from place to place behind the light of the fire which still licked around the engine of the first car.

"I am Suleyman," the man said.

"Well, I'm the Card Shark," Luke said, closing the gap between them. He watched Suleyman closer though, not wanting to be taken by surprise a second time. "And you have stumbled on to something that does not concern you."

Suleyman placed the door down. He looked sadly at the wreckage around him and then subtly towards the food store. Luke almost missed the glance.

"How many did I get, you think?"

There was a sound through the earpiece he shared with Lily, and Luke cupped his ear to cut through the static. It wasn't coming from his cousin though. It was closer. The sound intensified, the crackle becoming unbearable. Luke pulled it out of his ear and threw it to the ground after static energy burnt his fingers.

He shot a look past Suleyman into the fast food store.

"No way," he mumbled. "I didn't get them did I?"

"You got enough," Suleyman said. "Four dead that I can tell."

Luke punched the air and swore, spinning to look back down the street towards Chinatown. He knew that the Russian would be watching, and watching him fail to kill the celebrity or injure Dan in any decent way would be enough to bring shame down upon him. He could already imagine the stony look on his aunt's face.

"You have done quite enough," Suleyman said. Luke spun around again and leapt straight at the man, his legs pushing him with enough force to bring them both to the ground. But the bearded man took the fall well, as if he'd had practice, and then threw Luke to the side.

Luke snapped his jaws tight, grabbing the man's arm worse than any pitbull. But instead of calling out in pain or trying to shake his arm free, Suleyman brought his other hand down on Luke's head.

A flash of red mushroomed behind his eyes but he didn't let go.

Suleyman stood up, Luke still attached to his arm, but hanging limp, on the edge of consciousness. His eyes were bulging, he knew, and he wouldn't last long, but in the last moments he thought he saw Dan.

The kid was stepping his way over the rubble of the cars, the celebrity girl holding his hand and a third person struggling to push aside the doors to the fast food store.

Luke pressed his jaws tighter.

It was good to see Dan again. After all those years.

The Mad Russian sat again in front of the screen, his hands clutching the sides of the chair. There was a burning smell from the leather and he pushed the energy from inside himself down into the chair and further into the bedrock below. His eyes watched the scene a few blocks away. He could see Danya, scratched but healthy. He could see the girl, too, even less injured, and she was getting into a car, so close to escape again.

And the Russian felt anger like the old days, welling inside him.

The air thickened, a blue vortex swirling around him, pulling the interior of the room into the center, transforming it all into energy. The desk, the lamps, the chairs and wine were all consumed by the maelstrom.

He sat like a husk, his mouth open, his tongue thick and close to his lips. He couldn't stand it anymore, the sense of losing Danya to the world. And the world had already taken so much away from him.

He let his head fall backward and his eyes rolled with the motion, blacking out the room for a moment. When they came back into focus he exhaled slowly. As his body relaxed, the energy in the room centered in his chest and then lower, and finally he pushed it downward, through the chair, into the ground.

A wild thing, it thundered its way towards the streets above, punching through the rock like a wave, unstoppable. The world shook above and below the surface, and the Russian clenched his jaw, tasting blood, forcing it further and further, whipping it into a frenzy of mad energy.

When it erupted from below, the streets of Melbourne were bathed in a harsh, hateful light. It exploded through the streets, through buildings and brought everything undone.

"Yes," the Russian said. "Now it is my turn."

CHAPTER 16

DAN

MIRANDA WAS DOING well, considering she had just escaped a head on collision with two thrown cars. Dan pulled her up through the broken doors of Birdie's and down to the curb where Tabitha's car was waiting.

"Get in," the cleaner said. Her piggy tails had come undone sometime between Dan and Miranda crashing through the front glass-panes of the shop and then convincing her to help them get out of the city. Dan was amazed how unflappable she had turned out to be.

Miranda stumbled a little and then steadied herself against the car, giving a quick glance over her shoulder towards Sully and the Asian kid who Dan thought was probably Luke Ma. Sully was trying to shake the kid off his arm.

"We don't have time," Tabitha shouted. Miranda nodded and ducked her head to get inside. There was a link there, between Miranda and her bodyguard, and Dan wondered whether it might be better for her to stay with Sully rather than risk it with a hopeless guy like him.

Tabitha revved the engine and it bunny-hopped forward, letting out a bang from the exhaust.

Miranda fell into the seat and clutched her bag to her chest. Her eyes were looking forward, in shock. Tabitha regained control of her car and lifted her hand to Dan.

"Are you coming or not, Galkin?"

He stepped back, away from the car. Looking down at his hands he saw the bracelet on his wrist glow slightly. The hairs on his arms lifted. He felt a hum growing in his ears and as he turned back to the street he could feel the rising wave of energy unleashed from his grandfather. His fingers spread outward, his palms up. Above him the sky darkened even further and clouds started to flash with lightning, although it was so high up that no bolts could be seen.

The door to the car slammed.

Dan stumbled back to the street, his eyes still looking upward as his hands began to glow. It was as if the energy wave was honing in on him. The ground began to shift and then everything erupted in a white light. A column of energy shot all around him and into the sky, bathing him in electricity. It was like being born, he thought, losing track of everything else around him.

A second later it was gone.

Dan dropped to his knees and cleared his vision. The ground was jagged, the road ripped up and buildings all around him had been pushed backward by the blast.

Tabitha's car was gone.

He pulled himself up again and staggered towards where it had been only seconds before, but there was a chasm, a rupture in the street. Canyons criss-crossed all around him, and then he saw the car, its front section jutting out of the ground. Dan got to the car and grabbed for the door, but the rain made everything slippery. A tremor ran through the ground and the car shifted, precariously tilting. It was hard to see how far the fissure went, but darkness spread below.

Miranda's hands pressed against the window.

They looked at each other. Silent. Rain dripped off his face, but time stopped.

There was movement in the reflection of the window, a sliding object. Dan turned around slowly, his hands still gripping the door.

A tow truck turned sideways as it slid down the street, kicking up a spray as it swept through the flooded intersection. Dan pulled on the car door again, pressing his boot against the outside, his fingers slipping on the handle. The rain kept slamming into him, the wind whipping the trash and grit from the street. The truck lifted on to the curb across from Dan and collected the side of a sports store. More people spilled out on to the streets, part panic and part gawking.

Above him, Dan felt the rumbling of a helicopter but in a second there was a flash and a boom which flattened him against the car. The Russian was taking pot-shots at the media. Dan's breath fogged up the window and for a moment he came eye to eye with Miranda again. Her palms were still pressed against the glass. She wasn't screaming, wasn't losing it like he had feared. She just looked at him with her sad, brown eyes. The car lurched again and sank deeper into the fissure.

His fingers slipped back around the handle. The rain

seeped through his t-shirt and jeans and the electricity which hummed under his skin snapped and crackled. He had never been comfortable with using his powers in the wet, always worried that he'd end up short-circuiting his brain or detonating into oblivion like his father.

But Miranda was slipping away.

He released his hand, fingers not working, not getting any kind of hold on the slick metal handle. He felt the tingling crawl up his arm towards his chest, the electricity returning to the center, condensing, building upon itself. There was so little of the energy remaining in his system. Since the hotel explosion Dan had been drained and couldn't pull new energy into his body without immense pain.

And then Sully was beside him, his hands grabbing the car and lifting it back to the surface. Dan saw the bloodied mess on the man's arm where Luke had bitten him, but there was no sign of Luke anymore. Dan didn't ask. The bodyguard pulled open the door and Miranda spilled out into his arms. Tabitha crawled across the handbrake and stick to the passenger side. She looked up at Dan through her ruined hair, her wide eyes showing a hint of terror. He helped her out and then stumbled into the rain.

"I wasn't sure about that," she said. "We almost…"

They looked at the street but there was hardly anything to show what it had been like minutes before. Birdie's was on fire, cars were crushed and the power poles were sticking up at all kinds of angles.

"What's going on?" Miranda asked, her voice cutting through Dan's silent wonder as he looked around him. Sully wrapped a jacket around her shoulders but she couldn't keep still. Her face was streaked with black, but Dan wasn't sure if it was makeup or ash.

"We have to get you out of here," Sully said simply. He looked at Dan and then around at the devastation. Dan had the feeling that he was being judged. "It is not a safe place."

"I want to go home," Miranda said. "I just want to go home, Sully."

"They're after you aren't they?" Tabitha said, arms crossed, and looking at Dan. "You and the girl."

"It happened before," Sully added. "Do you have any enemies, Mister Galkin?"

"None that want to blow up Melbourne," he said, although he wondered whether that was entirely true. "It's got something to do with this." He lifted his hand and turned it so the bracelet could be easily seen, despite the fact his skin was now streaked with ash and grease and rain.

"It's him," Miranda said. "It's your grandfather, isn't it?"

Dan shrugged.

Sully didn't seem so sure.

"You have to get out of here," Tabitha said. "The big guy is right. The streets are not safe – for anyone."

She put a hand on Dan's shoulder and smiled a little. There was kindness there. Dan felt his throat tighten. It was like everything was falling away and all he'd be left with was some kind of crying mess. He sniffed and looked away, thumping the bracelet against the car.

"You have to look after her," Tabitha said. "You know that. I can tell."

"He's not looking after anyone," Miranda called out, checking her phone, cleaning its screen.

"You know that," Tabitha continued, ignoring Miranda. "Don't you have someone who knows about all this crap?"

Dan nodded. "But the people I know aren't the good guys," he said.

Almost on cue the world shifted strangely. It was as if they had blinked and in the short time their eyes had been closed, the world had changed subtly. Tabitha was standing slightly further away from Dan than she had been before; the fires licking through the cars back at Birdie's had leapt in intensity; and Sully was on the ground, head down and bleeding from a gash to his forehead which had dislodged his turban.

The world shifted again. Another blink.

Tabitha was covering her mouth, eyes wide as she looked at Sully. Dan had spun around and was looking away, Miranda had vanished. Sully had got to his feet again but his left arm looked useless.

A third blink, and Dan knew he was facing Grandfather Time: a drinking buddy of the Mad Russian. The man had appeared on the street, although it wasn't really in his character to be so bold. His legs were very thin, but long, and the tuxedo he wore seemed to cling to his narrow frame. The top hat which sat above the man's rather grey face, was tall and followed the lines of his body. He held a cane in his gloved hand and looked around the street with a casual air.

Dan felt Miranda bump into him, her hands holding onto his shirt as she kept close, keeping the chaos just out of sight. She was breathing hard, pulling on his shirt with each heave.

Sully wiped blood from his face and gave Dan a single nod of his head before turning to face the gentleman in the middle of the road. At first Dan had no idea what the nod meant, or even whether it was a nod or simply the man's way of shaking himself back into a clear state of mind.

Then Sully threw his fist in a wide arc and nearly collected Grandfather Time's head; but there was no chance of landing any blow on a man who could stop time. The air between the two men shimmered and Sully's fist slowed, almost frame by frame, until Sully was suspended in a frozen position.

Grandfather Time stepped around Sully and looked him up and down slowly, taking in the bodyguard's face and clothing. Then he stepped further past Sully and stood facing Dan and Miranda, both of his hands neatly clasping the cane.

"Good evening, Daniel," the man said, and he raised one of his hands to gently tip the brim of his top hat. "There is a matter your grandfather wishes to discuss with you... and the young lady in your custody."

Dan stepped back, Miranda so close that they moved together, fumbling over the broken road. He looked at Sully again, frozen and so vulnerable. Grandfather Time watched them retreat, his eyebrows raised only slightly.

"Do you expect to simply walk away from this discussion, my boy?"

"I don't expect anything," Dan shot back, still stepping backward. They were at the street corner next to a car park. He tried to pull his mind back to the electrical world, the second world he knew so well, but there was too much going on around him. The bracelet was sending a ringing sensation through his body and into his ears, distracting him from searching the surroundings for something to draw upon. There were electricity lines everywhere, of course, but he couldn't make a connection.

The air shimmered again.

A hand pressed down on Dan's shoulder and he winced under the pressure as Grandfather Time appeared suddenly behind him, his fingers digging in to Dan's skin. With a twist, the old man pulled Dan down to a kneeling position. He held Miranda around the wrist with his other gloved hand and she was pulling at him with both hands.

"It is time," he said simply. Dan looked around and up to the man's eyes and he saw the distinctive hourglass pupils. He had first seen them years ago and they had given him nightmares for weeks. He tried to twist himself free but the man held him fast.

And then there was a sharp crack and Grandfather Time staggered backward, his fingers lifting from Dan's shoulder and clutching frantically at his own. A second cracking sound followed.

"Don't just stand there!" Tabitha shouted as she leaned across her car, leveling a handgun over the roof. She fired a third shot and Dan dropped to the ground as he saw the flash, but the bullet went wide.

Grandfather Time looked at his hand, stained red from the shoulder wound. Dan had never seen the man pause for so long.

"Look after her Galkin!" Tabitha shouted and fired again, the fourth shot connecting with Grandfather Time's leg. He collapsed to the ground, his leg snapping out to the side.

Dan reached out and took Miranda's hand, pulling her quickly to her feet and then across the road to the car park. The two of them leapt over debris and through the boom gates, the sound of another gunshot behind them.

As he passed the second rate lighting in the car park, Dan ran a surge of energy through them, and then through the rest of the lights contained in the building; blowing them into darkness. His reserves were nearly dry. He'd never felt so hollow. They reached the stairwell and Dan pushed Miranda ahead, the heavy clank of the door closing behind them leaving them in total darkness.

CHAPTER 17
MIRANDA

M IRANDA FELT THE rough edge of the wall behind her as they stopped running. It felt safe, solid. The whole world seemed to be falling apart outside, with roads being ruptured by blasts of fire and strange people throwing cars and doing impossible things all around her; but now she felt like it was a whole other world away, somewhere out there.

The darkness wasn't absolute. As her eyes adjusted, she could see Dan's outline, listening for pursuit. He seemed calm. Her own breathing was erratic and she concentrated on bringing it under control, but it was hopeless. Her tai chi instructor never taught her how to bring about calm in such a crazy situation. It was all about controlling emotions before a concert, about channeling the nervous energy, harnessing the adrenalin.

"We can't stay here," Dan said softly. She felt his breath, they were that close. She nodded, watching his lips. It was only a matter of time before she would be running again, and without Sully to stop the threats she really didn't know what would happen to her. She was scared. Probably more than she'd ever been.

When she signed on to the international tour, her father introduced her to Sully. They knew each other, apparently, although how a family man from Riverside, California knew a Turkish adventurer, she never found out. Sully was very good at evading conversations when he wanted to, and her father was on the other side of the world. But in the first few days Sully put her at ease, being there as a stand-in parent as well as a bodyguard against the more intrusive demands of her manager and the local crews in each city.

After the protests in Los Angeles and Seattle, they made a pact to always be honest with each other, to be there no matter what the personal cost. At first Miranda thought it was more about making her feel comfortable, that the promises were really one-way. But Sully needed her too. He missed his own family: his wife, his two sons. Miranda didn't know where they were or why he couldn't be with them, but she soon learned that she made his life a little better just as he did for her. They went horse riding in the Rockies for three days before her tour left the United States, and during the long, anxious nights, she heard him speaking in his sleep.

His mouth twisted in pain and he shouted out to someone he couldn't see. Miranda didn't know Arabic but she could interpret the emotions. When he woke the next morning she made it her goal to keep him smiling as much as possible. Even through the stress of travel, the terror of Jakarta, Sully remained her keystone. But now he had been taken away, brought to his knees by a sinister man in a top hat.

"Who was that back there?" she asked as they waited.

"A bad man," Dan said, his breath still close, like he was watching her. She touched her cheek and felt it was wet.

"And what does he want?"

Dan pulled himself up and then held out a hand for Miranda to take. She had no other choice and he pulled her up and then pressed his other hand against a door. Shafts of muted light filtered in as the door opened. They were stepping out onto one of the upper levels. She heard a helicopter in the distance, and then an explosion like three popping firecrackers, all in a row. She held her breath as the silence returned, and then she heard the helicopter again. It was safe.

"Have you got a credit card?"

He pressed her hand gently, pulling her out into the open space. She could see him clearer now. His face looked so normal, like any other boy she'd known. He didn't look like he belonged to this kind of mess, like he'd be comfortable trading blows with supervillains, tossing cars, shooting out balls of fire. He just looked normal.

Maybe even cute.

A closer explosion rocked the building and she grabbed for his arm to steady herself. He looked towards the edge of the car park, a long way off.

"Come on," he said. "I need to get to the phone."

"I've got a phone," she said, instinctively pulling it out of her jacket pocket. She pressed her thumb to the side and the screen jumped to life. Dan's eyes widened and she felt a vibration in her phone. There was a bearded man on her screen looking furtively from left to right, his eyes digitized specks of light. The face pushed forward against the screen and it was suddenly a three dimensional image.

Dan grabbed the phone from her and turned it off.

Her hands were shaking, but he pressed the phone back into her palm and closed her fingers around it.

"Better put it away," he said. Then he tilted his chin towards a pay phone. "Needs to be ... anonymous."

She nodded. Her eyes blinked back tears as she dropped her phone back into her bag. There was a second explosion, closer, and she clamped her hands over her ears. The ringing was so intense, and the image of the holographic man seemed to yell at her even though it was gone. Dan mouthed something at her, pointing to the purse she had pulled out with her phone.

"Credit card!"

She heard him the first time but it didn't seem like it was important considering the amount of danger they were in.

"Why?"

"I need to use it."

Dan pulled the handset from the phone booth and listened for a dial tone. He pumped the cradle twice and then started dialing a number.

"If you're ordering pizza..."

She heard her own words, amazed at the way she sounded confident, flippant even, despite her heart racing against her chest.

"Have you got the card?"

She passed him the platinum piece of plastic and huddled down next to the wall, her hands over her ears but still watching him. He shifted the phone to his other ear and then lifted the card, squinting at the number.

"Bree, it's me," he said. Miranda let her hands slip from her ears. "I've got a problem."

He rolled his eyes and nodded, once, then again.

"Need an evac, not a lecture. Yes, there's a card here. It's good to go. I'm punching the number in now."

He looked quickly down at Miranda as she sat still beside him.

"No, it's not stolen."

Dan pulled out his own mobile and was entering numbers into it while cradling the other phone with his neck and pressing the credit card against the glass to help everything stay balanced. It was funny, or would have been, in a different situation.

"It's in," he said. "GPS co-ordinates too. We're on the third floor. Can you get us out now?"

He hung up the phone and stepped away from the wall, handing back the credit card and slipping his mobile back into his pocket.

"I thought you lost your phone," she said. "At the airport."

"This is my other phone."

"Uh-huh."

"It's the secret one. For superhero business."

"Since when are you a superhero?"

Dan looked around the semi-darkness, anxious.

"I was being sarcastic," he said. "She should be here by now."

Miranda stood up again. Her jeans were torn, her hair a mess. She needed to get back to Sully and then to an airport.

Dan started to chew his fingernail as he paced the lot. She smiled, despite herself, and realized just how much younger he was. As she pulled her hair back into a ponytail she turned around and saw a woman standing just behind her.

"I'm Bree," the woman said. "Your credit card checked out. I won't be able to give you a receipt though. The machine's down."

Dan pushed past Miranda, grabbed her hand in his and then held his other hand out to Bree. The new woman smiled at him and gave him a slow look from his trainers to his cut-up face.

"You've been having fun."

"Can we talk about this later?" he asked.

"Sure." She took his hand and Miranda watched in horror as first Dan, and then Miranda herself, began to dissolve into grains of sand. She opened her mouth to scream but nothing came. She lifted her hand but it was nothing but sand. And then everything was gone and she had the feeling of being whisked up twenty floors in an elevator.

There was a gritty feeling in her mouth and a tightness in her throat. She found herself on a polished timber floor, her legs splayed to the side and her hands rubbing her neck.

"It's psychological," a voice said. "There's nothing in your mouth. You're as I found you in the car park."

Miranda looked over her shoulder and saw the girl from before. She stood with a bottle of water in her hand and when Miranda's eyes locked on to it, the girl smiled and tossed it to her. Miranda caught it with two hands and hurried to open the lid, scarping down the water to ease the soreness.

"Thanks," she said.

"You're the paying customer, I presume," the girl said. "Dan's not the kind of boy who goes around waving exclusive credit cards."

Miranda took another drink and then helped herself off the floor, taking the time to look around her new environment. The space was obviously a loft of some kind, and there was a view which included an ocean, the lights of ships red, green and white. It reminded her of Christmas parades back home.

"I'm Bree," the girl said. "Your boyfriend's fixing his face."

"Miranda."

"I know," Bree said. "You're on the telly."

Miranda was impressed with the Spartan décor: wide spaces, minimalist style. She had the impression that it wasn't a room that was lived in. Bree gave a similar impression: practical, transient. She was Middle Eastern, or North African. Her hair was tightly braided in short stumps. Miranda felt for her own hair which was falling over her shoulders. There were times, she admitted to herself, where a team of stylists was a blessing, but she knew any contact with her tour team would likely end in more explosions, more blood and more clashes with things that were better off left to the imagination.

"What do you mean, fixing his face?" she asked, processing Bree's earlier words. The other girl smiled, but then Dan appeared through a door: shirtless with a towel over his shoulders, his hair partly wet after being hurriedly dried.

There was a gash across his forehead, another wound he'd collected in her service.

"You're okay?" he asked.

Miranda nodded and took another drink of water, pulling her eyes away from his fresh face, those green eyes, those abs. He walked past her and gave Bree a quick hug. Miranda turned to watch them, but they pulled apart quickly, almost like brother and sister.

"What now?" Miranda asked while Bree pulled away from Dan and leaned against the wall, a smile playing on her face. "Have you called the police?"

"You can't do that," Bree said, even as Dan was about to speak. "This is out of their league, and they know it. Even if you did get them to believe you, any help they sent would be fresh meat for the likes of the Mad Russian. You'd be sending them to their deaths."

"Dramatic, much?" Dan murmured, grabbing his t-shirt. "We better just keep out of sight, until I can work out what's really going on."

"You mean, whether you're the one they want dead or me, right?" Miranda asked. "Why don't you just say it? I think we're a bit past secrets, pizza boy."

Dan's face shifted from one expression to the next, as if he couldn't find the words or the tone to respond. She'd watched him enter her life as a cynical, hard-done-by kid and then some kind of weird monster who could survive being flattened by a hotel. She wondered how he would show himself next.

"It's Dan there're after," Bree said. "There, I've said it. Miranda can go home."

The words washed over her in a mixture of relief and

fear. It sounded so simple, like a rear exit from the stage. She could leave this mess, get on a plane and fly home to California. She could fade away. But she'd done that before, in Jakarta.

She didn't want to be that person.

"How do you know that?" Miranda asked slowly, and she could tell that's what Dan wanted to know too. "People have been after me as well, here and at the last few concerts overseas. A … a thing came out of my phone. How can you be so sure?"

"Because they approached me," Bree said. "Asked me to join the reunion tour, but I said I'd outgrown them."

"Who?" Dan asked, moving to her, moving back into the shared space with Bree. Suddenly Miranda wasn't even there as far as he was concerned. "Did *he* come here?"

"God no," Bree said. "Just a man, representing a man and so on. The Russian is never that direct. Besides, I think Grim is more involved with this thing. I see you're carrying his work."

Dan lifted his wrist, the silver cuff clear to the three of them.

"This is Grim's work?" Dan asked.

"He was commissioned by the Russian. Having trouble with your powers lately? It's a standard restraining device, probably calibrated especially for your DNA. I'm sure your grandfather was more than happy to oblige with a sample if Grim didn't already have it on file."

"So what did they offer you?" Dan asked, dropping his hand.

Bree laughed.

"The usual."

"And you said no?"

"Dan, I'm not going back to that world. You got out of it, so you know what I mean. But there're loose ends and they all wind back to you. You can't go to the police or the super heroes. They've been bought or scattered. Every inch of the city is under surveillance in some way or another."

"I've got people," Miranda said. Somewhere out there Sully would be looking for her. She didn't want to think about the man in the top hat, his gaunt face and blurring movements. Sully was unstoppable. He'd told her that the second time they'd met, and he hadn't been wrong about anything before.

"They've got your people," Bree said.

"That's not true," Miranda said, but she really had no idea. Bree ignored her.

"The only place left to you is the secret world, right under their noses," Bree said. "Those people are the only ones who can get you out of the city."

"Like you? People like you?" Dan asked.

"I'm not getting involved in this beyond what I've done already," she said. "You need to get out of the city."

Miranda wasn't sure she wanted to go back outside. A quick look out the window and she realized she was in some kind of apartment complex above a spreading series of docks. Melbourne was still out there, looming behind her.

"Can you get me to Grim's house?" Dan asked.

Bree shook her head and looked away.

"Please?" he asked, voice dropping.

Miranda felt sick, her throat tightening again, her heart rate thumping into a higher gear.

"I'll call you a taxi," Bree said.

CHAPTER 18

DAN

THE RIDE INTO the city was quiet. They scored a melancholy driver who seemed more interested in two photographs lodged on his dashboard than in opening up conversation with Dan and Miranda. They were photos of two children and the driver who was wearing cricket whites and smiling widely into the camera. Dan wondered whether Miranda had family, whether her father took time out for her. She was looking out of the window, her profile lit up every now and then with the passing headlights of traffic. Sometimes he wished he could steal a happy childhood.

But childhood really wasn't an option anymore. He was seventeen and there was nothing out there except the cold, hard world of adults. He didn't really have a plan, of course, but he knew he had to be proactive. If he waited then the Russian would catch him. His only chance was in getting out of the city, and for that to happen he needed help.

"Where are we going?" Miranda asked softly. She had her knees up to her chin, resting on the seats. She didn't look at him.

"To a friend's house."

She scoffed quietly.

"I didn't think you had friends," she said.

"A family friend."

It had been a very long time since he'd seen Gerhardt Eis, the man everyone called Grim. It had been just before everything fell apart, before the camping trip to the Grampians, before the unraveling. He was an uncle, of sorts. Good with machines.

Dan ran his fingers across the metal cuff. He couldn't sense the electrical world anymore, not in any distinct shape. There was a pressure out there, like a creature shuddering along its path, but he couldn't see or communicate with it. The metal cuff had messed him up somehow and since Grim was its creator, Dan figured he'd be the best one to take it apart. Once he was free and back in control of his powers, then they could sneak out of Melbourne.

As the taxi stopped at traffic lights Dan looked out and saw familiar houses and then a tacky fish and chip shop he had been to as a child. They were getting closer.

"This'll do," he said, tapping the back of the driver's seat. He passed the man some money and got out into the evening air. Miranda slid across the seat and stood up next to him on the curb. They looked at the flashing lights around the fish and chip shop and were greeted with tempting smells.

"Smells good," she said.

"I promise to get you chips later," Dan said. She shrugged and looked up and down the street. Cars sped past with the hum of engines and the spray of water from the road.

He took her hand. He didn't know why, but he did.

And she let him take it.

They walked down the street, anonymous but hunted nonetheless. At the corner they turned left and walked down a darker street.

"It's been a long time," he murmured. He could see the house, sixty feet away, windows dark and the aluminum cladding in a shabby state of disrepair.

Miranda squeezed his hand.

The poker nights had a sense of excitement about them, and even though Dan, at the age of ten, hadn't begun to manifest his sensitivity to the electrical world, he could almost hear a hum in the air as his grandfather scooted around his house making everything just right.

There was no real way for Dan to know that his grandfather was a supervillain, or that his poker buddies were notorious criminals with names like Yellow Peril or Grandfather Time. To Dan, they were Aunty Pearl and Uncle Jon-Jon, and compared with the shut-up life he had with his mother, who was afraid of everything, poker nights presented Dan with a glimpse at the wider, more exciting world of grownups.

His mother would retreat to the guest bedroom a little after seven and when the door clicked, Dan's grandfather would change gears, increase his agitation and move around in a manic way that often had Dan laughing, although never to the old man's face.

Dan could tell that staying in his grandfather's house was unnerving to his mother, but they had come to a truce especially while Dan's father was in prison. They moved in so Dan could be watched while she recovered from her breakdown. No one was really happy about the arrangement. His mother felt like the world was collapsing in on her and didn't seem to care enough to do anything about it, and his grandfather mostly felt embarrassed by his imprisoned son and, in his words, 'wanted to make sure mistakes weren't repeated'. Dan figured that meant his grandfather expected him to one day end up in prison as well.

It was funny how things turned out.

The poker game started after the sun disappeared, and Dan's grandfather cackled like a sideshow magician, laughing at the evils about to be unleashed. It was never so dramatic, and apart from the regular scuffles over misplaced chips or accusations of cheating, the games were really just about a group of old people gathering around to tell tales on each other and revisit old arguments.

After the initial excitement of the night, Dan usually ended up asleep in the door jamb between the living room and the kitchen, and the guests stepped over him to fetch refreshments, sometimes commenting on his resemblance to his father. When he was half-asleep during these times he usually heard the most interesting stories but the fusion between voices and dreams always made him uncertain about what he really heard.

One night, though, Dan was sitting out on the back veranda listening to mosquitoes when Grim scuffled out of the back door and coughed like he was choking to death. The coughing was usually followed by sneezes which verged on barks, and Dan looked up expecting to see the red face and watery eyes of his grandfather's German friend. The sneeze barks never came. Dan was a little disappointed.

"*Guten abend*," Grim said, sorting his handkerchief back into his pocket. He was a balding, rather round and red-faced man. Dan watched the dark hair on the back of Grim's hands as he pulled out his packet of cigarettes and lit one up, coughing again as he drew in the smoke.

"Are you winning?" Dan asked. It was his usual response, no matter which of his grandfather's friends appeared next to him. They usually grunted or smiled at him, and then went away.

"No," the old man said slowly. It was strange how long it took for him to release the word, like it was playing on his lips, refusing to make the leap. Grim's eyes closed and he breathed in the cigarette, his nostrils flaring a little. "No, *mein freund*, it is not a day for winning."

"Aunty Pearl said you were on a losing streak last month," Dan said. "Said you should stay home."

Grim shrugged.

"Pearl is correct," he said. "She's a crafty one."

Dan moved over to make room for Grim to sit down on the steps. He smelt of cigarettes and whiskey, and maybe wet hair. It wasn't Dan's ideal way to end the night, but he had been getting bored with listening for insects in the growing night.

"The days are not for us any more," Grim declared. "No matter what Galkin says, no matter the way the others protest. It is a certainty."

"It's just a game."

"Not any more."

"You'll be back next month. Luck changes," Dan said,

smiling in encouragement. Grim looked like a beaten dog and even though Dan didn't particularly care one way or the other, he didn't want to get caught on the steps with a slobbering wreck. If depression took a hold of the old man, Dan knew he wouldn't be leaving the steps for a long time.

"It is nice you say these things," Grim said and passed Dan the cigarette. "But you are young, not part of the old days. To you we are old men and women, playing card games in the living room."

He sighed. Dan took a tentative tug at the cigarette and coughed once.

"In our days we ruled the world," Grim continued as Dan took another breath. "But the glory days are no more, the rules they have changed and never go back now."

Dan had heard his grandfather complaining about the world, almost every day actually, and it had become a chorus alternating between his grandfather and his mother as they cursed the present and clung to the past. Dan didn't particularly like anything about the past. His hopes rested on the future, when he could do something and be someone, instead of the son of a blue-skinned freak-woman who didn't allow him to do anything the other kids were allowed to do.

"The past isn't so great," Dan said. He blew out the smoke slowly, enjoying the feeling of being mature.

Grim cursed in German and spat to the side before reaching out and snagging the cigarette from between Dan's lips. He gave Dan a look and then the cigarette, shrugged and sighed.

"This thing with India," he said. "It is no good when a

country acts like that, in that way. The conflict is global now, not our little games, our little … personal playground."

Later, Dan remembered that India had annexed Pakistan a year before in a bloody and bold show of nationalism, backed by what seemed like hundreds of uberhuman agents. It had been difficult to get impartial reports from the area and somehow the whole *invasion* had been and gone. The fall-out was reported less and less and it seemed even the world leaders had accepted that India was within its rights to expand its territory to combat terrorism. It had been exciting for the younger Dan, in the opening stages, but when the men and women in suits took over from the elephant-headed gods and living whirlwinds, he didn't see the big deal in any of it. Grim, on the other hand, seemed to be taking the whole thing personally.

"India is a long way from here," Dan said.

"Not so far."

"Uh-huh."

"You miss point, Daniel. The scales are not right any more, no room for individuals like us. Everything is now on world stage, with world media and power-brokers. Grim is just old dog now, and that lot in there are finished too."

He looked over his shoulder and sort of rested his chin there, defeated. There were sounds coming from inside, some glassware clinking and muted conversations.

"It's just a game," Dan said again.

Grim stood up, holding on to the rail as he did so, showing his age even more. He breathed deeply and stepped up to the veranda and then back inside the house. Almost immediately the sounds inside lifted and laughter rang out. Dan stepped off into the garden and walked to the gate, closing out the smells and sounds, and seeking out the insects again.

The gate was broken and weeds grew up through the iron-work. As Dan stood there looking at the front door he wondered whether the time had come for all of his grand-father's friends to fade away. There hadn't been any public news from them since the Mad Russian vanished, apart from some rumors about Pearl and her sprawling crimi-nal empire. Probably the world had changed, like Grim predicted. The Celestial Knights were bigger than ever, but they operated in global circles, rarely coming to touch the ground in Melbourne. And the threats had become more indistinct – secret cells of terrorists or the occasional mad science experiment rampaging through a city. America still had its fair share of costumed bad guys, but the rest of the world seemed to have moved on.

Until now.

"This is the house?" Miranda asked. She was still hold-ing his hand. He nodded and pushed the gate a little with his foot, the squeaking protest of the hinges making him wince.

They weaved their way through the gate and to the front door. Grim had moved into the old house after Dan's grand-father vanished. Theresa hadn't wanted it, so Grim crawled in and never left. There were no lights outside or inside. It didn't look promising. But even if the old man wasn't home, Dan knew there might be some way for him to break the cuff, some kind of device or instructions left behind.

Of course, he also knew that he could be walking into a trap. With a glance back to the street he wondered whether the house was being monitored.

Miranda rapped her knuckles on the door, giving him an annoyed look, but still she didn't let go of his hand. After her knock, she stepped back a little, and Dan gave her a smile.

"You'd think a pizza boy would know how to knock on a door," she mumbled, but there was a smile on her lips too. Dan tried the door handle. It was unlocked so he turned it and pushed open the door.

A musty smell greeted them as the door swung backwards, almost rolling out as if it'd been bottled for months. It was a mixture of swamp water and wet dog. Miranda covered her nose with her sleeve, but Dan stepped into the house with his full focus on finding out if anyone was inside.

He ran his hands over the walls, the limited connection with the house's electrical work drawing him to the light switch. Dan kicked the door closed as the hallway lights flickered on.

The place was full of junk. Even in the hallway, Grim had piles of magazines rising to an impressive height, stacked on side tables and even on the floor. The first room to the right was full of boxes overflowing with papers and schematics. Disused and outdated computer monitors punctuated the boxes, their screens intact or broken, but nonetheless useless. The other front room was full of furniture, piled up like a road accident. They moved to the living area and found it had been fitted out like a workshop. Benches were crowded with machines and power tools. Working computers blinked softly in the background.

Dan's fingers closed over a lighter sitting on the kitchen bar. He looked at it, his thumb rubbing over the wolf logo. It had been Grim's favorite thing, his keepsake. But it wasn't just a lighter.

"You're a sight for sore eyes," a voice called out. Miranda had wandered to the back door in the kitchen. Dan turned around, already knowing the voice.

He slipped the lighter into his pocket.

It wasn't Grim.

The young man was leaning against the door to the back rooms. Behind him was a glow, probably from a laptop. He wore a fur-lined hooded jacket over a singlet and jeans. Gold sparkled from his neck.

"Halo," Dan said.

CHAPTER 19
HALO

H E WAS ONLY a child the first time he heard another person's thoughts inside his head. His mother lay with her head in his lap, gasping through blood which bubbled over her lips. Her eyes held him in place, refusing to let him see the wreckage of her body. Bombs exploded up and down the road outside. The sun filtered through the crumbling wall, making him blink in the harsh light and dust.

Mujhe tumse mohabat hai … Mujhe tumse mohabat hai … Love you, love you…

And she taught him a valuable lesson that day. Everyone dies. And when they do, there is no dignity, no graceful passing from this world to the next. There's blood and desperation, a clinging to anything solid while the heart betrays the brain, refusing to pump the oxygen to keep the darkness at bay.

Even before his thirteenth birthday, Sohail Pirzada was forced to flee his home in eastern Pakistan, along with his father, cousins, and thousands of other refugees. When the shadow of India stretched across the land, few alternatives were offered to his people, other than to run.

And running became his vocation.

Moving from one refugee camp to the next, often in the middle of the night to avoid the authorities or ruthless gangs, Halo found his way to Australia. And the running continued, only now it involved keeping one step ahead of the law as he turned his hand to shoplifting and small cons. His father was harsh, but the words and hand of a broken man were never enough to keep Halo standing still and compliant for long.

He withdrew into his own world, not trusting anyone. He could read what they really thought, sometimes things that they didn't even realize they were thinking. School teachers with cruel thoughts hidden behind empty but smiling praise. Uncles who hated to even look at him, or wished he was dead. Men of faith who cheated and stole. No one had a clear conscience. Everyone hid a dark stain.

It wasn't until he stole a necklace from an old Russian man that Halo met a force able to stop him in his tracks. And even now, years later, it was the Russian who was threatening to undermine everything Halo had built in the man's absence. For five years, he moved his way through a series of underworld cartels, offering his services here, impressing the right people there. At each point he would glean information from his new employers without them knowing. A single look in their eyes and the whole network opened up for him: secret dealings, alliances, important names and numbers, locations of caches, passwords.

But the Mad Russian had returned.

And he had demanded unbroken allegiance.

"You are my hands in this," he said. "The little god of vengeance."

Halo wanted to say he wasn't so little anymore, but his pride was held back by survival instincts. The only way to stay alive was to stay useful, and so he had been deployed to the old house with a simple instruction and no room for negotiation.

The house was rancid.

Grim sat in a cane-backed chair, rubbing at himself, his skin red under the thick bush of hair which ran the length of his arm. He offered Halo a coffee but the mug remained untouched on the kitchen bench.

"You have something for me?" Grim asked with a voice one step away from panic. "Something from Galkin?"

"You haven't been a very good soldier," Halo said.

"I have," Grim barked, rising a little from his chair. Halo raised his finger and the old man sat back down, his hands now in his lap. "I have always done what was asked, always."

"In the old times, probably, but with the Russian out of the picture you got a bit sloppy."

"I thought he was dead."

"We all did," Halo said. "Some of us got a little carried away with it though, wouldn't you say?"

"I only wanted to retire, to leave this mess."

"Come here," Halo said, and he stepped closer and took the man's chin in his gloved hand, pulling it up so he could look into the old man's eyes.

"Halo... I only wanted it to end."

"And it will," Halo said.

There was a brief flash of light, bursting from within

Halo's eyes, and the old man relaxed a little, held by the power of Halo's mind forcing its way inside his own.

Forgive me Father, for I have sinned…

Three seconds…

He'll kill us all… the world will burn if he's not stopped…

Four seconds, and it was done.

Grim's head slumped backward, his glassy eyes looking to the ceiling.

Halo slid the knife out from under Grim's ribs, and wiped it on the man's pajama pants. Two wipes, one for each side, and the blade was new again.

"The Russian doesn't like strays," he said softly. "You knew that, just as well as I did."

There were noises from the front of the house and his fingers tensed around the blade's handle. Three knocks and he knew he had to move quickly. He tucked the blade into a sheath hidden under the waistband of his jeans, and grabbed the back of Grim's chair. With a quick kick, the chair tilted to lean on its back legs, and Halo dragged it to the walk-in pantry, pleased with himself that blood hadn't leaked out to the floor.

The front door opened.

He pulled the chair right into the small room and jammed it against a wall of shelves. Grim's body slumped to the right but remained wedged there and safe from discovery.

Halo stepped around the chair and listened at the door.

There were voices, and as he recognized Dan Galkin, a smile crept across his face. He looked back to the dead man and shook a finger at him.

"You sly old dog," he said.

He opened the door and slipped quietly into the room. He saw the girl first, but Dan was there in the room as well. He looked fresh enough, which was surprising, considering the damage done in the city. He pulled off his gloves and tossed them into the pantry.

"You're a sight for sore eyes," he said, closing the door behind him.

Miranda Brody looked at him wide-eyed.

Dan seemed a little surprised as well.

"Halo."

Halo smiled and leaned against the door.

"The same," he said. "Although I've got to ask what you're doing here."

Dan walked closer, coming to a stop about the place where Halo had killed Grim. Miranda stepped back until she was beside him.

"Where's Grim?" Dan asked, although his eyes were trained on the floor just in front of Halo. Dan remembered what Halo could do.

"I don't know," he said. "I was hoping you two were him, actually." He cocked his chin towards Miranda. "Who's your friend?"

"Elley," she said quickly. Halo smiled.

"Funny, but you look like Miranda Brody."

"I need to see Grim," Dan said. "Do you know where he could be? It's kind of urgent."

"Has this got something to do with our favorite psychopathic grandfather?"

Dan didn't say anything, but he didn't need to. Halo looked to Miranda but she wasn't looking at him either.

"Thing is, you're a wanted man. A guy called Curtis

came and offered me money to tell him everything I knew about you."

"Typical."

"I didn't tell him anything," Halo said. "But I found out a lot when we got close enough. Guy didn't even wear shades, like some amateur sent to the slaughter. The thing is, this Curtis guy, was hired by Grim. Mad Russian is back and he's got this idea to get his mates back at the table so they can run the old games, as if nothing's happened, you know?"

He stepped away from the pantry door, towards the kitchen basin.

"Imagine sending someone to me for information and not protecting themselves," he said, with his back turned. "So I figured it was a trick."

"They tried to kill me," Dan said softly.

"I know. Seraphima and explosives from your pop."

Halo turned around again. Dan was standing closer, along the bench, but still not looking his way.

"What did you do to the Curtis guy?" Dan asked.

Halo laughed and play-punched Dan on the shoulder.

"I stabbed him in the guts and hid him in the pantry."

Dan smiled.

"I'm not kidding," Halo said. But then he smiled widely and grabbed Dan's shoulder, turning him around and wrapping his arms around him, pulling him into a hug.

"It's good to see you," Dan said and then pulled away.

"Liar," Halo said, smiling again.

"Have you seen my grandfather?"

"Not for a while," Halo said. "Not since he died. Still, I don't think he'll give a toss about me anymore. You're the prodigal grandson, so with you in the picture I figure I can do whatever I want. He probably doesn't even remember me."

He pulled Dan's hand up and studied the metal cuff.

"That's Grim's work."

"I know," Dan said. "I need to get it off me and then get out of Melbourne."

"I need to stay alive," Halo said. "Helping you can get me noticed. My life's my own."

"We've got money," Miranda said.

"So have I," he said. "Thing is, I don't like the fact they sent this Curtis guy to shake me down."

He looked at Miranda and she smiled under his scrutiny.

"Tell you what," he said. "I'll take you to people. They can make anyone disappear, and all it'll cost you is a bit of time with your friend here. Elley is it?"

She nodded.

"You look like Miranda Brody."

"You look like you listen to her music," Miranda said.

He laughed again.

"Where are these people?" Dan asked.

"Chinatown, of course," Halo said. "But it's not about going straight to the source. There's a dance to it, a weaving through place to get to the final destination."

He was talking to Miranda now, always to the girl.

"So, Elley, do you wanna see the real Melbourne?" he asked her.

CHAPTER 20

DAN

HALO WEAVED MIRANDA through the night, sweeping her into alleys with live music and then out again into night markets peppered with Asian cuisine. His voice was smooth and assured, even more so than his movements which showed that Melbourne was his town, and it unfolded according to his command.

Dan hated him.

In fact, as Dan trailed behind the laughter and animated critiques of the world of food and music, he admitted that he'd always hated Halo. He'd hated him on the first day, back when they were brought together under the pretense of becoming the next generation of heroes. For years he'd put up with Halo's desperation to come out on top. It didn't matter that no one else was playing the game. Halo made sure he was the winner and that everyone else around him was crushed in the process. The Mad Russian often compared Halo and Dan, and no one was ever left with any doubt about where the old man's favors fell.

"This isn't your lucky night is it?" Halo's voice reached Dan and he looked up to see Halo leaning against the brick wall, his head angled down towards Miranda who looked up at him like some groupie. There was something wrong with the image: the loud, cocky and rude Miranda suddenly being tamed by Halo of all people.

Dan hated mind powers.

"It doesn't bother me," she said. "Luck changes all the time."

Halo took on the look of being impressed by her insight, his eyes flashing in the semi-darkness, but Dan knew it was just another strategic move. He caught up and looked around, noticing that the alley had been done up in various tags and graffiti. He traced a Lizard Boy tag with his finger. It was fresh.

"Nice dead-end," he mumbled.

"I've got to show you this one last place," Halo said. He turned around and the afterglow of his powers was still in his eyes, sinking back into his head. Halo could steal ideas, memories and feelings. All he had to do was flash his eyes at you and he'd gain access to every one of your secrets.

The way he moved should have given Dan a warning; like a panther casually leading prey to a clearing. Dan didn't really know whether panthers led prey to clearings, but when the three of them slipped through an old door in the alley and then down stairs to a basement, it was the first image that formed in his head.

"Bastard," he breathed.

But behind the heavy door was a thumping cocktail of light and sound. A bouncer gave Halo a thumbs-up and let them inside. Dan pressed his hand against his temple, pushing back the throbbing pain that lingered there. The bracelet was making him feel sick.

Miranda appeared in front of him. She smiled widely, almost as if she had no problems in her life. He felt bad that he'd let Halo soften her anxiety, let him take away her fear with his golden eyes. But she was out of her depth and he had to keep her protected until they could get out of the city.

"Come on," she said, and pulled him towards a booth where Halo was waiting with his arm along the back, waiting for Miranda to return. Dan nodded and let himself be dragged deeper inside.

Drinks appeared as he fell into the seat and he mouthed a thanks to Halo. His arm was around Miranda's shoulder now, but his eyes were on Dan. Even in the pulsing light and shadow of the club his eyes were golden. He was weaving his magic.

"You still like the brain dead girls?" Dan asked across the noise. Halo laughed. Miranda didn't seem to understand.

"It's my specialty, Dan," Halo said. "How often do you use the TV remote?"

"I don't think it's the same thing," Dan said.

"I think it is."

He pulled Miranda a little closer, although she seemed more drawn to the dance floor. Dan felt a tremor of hope that Halo's influence wouldn't stick forever.

"Hey," Halo said, close to her ear. "Have a look at this guy."

Miranda turned and looked at Dan. She had relaxed. Any threat she felt an hour ago was gone, and part of Dan wished they were still running for their lives. He would prefer the barbed comments to the honey-glow of infatuation that Halo dripped over her.

"Have you noticed how much this guy talks?" Halo asked.

Miranda smiled and sipped from her drink.

"All talk," Halo added. "You know the rest."

"Yeah," Miranda nodded.

"He's not really your type, is he? I mean, the boy scout thing gets a little dull around the age of, what, twelve?"

Miranda laughed and Halo leaned closer to her. His fingers were playing with hers in her lap, intertwining. Dan felt a wave of nausea again and sat back.

"He's a special guy, though," Halo continued. "Special, like freak show special. The boy's mum is his aunt, his uncle's his dad, classic fucked up genes."

Dan wished he had access to his powers. As he forced himself to breathe deeply he imagined Halo being thrown backward across the floor, arcs of electricity feeding on him from all directions.

Miranda looked confused, as if she were calculating something in her head.

"Is that true?" she asked him, leaning away from Halo, across the table, where her hands cradled his glass. Halo gathered her hands again and brought them back to her lap.

"His grandfather's a great man, Miranda, but he's a villain: a calculating cold-blooded, whack job villain. What'd you expect?"

All Dan could see was the wideness of Miranda's eyes. He'd let her become duped by Halo just so he could have the time to work out a solution. And it wasn't working. It never did.

"Let's get out of here," Dan said and slid across the booth's seat.

"Dan, wait," Miranda said, grabbing his arm. "I'm not judging you."

Dan pulled himself free.

"Of course not. Who would judge this crap?"

As he stood up, he nearly collected a waitress. She was suddenly right there in front of him. He started to apologize but then saw who it was, and stopped.

"Hello Dan," she said. Her face was porcelain or ice, and he could feel the coldness cascading off her. They were too close, and she stepped back, her face remaining politely impassive.

"Her name's Lily," Halo said, his arm draped over Miranda's shoulders in the booth. "We go way back. Sometimes Danny forgets about that, forgets about who he is, where he comes from."

"Come with me, please," she said softly, bowing so that her sleek black hair fell to the sides of her face. She raised her head again and turned, walking back through the club, her black dress swishing elegantly in her wake. Dan shrugged his way into the crowd after her.

"Don't worry," Halo called out. "I'll look after your celebrity girlfriend."

CHAPTER 21

HALO

HALO WAS OLDER than Dan, so he knew how the world worked and wasn't blinded by optimism. It wasn't that he'd sunk into a grey world of helplessness and despair – no, he had more self-respect than that. Instead of optimism, Halo employed an active self-interested view of the world. He worked hard to get what he wanted, and didn't worry too much about the journey.

Sometimes though, the journey was interesting. Like with Miranda Brody. The fact that Dan was obviously crushing on her made it all the more satisfying. The kid needed to harden up and fast. The future had no time for a Dan Galkin who was afraid to unleash his birth right.

The Mad Russian would either have his version of Dan or there would be no version of Dan. The fact that the kid remained clueless was slightly amusing, although the amusement would only last a few more minutes. Fate was waiting in Chinatown.

Halo pulled Miranda to her feet and led her to the floor, the girl's body already shifting to the beat. Miranda squeezed his hand and he let it go so she could surge forward and show him her moves. She was a professional, he had to admit. Probably been taking lessons since she was born.

Behind the whirl of Miranda, Halo watched Dan and Lily. The quiet girl had always been a stranger to him, but with Dan it was different. He grinned. Somehow Dan was able to melt the ice princess's heart. He watched them disappear through a door on the other side of the club. As the door closed behind them he let out a low whistle.

Things were closing.

"What are you thinking about?" Miranda asked, smiling. She probably thought the whistle was for her, and in a way it was. Her whole life was about to come to an explosive end. It'd probably increase her sales, make her an icon for the ages. Halo reached his hands around her waist and pulled her closer, noticing the eagerness in her eyes and the shuffle of her pumps.

"No thinking here," he said.

Their eyes met and he pushed himself into her, pressing his lips and body against hers, even as he pushed past the paper-thin barriers of her mind, plundering her surface thoughts, her various numbers and psychic knickknacks. She had a nice mind, he noticed, his excitement building. It wasn't nearly as vague as her celebrity image suggested. She loved music, loved her home and family, the sunshine, the mountains.

Dan... Dan... where are you?

He slipped around her annoying pleas and picked the bank account details from her mind, storing them safely away for later use. He parted her thoughts a little to glimpse her childhood. A father and daughter riding through mountains on motorbikes; young Miranda singing in a cubby house with her sister. He paged through them with bored ease. It was a rush slipping into someone else's life, enjoying the emotions, the fractured essence of a person, but he'd never found pleasure in the family flashbacks. Halo sought drama, weakness, dark secrets which he could twist and turn back on the person in the real world. He pushed aside the memories of Miranda's childhood.

And then there was a burst of fire. It was so sudden and so complete that he stumbled. His mind withdrew a little, nearly forced out entirely. But he recovered and focused on the flames.

There was death. He could sense it, taste it, feel it, smell it. Miranda was hurting, he could tell, and the details of the boy's face would stay with her forever.

I am fire.

The voice was there too, small and bright. Her memory would have altered it, shaped it to suit her torment. Everyone made things out to be worse than they were. He hesitated before withdrawing. With a little pressure he could wipe the memory away, or dilute it, perhaps let it fade a little so she would be more able to live with herself.

Time seemed to stand still.

I am fire.

I am fire.

The words would stay.

She wasn't his responsibility.

He pushed her against the bar, kissing her deeper as he let go of her mind, allowing the music and half light of the club to reclaim him.

She seemed surprised. Pleased, but a little unsure of what was going on.

"You want another drink?" he asked.

He knew she was marked – a necessary sacrifice for everything else to come together. But she was attractive, in a manufactured American kind of way, and while she was his he didn't really care about what the Russian's plans were.

Miranda turned her head and stumbled away from him. He wondered whether she had felt the telepathic intrusion, but there was no need to worry even if she had. What was she going to do about it? She was only human.

Halo smiled. She moved well.

Like she had practice.

"What was that?" Halo asked, watching her stumble back. "You forget something?"

"Where's Dan?"

Her concern was a surprise. Halo's fingers hardened around the edge of the bar and he wondered how the Russian was going to kill her.

"Where's Dan?" she asked again.

CHAPTER 22

DAN

THE WALLS WERE close on either side and Dan ran his finger along the royal purple surface as he walked down the stairs. The lights were subdued, almost golden, and as they moved down it was like a whole new world was unveiling itself. Behind them was the rave scene, bass suddenly absent once the heavy steel door closed at the top of the stairs. And ahead of them was a darker, lower, but altogether more civilized place. For a moment, Dan wondered whether he would have been better staying with Miranda and Halo, drinking away their anxiety, dancing through their fears. But then Dan knew who was behind the attacks, he knew it was a matter for family, and you could never escape that. It had nothing to do with Miranda, nothing to do with the way her fingers brushed against Halo's waist, the way she listened to him, breathed him in.

They were made for each other. Halo and Miranda: two shiny surfaces, reflecting their own splendor, nothing more than manufactured poses and clever rehearsed platitudes.

He hit the wall with his fist, and then again, but it didn't clear the images from his mind. Her smile for Halo. Her tinkling laugh for Halo, the tossing of her hair. He didn't even want to like her, to be so suddenly obsessed with her. He didn't want anything except to get away from her, back to his life, his meaningless, empty life.

Dan forced his mind back to the present, to the swishing dress ahead of him, the sweeping dark hair and the subtle chill in the air. Lily welcomed him with an enigmatic smile and the doorway to this secret basement. Her movements were smooth, her poise perfect, and Dan followed her with a growing sense that he was walking into a trap. Lily was the lure. She always had been, even before the sundering, and it seemed she hadn't strayed too far from that original arrangement.

"Has my grandfather been in town long?" he asked, watching the liquid movements of her dress as she seemed to float down the stairs. He wondered what she would have made of herself if she never met the Mad Russian.

She didn't answer. Lily wasn't the talkative type.

"I know he's behind this. I can feel him."

And it was true. The further he walked down the steps, the more confined he felt. The walls were still close but they hadn't narrowed. It was the gradual silencing of the electrical world around him that caused the growing unease.

The Mad Russian, and that's how Dan referred to his grandfather now, was a scheming old man with the power to manipulate the world around him, to bend it to his will. Dan could picture him mentally switching off the lights, the power, the connections, like a meticulous gentleman closing up his house for the night.

"You are our friend still," Lily said when they reached the door at the end of the stairs. Her black hair fell across her face and shielded her features. Dan had given up trying to tell whether someone was lying to him, so her attempt at hiding was wasted on him.

"You don't write, you don't call. I think friendship's a little more than memories, Lily," Dan said softly, leaning down so his lips were close to her dark hair, the ear hidden but as sharp as ever. "And I don't forget."

"Like the grandfather," she smiled, head still tilted to hide her eyes.

"Afraid so," he said, straightening and looking at the door. There was a small, golden security camera peering down at them, but Dan's senses couldn't detect anything about it. The numbness was infuriating, like he was being kept away from something, a secret that everyone else knew.

"Not a very bad thing, Dan. To be like our elders."

"Depends on your perspective, I guess."

Lily's grandmother was a match for the Mad Russian. She was known as Yellow Peril, but only during the crass years of the 1970s and 1980s. She was less dramatic than the Russian, more prone to work from the shadows, pulling strings, and she'd been manipulating the world since before the Second World War. Pearl was still influential now, although she had been forced out of her homeland decades ago by newer generations of crime lords, and relegated to the shadows of the Melbourne underworld.

Dan pushed the door with both hands, tired of being watched by the camera, but it was locked. He pushed again, harder, heard a solid click, and the door opened. He walked past Lily, his bare arm brushing against her dress. It was ice cold. He could feel the chill rolling off her in invisible, glacial waves. He realized some other things never changed either. She hated being touched. It was the only way to tell she wasn't normal, wasn't a real woman, but instead some freakish simulacrum of ice and blood.

Dan dismissed her entirely as he walked into the small office. She had made her decisions, chosen sides, long ago. The room, although small, seemed to unfold ahead of him. He knew that somewhere above him were the bright lights of Chinatown, the clusters of tourists and family groups, the smells of the Orient mixed with the relentless beats of nightclubs and the bass of circling Commodores. But looking around the office, it was as if he were in another place, another country, entirely.

Three of the walls were lined with books, leather and cloth bound, spines sorted according to color. Knowing his grandfather, Dan knew the books were more than decoration though. Each one would have contained knowledge carefully chosen and methodically absorbed. The wall directly opposite him, and the entrance, was dominated by a thick-set desk, black and lacquered, behind which sat the bearded man known throughout the world as the Mad Russian.

Dan's grandfather looked older, especially around the eyes which were now clearly marked with dark circles. His beard had given up its jet black color and was replaced with wiry grey wisps, although the hair on his head was still a tousled mop of black. Despite the physical changes that had perhaps stolen a little of the man's vitality, it was clear that the Mad Russian was still a man in possession of unnatural power. His eyes were filled with an elemental fierceness: black voids churning with flashes of light.

"Leave us," the man said, his hands flat on the desk in

front of him, his new posture suddenly reflecting the absolute influence he wielded in that place.

Lily closed the door as she bowed away.

"You are well, Danya," his grandfather said, although the voice held a question in the air. Dan moved along one wall and looked at the books, knowing his grandfather's eyes would be tracking him but that he would have been otherwise impeccably still.

"You didn't kill me, if that's what you mean," Dan said, stopping as he pulled out a Dostoevsky.

"A message," the man said, and then switched to Russian. "You are here now, grandson, and that is all that matters."

"Why are *you* here?" Dan asked, sliding the book back quickly and folding his arms across his chest as he stared at the old man. He deliberately spoke in English.

Anger flashed across the Mad Russian's face, those dark, dark eyes narrowing slightly. Dan felt his throat tighten and knew the danger.

"You are a man, almost a man," his grandfather continued, his English stilted. "Guidance is needed now, to move into manhood, yes. And here am I to assist."

The Russian's face was suddenly overtaken by a smile, the fragility gone, flakes of fatigue stripped away by an almost insane grin. Dan couldn't look away and the tightness in his throat intensified, crushed him. He reached his hand up and pressed against the skin there, massaging it, but the tension grew.

The Mad Russian stood from the desk, revealing his slender black suit and deep scarlet tie. As he walked around the impossibly long desk, he kept his eyes on Dan's, the smile slipping into something more serious.

"You speak no more Russian," he said. "You respect no thing but this consumer god, like all Westerners. You are my blood, my powerful blood, Danya Petrovich Galkin."

He stood in front of Dan, their eyes level, although it had been different at their last meeting.

"You will not be disappointment to me."

And suddenly the pressure was gone and Dan looked away, trying to slow his pulse and breathe deeply without betraying himself, his weakness. He was nothing in the presence of the Mad Russian, and both of them knew it.

The old man returned to the desk and sat down, resuming his original position. Dan settled into a chair opposite his grandfather, almost stumbling as he attempted to recover. His hands folded into his lap but he wasn't comfortable. The man's eyes were pinning him there, dark orbs which had no soul, no light at all now. They had always captivated him, frightened him, even as a boy.

"What do you want, grandfather?" he asked in Russian.

Dan's words seemed to please the older man, who nodded his head twice as a smile spread again across his face, although this time without the hint of mania.

"You have been hired to kill this Miss Brody superstar," he said, and slid across a photograph of Miranda. It was a publicity still and looked eerily familiar, a copy of the one Alsana had shown him a few days earlier. Her face was airbrushed, the smile impossibly white, but it was Miranda.

"No, I haven't," Dan said, and slid the photograph back. He felt his body surge, electricity fighting against whatever it was that had been holding him back since the hotel, fighting to rupture through his skin and into the air. But the metal casing attached to his wrist hummed and the surge was gone.

The Mad Russian watched Dan's struggle. He refused to take the returned photograph, but held his grandson's gaze.

"You have, yes."

"Who? Who hired me?"

"Me. I want you kill this girl."

"What? No."

"Yes."

Dan gripped the edge of his chair. His vision flickered a little and he caught glimpses of the circuitry entwined in the walls around the office. He sensed his grandfather's power, dark and dangerous, swirling inside the old man's human casing. It was returning to him, angry, crazy lightning that wanted to consume and liberate all at once. He stood up and felt a rush of blood to his face. Strobes of light crossed his vision and he clenched his jaw.

The old man simply smiled at him.

And then the power was swamped again by the numbness.

"But why?" Dan said, licking his dry lips, exhausted.

"You make good money, Danya. Good money on this. And you be someone again. A good boy."

CHAPTER 23

THE MAD RUSSIAN

GALKIN WATCHED HIS grandson across the room. He could sense the boy struggling against the restraining band, the energy spikes playing havoc with the overhead light. With a wave of his hand, Galkin pushed Danya's powers back, restoring the room. He pushed a little further, compelling his grandson.

"Sit."

The boy collapsed into the chair, his head falling forward, blood dripping from his nose onto the thick carpet.

When the Small Gods had thrown aside their coats and stepped out into the Melbourne sun, so many years ago, Galkin had watched them through a monitor. He had other business that day, in another State entirely. But before he attended to his own business, he made sure he watched the children's debut.

Danya had been twelve; skinny but keen to step into an adult's world. The five of them had been wearing sleek black costumes, with red and white highlights. Pearl had sourced the material from her Chinese contacts, an elegant Kevlar-blend.

Sebriya had lifted into the air, as instructed, whipping up a storm across the paved pedestrian area, confusing the people and drawing everyone's attention to the central fountain.

Halo flashed his eyes at a group of shoppers and they dropped their bags and waited for his commands. He sent them at each other's throats, clawing with manicured nails, butting each other with styled heads and kicking wildly. Galkin remembered how he had been so pleased, how he clapped his hands together with glee while watching the screen.

And Lily had fired shafts of deadly ice into the shop windows, lancing right across the mall to each side, shattering ice and glass in beautiful explosions.

Danya joined the chaos by blowing the lights up and down the lines of shops, frightening the shoppers and staff who ran into the mall. The boy was so excited, his little legs almost dancing as he let loose in a public place.

But then there was Nico, Danya's father, who was brought in to help shape the Gods and who was to be the de facto leader as they ran wild through Melbourne. Nico had shaved his hair to the scalp and painted red streaks across his skull. As he whipped his hands around in front of him, fire erupted outward, scorching the air and anyone who stood before him.

Burning so bright, but without the purpose Galkin had hoped to instill in him. The display was meant to draw the Celestial Knights into the open, but the way Nico was burning the world around him, Galkin knew it might be too much power too quickly; and like any dying sun, the bursts of heat and flame would burn brightest before the fall.

The Celestial Knights did arrive.

Galkin had planned it a fortnight before; a discreet conversation with an associate in Prague who fed the information along to its ultimate end. Most of his network operated out of Russia or the former Soviet states, but through the gradual drift of agents he penetrated the West, having important contacts in most developed countries. After five years of exile, the Mad Russian's networks were still surprisingly well established. Galkin wondered whether that was a reflection on his power and influence, or simply the fact that the people he knew had all grown equally old and useless in the modern world.

In the end, things turned out as planned, in a broad sense.

Six Knights appeared in the skies, appointed above like they always were, dominating the scene immediately. There was the imperious Parhelion leading the charge, flanked by Castus and The White Rabbit, who leapt to the ground with tremulous effect. The wily Inconnu held back, floating in the air, assessing everything, and Atomic Girl grew to enormous size and landed gently at the far end of the mall.

Galkin had turned away from the screen at that time, leaving through the hotel window where he was staying and drifting across the Sydney skyline. He would later hear about his son's spectacular explosion, which brought down half of the Knights at the cost of his own insignificant life. And the children had tried their best.

But they were the distraction.

He had moved down from the sky into a government laboratory, parting the walls as if they were wax paper, and then through two floors of research rooms until he found the core chamber, bathed in a purple glow.

"Good evening," the scientist had said as Galkin's feet touched lightly to the floor. "This is an important time."

"Perhaps the greatest," Galkin said, bowing his head in greeting.

The two men looked to the core which levitated in the middle of the room, held by invisible energy which seemed exotic and ever-changing to Galkin. He felt his hands rise, the fingers reaching for the mesmerizing, yet quite alien, energy.

"It will only remain stable for a moment…" the scientist said.

"Ah."

The Mad Russian was needed to stabilize the fields and he did so, shaping it with his mind, re-working its patterns and bending it back upon itself until it retained the strength enough to remain in this reality.

"It is beautiful," Galkin said.

And it was.

Five years later, Galkin watched his grandson bleed into the carpet.

The scientist had tricked him, had played to Galkin's

arrogance, and shunted him almost out of existence. It was not death or an endless loop of stasis which stared back at him as his body was ripped inside the energy portal; it was life. A whole new world, but a different one, without allies or family. He had been betrayed by his own double-agent, almost like some fool's pulp novel. The anger raged in him but in the different world his rage had no power, his body was no longer able to harness the devastating energies which he had been born with. And in time his body began to fall apart, to fight itself in search of those lost energies.

The scientist had trapped him in a new world and it had nearly killed him.

Galkin would have his revenge.

He pressed his fist against his chest. It had taken five years to return, but now his body had weakened to such a point that even back in his own world he could feel it breaking down further every day. Like Nico, perhaps, his body was about to enter its nova-phase. Perhaps death was imminent. Perhaps it would be lingering. Whatever it was that had begun consuming him from within, Galkin knew that it was not a thing he could fight, not anymore. At one time he may have been able to, perhaps, but those days were centuries past. As the modern world had replaced the old one, the Mad Russian had been stripped of his godhood.

Danya sat back on the chair, his eyes raised to Galkin's. A splash of scarlet ran across the right side of his face in a violent streak.

"This is the future," Galkin said softly.

Danya nodded, and Galkin felt like a change had taken place in the room. The boy's movement could have been from weariness or defeat, but the energy swirling under the boy's skin seemed to call out to Galkin, to reassure him that even if he was to end his reign on this world, the successor was ready, or almost ready, to take his place. The old man's eyes flashed.

There was a knock at the door, and through his extending senses, Galkin identified Halo and Lily on the other side, and with them was another woman. It was time for the transformation, he thought, looking back to Danya. The locks slid apart and Halo turned the handle before opening. There was hesitation there and for a flicker of a second, that bothered Galkin.

What was the point of hesitation?

Halo pulled Miranda Brody into the room and she stumbled, pulling against the hand that gripped hers. Lily came in last and closed the door silently behind her before turning and taking up her place against the wall. She was always keen to wait and watch. More hesitations, Galkin thought and his body surged with power.

"Welcome, Miss Brody child," he said, and lightning burst from his fingertips and crackled into the air leaving the smell of ozone. Halo let her wrist go and stepped back, clasping his hands in front of him, his delivery complete. "And a return greeting to you Sohail, my son who is not my son."

"You've got balls," Miranda said, her chest rising and falling even as Galkin switched to seeing her as impulses and nerve endings. Her eyes shot to Danya, widening as she took in the blood which still marked his features.

"Ah," Galkin said. "Perhaps my grandson, now will show his true self."

"What?" Miranda asked. He could see the conflicting emotions play themselves out in her body, the contradictory messages she was receiving. Halo's influence had soothed her perceptions, muddled her mind, but underneath she was fierce. Galkin allowed himself to watch the impulses rush around her body, the bright lights only he could see. She truly was a star.

"Your death will bring him back to me," Galkin said, baring his teeth in a too-wide smile. "Your death is the … the …"

"Main event?" Halo offered.

"Tonic," Galkin said, narrowing his eyes at Halo who smirked and looked down at his feet. "Our blood is old, ancient. But too much is wrong between the boy and his grandfather."

He sat down in his chair.

"I blame myself," he continued, looking to the roof and sighing. "And the years have not been kind to him or to our family. So. So. You, Miss American Brody, will heal the poison. The boy will serve the grandfather by killing you for all world to see."

Danya turned his head to look at Miranda. Galkin watched the movement, savoring the slowness and the way the American's face changed. Confidence was such a fickle liquid, drained in seconds, difficult to replace.

He clapped his hands together suddenly and Miranda jumped. It pleased the old man, no end.

CHAPTER 24

DAN

DAN SAW THE anger rush out of Miranda's eyes, leaving her with nothing but fear and uncertainty. He wiped his face with the back of his hand, and then stood up with the help of the old man's heavy-set desk. His back was to Miranda again, and he looked directly at his grandfather.

"Make choice," the Mad Russian said from the other side of his desk, fingertips coming together under his chin. Dan could feel the centering of power there at those tips, like a simple lock holding back a monstrous force, just hidden out of view.

Dan turned his head and looked back at the others.

Miranda looked very thin beside Halo. She was used to presenting herself to the world, forcing herself upon the paparazzi and the hordes of fans who flittered from one new pop sensation to the next, but now she just looked scared. And alone. She was the only normal person in the room and the topic of conversation was her death. Dan couldn't help but feel a little irony in there somewhere.

"Come on, man," Halo said, prompting him to make

that choice. "It's not like she'll get out of this anyway. It's dead with you or dead with us."

"He is wasting time on purpose," Lily said, not looking at Dan or Miranda.

"Playing the game?" Halo suggested. "Not likely. Dan doesn't make decisions. He just lets them take over, isn't that right, mate?"

Dan ignored Halo and leaned against the desk with his grandfather, looked the old man in the eyes. The metal clasp on his wrist throbbed but he knew he couldn't do anything about it, couldn't muster his powers to overcome its dampening effect. Only the Mad Russian could do that.

"Alright, grandfather," he said softly. "I will do it, but I will do it for you, for the family. Not for the idiots you've got here."

The Mad Russian breathed in, eyes fierce but now with a new kind of light.

"I'm not going to join the Small Gods again," Dan said. "I'm not going to be a toy soldier, so if I do this I'm with you. You've got to accept me as your apprentice, your grandson. Get rid of these clowns."

And there it was, Dan realized. Halo, Lily and whoever else the Russian may have brought out of the obscure past was nothing, just window dressing.

"It'll be just us."

The Russian nodded.

"What?" Halo pushed forward, demanding space next to Dan. "That's not the deal. You said you'd take me."

The room's temperature dropped as Lily also showed her displeasure.

"This is no discussion," the Russian said, standing

slowly as he thought through the new situation. Dan had seen him go through the same process dozens of times and he wondered just how much the old man was aware of his own affectations.

Halo folded his arms and stepped back next to Miranda who was leaning heavily against the bookcase like she might collapse. She wasn't looking at him, but he could see her body shaking, her arms wrapped around herself. The room's temperature remained frosty, mirroring Lily's silent glare.

"You kill this girl, you kill this girl."

"Yes," Dan said, and he turned to follow his grandfather's movement from behind the desk. He was walking slowly with his hands behind his back, bent slightly, perhaps showing his age at last. Miranda looked at Dan with wide, disbelieving eyes and he held the gaze for a second. "I'm with you."

Miranda shook her head.

"We do this tonight, now, yes," the Russian said.

Dan shrugged, still keeping his eyes on Miranda who had covered her ears with her hands and was shaking her head silently. He could see the wetness on her face and he wanted to shunt everything else away, all the messed-up people in the room, to protect her, to make amends.

"Sure," he said. "But not in the city, not here."

"Maybe the Federation Square, yes?" the Russian said, smiling and not listening. "Full circle. Or the bridge."

"How will he do it?" Halo asked suddenly. "He can't even open an automatic door tonight. Hey, maybe he should go old school and just strangle her."

"Enough." Without even moving his hands, the Russian lifted Halo off the ground and then hard against the wall of books, shoving him against the shelving twice before letting him stumble to the floor, clutching his throat. "You shall speak no more on this, Sohail."

The Russian looked at Lily and she averted her gaze, head down in subservience as usual. He didn't even bother to look in Miranda's direction, but his gaze came to rest again on Dan.

"Outside," Dan said. "It needs an audience."

"You are certain about this?"

"I don't have a choice."

"We go up," the Russian said. "And you, Sohail Pirzada, shall follow. Bring the girl."

The door swung open at the Russian's command and, with his grandfather's hand on his shoulder, Dan was moved back into the stairwell which had seemed so constricting the last time he had been in it. Now it just seemed like a dream.

He'd woken suddenly, with panic in his chest, heaving for breath in the darkness of the tent. He couldn't breathe. His eyes widened in desperation, his hands clutched at his neck, trying to unwrap the invisible hands he felt there.

"Da," his grandfather had said, his face half lit by the moonlight as he knelt at the tent's entrance. "Remember this feeling, Danya."

And then he had vanished and the grip had loosened.

Dan had been nine years old.

For three weeks, Dan had laid awake for hours in his bed, afraid of another visitation. His grandfather never spoke of the night in the tent, but Dan could feel him watching him closely whenever he was at home. Those hawk-like eyes, bright under thick brows, followed him from the breakfast rituals until he left for school each day. And when Dan returned home, usually late on purpose, the grandfather waited in his arm chair, the eyes watching, waiting for something.

It turned out the old man wanted to jump start Dan's powers. He knew the pedigree was strong, that power was there, ready to blossom. With his father in prison and his mother crumbling into insanity, the old man was restless for results.

"Fear is good teacher," he had said later, as Dan's world exploded with possibilities, his mind suddenly connected with the electrical world around him. Thoughts of the bogeyman strangling him in his sleep vanished as his grandfather taught him to control and manipulate the circuits.

They grew closer like co-conspirators, leaving Theresa to wander the house like a ghost. From bogeyman to teacher and mentor.

Dan couldn't believe how much he had been played, but manipulation had always been an intrinsic part of the Galkins' genetic makeup.

The desperate, conniving old man was still there in his thoughts, though: dark shapes in the night, just waiting for the moment to screw him up more. Dan knew that everything came a distant second to what the Mad Russian wanted.

"You told me once that fear was a good teacher," Dan said, as they left the basement club and re-entered Chinatown. He didn't know where they were going or how much time he had left before he and Miranda would have to face the Russian's wrath.

"That is good," the Russian said. "Remember the old times."

And forget the mistakes, Dan added silently. In his own eyes, the old man must have thought he was right, that there could be no other course of action, no other possibility. And that had to be a flaw.

The air around them shimmered and Dan felt his feet and body pulled up from the ground. The Russian lifted the four of them into the night, right in the middle of the crowds. Cameras flashed, people scuttled away in different directions, but the Russian paid them no attention. Dan looked sideways at Miranda and wondered how she felt, which was worse: the terror of flying for the first time, or knowing that she was going to be executed. Her head was against Halo's chest, his arms holding her steady. Dan turned away again, eyes to the front so his grandfather would see the little soldier in him, not the heartsick teenager.

They curved over the city, moving south towards the bay. Within a minute they saw the Westgate Bridge with its streams of car head lights coming across and leaving in equal numbers. It would be the bridge then, Dan thought.

The air was cold and rain fell from the dark clouds somewhere high above, but no water touched them. It was deflected by an invisible bubble as the Russian pushed his way towards the two barriers separating the incoming and outgoing traffic. The four of them set their feet down and the air shimmered with a light as the field dropped.

The rain and wind immediately whipped their faces and drenched their clothes.

Miranda stood with her arms wrapped around her body, her hair blowing away from her, leaving her face clear and white. Halo stood beside her, holding her arm. And that left Dan and the Russian together, the old man still touching Dan's shoulder in an act of tenderness or ownership. It was difficult to measure.

Cars slowed or swerved on both sides of the bridge. Across the city, images would already be zipping through social media sites and phones. He had asked for an audience, and now he had one.

"You with me now, Danya," the Russian said, releasing Dan's shoulder and pushing him gently into the rain. Dan moved forward two stumbling steps. "You with me now."

Miranda let out a choking sound and her body half-collapsed only to be yanked upward by Halo. Dan hadn't seen her so terrified, so violated by circumstances beyond her control. She pleaded with him, shook her head against the future and sobbed loudly. The Mad Russian grinned widely, his arms crossed together in anticipation. Dan's hand slipped into his jeans' pocket and closed over the lighter he'd picked up from Grim's house. He could feel the embossed wolf's head with his thumb.

"What did you do to Grim?" Dan asked, turning back to his grandfather, his own hair plastered to his face.

The Mad Russian looked surprised. The rain wasn't affecting him at all, locked away in another protective field. His face contorted, shifting to show confusion.

"What do you say?"

"I said, what did you do to Uncle Grim?" Dan repeated, turning fully around and pulling out the lighter so his grandfather could see it.

Dan knew he was already being too reckless, allowing himself to ask the question in the first place. He flicked the metal wheel and pressed the smooth embossed wolf's head. Instead of a lick of flame there was a solid pulse, punching outward towards the Russian.

The energy hit him and shattered the field into sparkling shards, coursing through and collecting the old man in the chest. He fell backward, arms flailing as he lost his footing and crashed against a pillar.

Dan held the lighter out in front of him and stepped after his grandfather, flicking his hair out of his eyes as he struggled to gauge the Russian's remaining power.

"Is it gone?" he asked. "Is it all gone away now, you think?"

The Russian looked up at him, surprise and anger etched on his face. The rain had soaked him already and his expensive clothes clung to his body making him look like an old man, an old scarecrow.

"I thought you made sure he didn't keep any of these," Dan said, standing over him, waving the lighter in his face. "I thought you kept him on a leash."

The man shook his head.

"I guess you missed one." Dan wondered whether Grim knew what was coming to him, and whether this was his only way to take a final shot at his old comrade. It probably didn't matter now anyway, he knew. The dampener had hit the Russian and robbed him of his powers, at least for a short time. Monsters like his grandfather never stayed down or dead for long. Dan knew that from experience.

"You say you with me, you make the promise," the Russian said, although it was difficult to hear him through the rain and emotion. There was confusion there, utter disbelief, pain, abandonment. Dan had seen those changes in his mother's face as well. And probably his own. "Why? Why you do this?"

"I'm a liar," Dan said, and he stepped back a little. "It's in my blood."

The traffic was still crawling past, although there was less of it on the outbound lanes. With little time remaining, Dan jumped onto the road and held his hands up to the oncoming traffic.

"Jesus," Halo called from behind. "Are you nuts?"

Dan waved the lighter back at Halo and then stepped out of the way of a sedan. The third car to pass was unlucky, and Dan got a hold of its door handle and pulled it open. The driver was a woman in her early twenties, eyes wide behind fashion spectacles.

The car swerved as she lost control of the steering wheel, but Dan lunged inside and stepped on the brake, stopping it and the traffic behind. The woman screamed but Dan ignored her and pulled out the keys.

He jogged around to the back of the car, headlights from the cars stopped behind the woman, blinding him temporarily. He shoved the keys into the lock at the boot and pulled it open.

He was running out of time.

When he grabbed his grandfather, Dan could see the arrogance and power had leeched from his body, and it didn't take much to lift him up and dump him into the car's boot. He saw the man's small, startled eyes for a second before he slammed the boot shut.

"What are you doing?" Halo asked, bringing Miranda closer, keeping her in between the two of them like a hostage. "Are you crazy?"

Dan hesitated when he saw Miranda, face streaked with tears, her lips still trembling. But then he threw the keys down between the two sections of the bridge and they disappeared into the darkness to be consumed by the river below.

"You'd better get away from here," he said to the terrified woman driver. He turned around to look at the cars stopped or moving slowly around him. "Everyone should get the hell out of here now!" he shouted. "There's a dangerous maniac in the boot."

"They won't listen," Halo said.

"I can't help that," Dan said and turned fully to face off against his former team mate. Miranda looked confused, but a light of relief had crept into her face. She pulled away from Halo and shook her jacket back into shape before pulling her hair into a pony tail.

"Are you..?" Dan asked. She nodded her head but wouldn't look at him. Instead she walked a bit further and leaned against a pylon, soaked but alive.

"Well that was interesting," Halo said.

"You want to give up yet?" Dan asked.

"I never give up," Halo said, stepping back away from the car. "You should know that by now."

Dan shrugged.

"Thing is," Halo continued as he walked backwards,

putting distance between himself and Dan. "Everyone wants to be somebody. Even me, even you. That guy in there, he didn't understand that other people have ambition too, that not everyone is a puppet."

He suddenly stopped moving and a smile broke out on his face as he pulled out a silver keycode device like the one that had originally been attached to the briefcase.

"You were never going to kill her," Halo said. "Everyone knew that, except the old man. And none of us wanted you to kill her either, if you're wondering."

"What are you saying?" Dan asked.

"I'm not the enemy. Here," he said, tossing the keycode device to Dan. "I took the combination from Grim's head before it was too late. It's set to deactivate your bracelet as soon as you connect the two."

Dan looked at the silver box, red lights blinking rapidly in a cycle. It was Grim's work and identical to the briefcase code he'd had earlier.

"I don't get you," Dan said.

"No surprise there," Halo said. "Get your powers back and get out of here."

"And what do you do?"

"I stay here with the old man and plot your death, keep him angry and off your scent until you're ready to take him down." Halo shrugged and looked back towards the city. "Or until the Celestial Knights come back."

Dan touched the keycode to his wrist and there was an audible click.

A wave of freshness blew through his head, like water, and in its wake he could see the shots of electricity and signals which fired in all directions. He closed his eyes and he could still see how everything was connected. The bridge was linked to the western suburbs and the blinding light of the city.

When he opened his eyes he could feel the hum in his mind again and marveled at the world.

"You don't have to look so satisfied," Halo said.

Dan lifted his hand towards the car parked to the side. The woman was gone now, running down the sloping road. With only the smallest of urges he pulled the electricity from the car's battery, whipping it out in a blue lightning bolt which lifted into the air and flew into Dan's fingertips. He moved his hand across to the other cars which had stopped and their energy fed him as well.

"Always keep an angel in your pocket," Halo said. He sat down on the curb, his face smiling as the electricity flew into Dan and made him stronger. It was a saying Dan had heard before. Halo used it on the girls, a smooth opening. Dan's senses were softened, out of focus with the new lines of energy feeding him from the cars and grid around him. He felt like he was floating, drifting away from the cold and the rain.

He saw Halo's self-satisfied smile but then it changed, replaced with shock. Something stirred behind them, pulling Dan's attention back to focus.

Miranda screamed.

Dan spun to look at her but she was already gone. He reached out with his powers, flaring the lights which lined the bridge, throwing the whole space into an overcharged glow.

He could see the ice trail, like a skateboard ramp rising over cars and then across to the other side. Dan jumped from one side of the bridge to the other, pulling himself across the gap which led to the river below. He narrowed his eyes and flared the lights again, but he couldn't see where she had gone.

And then he saw his breath mist in front of him and he felt the temperature drop.

He turned and saw a dozen spikes of ice lancing towards him. Some collected cars but enough made it to strike Dan, knocking him backward and onto the ground. A second wave of spikes smashed the pylon he had fallen against, broken metal jutting out from where the ice cut through.

A flash of white crossed his field of vision as another ice trail propelled Lily and Miranda over the bridge and back towards the city.

"Now that's a complication," Halo said from somewhere.

"Shut up," Dan spat back at him as he stumbled to look down the road again, pulling shards of ice from his t-shirt while others melted from the ambient electricity in his body.

The streak of white zigzagged ahead, ricocheting from courier vans to buses as it sped away from him, leaving him gasping on the road, not quite connected to the flare of headlights and traffic all around him. The red brake lights of cars and the overhead street lights weren't enough to capture Lily's features, but the swirl of ice and cold, angry air in her wake were clear signs that Miranda had been grabbed by his one-time friend.

Dan's breath blew out in short explosions of mist. His chest was tight from the sudden drop in temperature, but otherwise he was unhurt, and that meant he had to move. There wasn't time to tantrum, to hate the world for always dragging him down. He stepped on to the road and picked up a flared piece of metal from the shattered pylon. A car careened past him, horn blaring, followed by a truck and the buffeting wind of speeding vehicles.

Three steps towards the side and Dan was charging up, channeling electricity into the metal, changing its properties. The lights on the bridge flickered and then burst, one after the other down both directions. Their light extinguished, the power arced across the darkness and into Dan. He fielded the energy from all around him. Drivers swerved to avoid the flashes of blue-white energy, even as their radios flickered and their car batteries were sapped. It didn't take long for Dan to feel the pressure in his arms and legs, his whole body brimming with power. He slid the metal fragments under his shoes and they clamped on like metal soles.

He hadn't felt that fullness for weeks, the danger and the warmth.

But Miranda was gone, spirited away and getting further and further into the night. He turned back to the highway, knowing his body was glowing with the power, knowing that the drivers who changed lanes with sudden jerks and screeches of rubber were seeing something monstrous.

They saw death swathed in blue lightning.

A truck side-swiped a little sedan, sparks flying into the night. It righted itself quickly, coming close to Dan, close enough for him to leap at it. With his whole body charged, Dan could do things that other young men couldn't do. His body hit the side of the truck, arms out wide, hands plunging into the metal. His shoes magnetized and clamped hard against the truck's side. He carefully pulled himself up to the top of the truck's container, the metal from the pylon helping him keep attached, serving as a third magnet.

He had practiced magno-hopping the year before, more out of boredom than any sort of training. He'd started by magnetizing Noah's frying pans and then using them to leap from one level of the fire escape to the next. Somehow he'd progressed to jumping on trains and trams.

He stood up on the truck, scouting ahead. It moved alongside a utility and Dan leapt down onto the tray, stopping only to engage and disengage his magnetized shoes, before leaping on to the next courier van. He made good progress but Lily was already off the bridge, which meant he needed to employ more indirect methods to stop her from getting away.

As he leapt to the next car, landing with a thud that sent the driver swerving in alarm, Dan pushed his mind outward, along the power lines. While his consciousness sped blindingly fast into the city, he picked up phantom images of everything he passed. Hotels, nightclubs, traffic lights, darkened department and retails stores, museums and finally a dark space in his pseudo-vision.

Lily was cold. Heartless, perhaps, but definitely cold. The absence of warmth was easy to pick up and he reacted to it without thought. Bestial reflexes, not thinking of consequences. Not even thinking of Miranda. His consciousness burst out of the power lines just ahead of Lily and struck her from her ice sled down to the street. Power surged out from blocks around, channeling into the dark space until it fractured and fell away.

Back on the bridge, Dan shook his head to reorient himself in his body, but he caught the second or third burst of light from up ahead. Something ignited where Lily was. He could see the flickering of flames.

With another leap into the traffic, Dan caught a ride on the bonnet of a BMW, but only stayed long enough to leap onto a truck heading for the city. Within minutes he came to a road block, police already on the scene to keep traffic from getting close to the explosion.

Dan didn't waste a second. He leapt off the truck and helped himself to a motorbike which stood idle while its owner talked with police. The engine hummed into life at his touch and he weaved his way past the police van and closer to the intersection where he'd managed to stop Lily's escape.

Dan expected another fight.

He came prepared, his body still glowing blue with the stored energy, but Lily wasn't moving. She lay on the road surrounded by what looked like an ice web pattern stretching out in all directions from her at the center.

He knelt down next to her and touched her skin.

It was cold.

"I'm sorry," he whispered.

Her eyes opened halfway, the darkness behind the lids showing only a little recognition. Dan stroked her black hair and looked up and down her body but there didn't seem to be anything obviously broken.

"I think it's concussion," Miranda said from the side of the street. She was holding a metal pole, perhaps three foot long. Dan wondered where it came from, and then he saw the demolished café and imagined Lily had crashed her way through it after he'd struck her with the lightning blast.

"Are you okay?" Dan asked, looking back at Lily once more before he stood up.

"I'm the one holding the bat," she said, and tapped it into her palm twice.

Dan wasn't sure he understood what she meant. His body was getting cold. He felt the bruises suddenly, the battering he'd taken that night. And Miranda looked a little torn as well. She'd tossed away her jacket and her cheek was bloodied.

"We go now," she said.

Dan nodded.

CHAPTER 25

THE SMALL GODS

The Grampians, Five Years Before

DAN SAT WITH the handkerchief pressed hard against his nose, the blood turning it a dark red. He could hear the ringing sensation in his ears and looking across to Halo, he could still see the scowl on the Pakistani's face.

It wasn't over.

Ever since their first night at the camp, Halo had been pushing Dan. Tripping him on hikes or shoving him into walls, it didn't seem to matter. Bree had tried to play peacemaker, but Dan's grandfather ignored the growing animosity. Dan even thought that maybe his grandfather was pleased with the bullying.

Halo pulled his arm away from Bree who was wrapping it in a bandage. He shook it hard and then pulled on his jumper, hiding the bright red electrical burn Dan had whipped across his skin.

"I'll kill you," he said, pointing at Dan. "Next time I'll kill you."

Bree shot Dan a worried look but followed Halo as he left the clearing. She excelled under his grandfather's teaching, moving earth and rock as if it were simply extensions of her imagination. Halo was also making the old man proud.

A shadow passed over Dan's face and he looked up to see the wild-haired man who had brought them all to the mountains. His eyes were intense, crazy.

His grandfather placed a hand on Dan's shoulder and then carefully used his other hand to pull away the bloody cloth. Dan winced as the blood gushed again. He tried to pull the handkerchief back but the old man held it away.

"Our blood is strong," his grandfather said.

He breathed in, and the gnarled hand tensed slightly. Dan felt a warmth rush through his shoulder and then up his neck to his face. Everything seemed to be suddenly clearer and he blinked hard against the bright light of the sun.

His grandfather nodded and stepped back, breathing through his nose. The blood had stopped flowing and Dan felt stronger.

"I hate him," Dan said. "I hate Halo."

"No," his grandfather said. "You all must live together. Constellation is not made by a single star, Danya."

"He hates me."

"He wants to be you."

"He kicked me in the face," Dan said, standing up, looking towards the cabin where Halo and Bree were probably talking about him.

The old man chuckled.

"You burned him," he said. "A thing he will never forget

now. A lesson most valuable for our Halo. His power is of the mind, but you are of the world itself."

Dan grinned, looking down to the dry grass. He lifted his eyes and met his grandfather's gaze.

"Did you see it?" he asked. "Did you see what I did?"

The grandfather smiled widely and slapped his hands on Dan's shoulders again.

"I saw it, I did. And I felt it, here." He balled his hand into a fist and thumped his chest. "When you call the sky to open, you call to me as well. You and me, we are the same."

Dan reached forward to hug his grandfather but the old man stepped back, his attention moving to the household. Dan stumbled after him, kicking up dust and grass and he shuffled along. He could hear Halo shouting in the house.

"What has our little angry god done now, I wonder?" his grandfather asked, another chuckle in his voice.

CHAPTER 26

MIRANDA

"I JUST WANT TO rub it all out," Dan said, sitting on the dumpster with his knees drawn up. Miranda sat next to him, listening to the distant sirens, her eyes hidden again behind the dark shades. It was a miracle she hadn't lost them, or her bag. When it was a Gucci, she guessed you just didn't let it go. She looked up at the night sky, squinted and imagined she was sitting back home in California. The sky didn't look all that different, she figured. Stars all looked the same to her.

Beside her, Dan rubbed at his wrist again. The bracelet was gone but it'd left a mark. His skin was red. It reminded her of burns.

"So that was your grandfather?" she asked. She didn't know where to start.

Dan shrugged.

"And your friends?"

He shrugged again. She was getting good at this, she thought. He was really coming out of his shell.

"I guess you really are messed up then," she smiled, checking her left shoe, running her finger over the snapped heel.

"Sorry about that," he said softly.

"Oh, is it your fault?"

"Probably." He shrugged again.

Miranda leaned forward and looked to the end of the lane. Dan followed her gaze and they saw a few people, normal people, walking in the lights of the street. They had decided to wait ten minutes and she knew it was running out. They'd have to move again soon, and that would mean getting themselves back into the world, and probably back into the Mad Russian's sights. Unless he'd been killed. She told herself it was a possibility.

"You know, I bet you would have been a really boring kid at school," she said.

Dan shrugged again.

She stood up and awkwardly put her shoe back on, hopping a little and having to rest her hand on the dumpster to steady herself. Dan slid to the ground too, his trainers splashing a puddle as they landed.

They walked to the end of the lane, quietly, neither of them really excited about the prospect of moving into the city streets again. But there was no choice, she knew. The Mad Russian would be back to his crazy self in no time, and from what she knew of him, he was probably going to pull up the skyscrapers one by one to get to his grandson.

"Let's go," she said.

It didn't take long for Dan to find a car. Three steps, in fact. It was a blue sedan with a baby seat in the back and family stickers plastered on the rear passenger window. He looked around and then pressed his hand against the door. Miranda heard a clicking sound and the car unlocked.

She wondered whether he'd let her drive, and was relieved when he slipped into the driver's side. She hobbled around the front of the car and got in beside him. The engine was already humming when she closed the door, and he moved smoothly into the traffic.

She smiled to herself, looking out the window with her head leaning against the headrest. She wasn't worried about the owner of the car. Her people would get money to whoever they were and Miranda would make sure it was more than enough to replace the car. She smiled because Dan was really good at breaking the law when he needed to, and he did it without thinking.

He did a lot of things, she figured, without thinking.

"Do you hate your powers?" she asked as they moved onto the highway.

He heard her, but he didn't reply.

She reached out and turned the radio off.

It leapt back on without Dan moving.

"I don't think so," she said and turned the radio off again. "Seriously, do you wish you were boring like me?"

He smiled at that. She hit her mark. As usual.

"I don't know," he said, checking the rear vision mirror. "It's not something I can choose."

"But do you dream about being normal?"

He still wouldn't look at her.

"I try not to dream at all," he said. "Saves complications, saves disappointment."

"Very deep, Galkin. I just wondered, that's all. I know people who would... who do things to be like you."

She didn't shy away from the memories of the boy in Jakarta. She kept him vivid in her mind's eye, his oily skin, the shine of his eyes and teeth. The smell of gasoline.

"Some people think we're different species," Dan said. "Like a whole new race, or whatever."

"Did you even go to high school?"

"What?"

"You're mixing up race and species, but I guess it doesn't matter."

Dan curled his lip up and seemed amused.

"You're full of surprises," he said. "I'm saying there are people out there who see themselves above the rest of the world just because they've got freaky powers."

Like his grandfather, she guessed, but she didn't want to bring it up or break his conversation. He seemed to be relaxing a bit now they were on the highway.

"But I don't think we're any different, apart from being able to do things a little differently, or looking a bit different. We're still all just people, stuffing up as we go along."

"Still, there's something about ubers that makes us think of different... better futures." She paused and looked away. "There was this boy."

"Is this leading to some romantic confession?" Dan said, changing lanes. "Because I'd prefer not to know."

He pulled the car back into the left lane, overtaking an SUV. The motion was hard and Miranda braced herself against the dashboard. She shot him a look, hated him suddenly for not understanding her words, for cutting her off.

"You idiot," she breathed softly.

"I've got problems, that's all," he said. "I don't need to hear about your boyfriends."

The boy from Jakarta vanished, slipping back into memory, as the sultry Robbie Rogers replaced it. She screwed up her eyes and switched the radio back on, half expecting to hear one of Robbie's songs. She gave up and turned the radio off with a bang.

They travelled for a minute in silence, although Miranda was still churning inside. She hated the way he could slip into the adolescent boy mentality, the way he acted his age. He was seventeen. She expected so much more from him.

"You slept with Evie," she said suddenly. And regretted it instantly.

"Who?" He didn't even look at her.

"My backup singer."

Dan shrugged.

"The blonde. Small tits."

He looked at her then, and there was recognition in his eyes. She caught it just as he dipped them and looked away.

"You don't remember? Christ Dan, it was two nights ago."

"I could say sorry," he said.

"So why don't you? Why don't you say sorry?"

He shrugged again.

"You are such a bastard."

The car fell into silence again. Miranda wished that she could replay time, not say the words. It was his fault, of course. He had ruined the moment. She pulled out her phone and flipped the cover up and down, over and again.

"My father killed a lot of people," Dan said in the darkness.

She stopped fidgeting.

"What?" she asked, although she heard him clearly. You couldn't not hear those kinds of words.

"Twenty-nine, actually," Dan added. "Maybe more."

Their car passed under a bridge, speed cameras positioned to catch offenders. She wondered whether the Mad Russian had access to them, wondered whether they would be careening back into that crazy world of killers.

"They couldn't identify all of them because of the heat of the fire and the… you know… the rubble."

She put her phone away. He needed her to say something, she knew, but there wasn't any way of comforting him.

"People were just out shopping, you know?" he said. "He's got a following, my dad; these little sickos that discuss his career online and send him cards and letters."

"He's alive?" Miranda sounded disappointed, even to her own ears.

"No."

"They executed him?"

"Are you telling me or asking me?" Dan shot back. But then he banged his hands on the steering wheel and rested his head back. "Sorry, you're not the problem. We don't kill criminals here in Australia. No death penalty, not that it mattered."

"But he killed all those people."

"Yeah."

"That's horrible."

"Yeah."

They sat quietly. Dan tightened and loosened his grip around the wheel and Miranda just breathed slowly. Dan's father was dead, that was clear. She wondered what happened and the possibilities flittered through her mind, sometimes the face of the man who could have been Dan's father, was Dan himself.

"Stop the car," she said. "Pull over here."

He did as he was told, surprised at her words and probably too tired to resist. As the tyres slowed to a stop, she got out and walked to the driver's side.

"I'm driving, you rest. It's a straight road, I promise not to kill us."

His eyelids were heavy. He nodded and crawled across to the passenger side, his arms and legs everywhere as he practically fell into the seat.

Five minutes later he was asleep, with his head backwards, eyes closed and lips slightly parted. His fringe fell to the side, revealing one of the scars he'd collected recently. She reached across and let her fingers touch the skin.

His head was warm.

She stroked his face.

"You're so young," she whispered. And inside she knew that things between them were different. He was a boy she could like, a boy with charm, a boy with complications. But then she knew it wasn't ever going to happen.

There was just too much in the way.

Miranda checked her phone as she sat on the grass overlooking a river.

No messages.

No phantom techno-images of The Mad Russian, either.

The ground was wet, but it wasn't moving. It was wet and normal and real. She dropped her phone back into her bag and lay down, looking up into the sky. It looked different to home, but she'd already got used to the shifting world. Cities changed, skies changed. She breathed in and let her fingers spread out either side of her, pushing outward into the grass.

"Got some chips," Dan said as he walked up to stand over her. "I keep my promises." He'd only been gone for fifteen minutes. She could smell the fries and smiled. Dan stood there looking uncertain. His shirt was torn from the fight in Melbourne. She noticed the scratches on his arms and face.

"Come on, then," she said.

He grinned and sat down, quickly unwrapping the white paper, unleashing more of the smell.

"What's the plan?" she asked, enjoying the sensation of food. She couldn't remember the last time she had eaten.

"We get out of here," Dan said, not meeting her eyes. "There's a place west of here. Should be safe enough and far enough away."

"So we run?"

He shrugged.

"I was hoping we'd drive," he said. He looked exhausted.

"What about tomorrow?" she asked. "I've got a concert, you know. There are people out there who need to know where I am." Dan didn't say anything. He sat with his face looking out to the river. "We need a plan, Galkin."

"It's just that, plans aren't really my thing," he said. "I don't do this kind of stuff everyday."

A few gulls circled above them, their shrill calls piercing the air. They settled close to Miranda, white feathers almost glowing in the moon light. They hopped closer. Dan threw them a chip and they spiraled upward to catch it, shrieking with hysteria.

"I just want to be normal," he said, throwing a second chip further down the slope towards the river, drawing the birds away.

"I can call my people," Miranda said, although she knew that Sully wasn't going to be able to answer her. The others: the management crew, probably weren't going to be much help either.

"Bree said they're compromised."

"That doesn't mean anything," Miranda said.

"Let's just keep our heads low for a bit," he said. He turned to look at her, his whole face pleading with her to drop it.

"We'll need a new car," she said.

Dan bit his lip and looked down, his familiar smile already dancing on his face.

"Already taken care of," he said.

"You are a little villain."

She stood up and brushed off the grass which was everywhere, looking down at the river which now looked like a dark oily road. The hint of gasoline caught her on the light breeze. She closed her eyes, forcing down the memories again. The birds crept forward, chattering like devils, but apart from the gulls, they were alone. It was just her and Dan. She picked up her shoes and bag, already looking back up the hill.

Dan touched her shoulder and she felt a little shock at his touch. He rubbed his hand down her back and the grass was gone. Some kind of electric shock. He was full of surprises.

"I don't want to know what you just did," she said. "You need to come up with a plan tomorrow, because I've got fifteen thousand fans coming to see me." She reached her free hand back for Dan and he took it. "I don't care how mad the Mad Russian is, Dan. He's not going to stop me from getting to that concert. And neither are you."

"Maybe."

"Whatever," Miranda said, taking the lead. "And I'm driving again. You still look like crap."

"Fine, get us out of the city."

They walked up the hill. Behind them, the birds crashed down onto the paper and chips, screaming their rights and nipping at each other as they feasted.

Dan raised his eyebrows, looking down at Miranda's hand as she shifted gears and accelerated back onto the highway. She caught him smiling, but ignored him and passed the slower traffic, heading out of the city. It didn't matter which side of the road was the right one, and that's why she liked double and even the triple lane roads. It was all about the slipstreams, moving ahead like she would back home on her trail rides, navigating her way forward.

"You can stop smiling," she said, finally. A quick glance at him reassured her that he was going to live. The cuts on his face were almost fully healed. He looked exhausted still, but that wide, white smile was still there. "You told me to drive. Back there, you told me to get us out of the city."

"I guess," he said.

"You did."

"I just expected a bit more jerking around," he said. She cut him another glance and saw the mock-innocent eyes now.

"Are you flirting with me?" she asked.

"Hell, no," he shot back, finally looking away from her. He rested his feet on the dashboard, hunched up like a teenager. Miranda enjoyed the shift in atmosphere. Dan was arrogant but he had a lot to learn.

She sighed, easing ahead of another car. The lights of the city were behind them and a calmness spread through her mind. No more of these extraordinary people with their unbearable, convoluted plots. She thought of Sully and her manager. She thought of the fans and the media.

Everyone would be wondering where she was.

"My dad taught me to drive stick," Miranda said.

Dan shifted his legs. He ran his hand through his hair and raised his eyebrows again.

"I said, my dad taught me to drive stick. Back home," she said again.

"I thought you'd have a chauffer."

Idiot. She smiled, despite herself.

"Seriously? I'm not that girl."

Dan smiled too. He shrugged.

"My dad drove a truck," Miranda said. "Okay? Deliveries and stuff."

"Fair call," Dan said.

"What's that supposed to mean?"

Dan shrugged again.

"Can you stop shrugging?" she asked. "Seriously, can you not do that so much?"

He sat up and picked off the GPS unit from the stolen

car's dash. Short flashes of blue light arced from the device and up along his fingers. Miranda watched them, like little flecks of lightning. They started bright but faded quickly as they vanished up his bare arms. She noticed his eyes were closed. After only a few bursts of electricity, Dan dropped the GPS over his shoulder where it clanged to the floor in the back. Useless.

"Does it hurt?" she asked.

She could tell he was about to shrug, but his body straightened and he took in a breath. She watched his chest lift. He seemed like he could go to sleep. Behind them, his grandfather was probably being helped out of the boot of a car, furious as Hell.

"No," he said.

"Would it hurt me, if I touched you when you did that?"

"You wanna try it?"

Miranda shook her head. The traffic was thinning out. Beyond the lights of the highway, darkness swept across the land. The ocean was out there somewhere, and houses and farms, and normal people.

"Would it?" she asked again.

Dan let his hand slip to the gear stick. His bare skin lay warm against her own. It was a normal kind of touch and she surprised herself when she didn't flinch. He strummed his fingers and she slipped her hand around his, squeezing it gently.

"Thanks for saving me," she said softly.

A sound escaped his mouth, something like a half-laugh, but his breathing had slowed. He squeezed her hand back, but said nothing.

CHAPTER 27

DAN

THE SOUNDS OF the highway were well behind them, muffled by the rain and distant rumblings of thunder. Dan knew the storm would hit soon. He could feel the fury building across the bay behind him, hidden by the trees and the darkness of night. Ahead of him, Miranda held her shoes by her side as she walked barefoot towards the light of the house. Her pace hadn't changed at all, despite the mud and uneven road surface. She hadn't really said anything since leaving the car. Dan followed behind her.

The house was his house. Once upon a time.

Miranda stopped at the gate and looked around, pushing the strands of wet hair out of her eyes. Dan looked past her to the house. He could only see the one light on, the one in the laundry, but he knew she was home. The garden either side of the path was wild with herbs and discarded junk. He was embarrassed by the sprawl and hurried past Miranda, striding towards the door and hoping the whole night would hurry up and move on.

He rapped on the security door.

Eyes closed, he waited. How many times had he tried

to get away from this place, he wondered. How many times had he dreamed of running away, of pretending to be someone else, living a normal life?

Miranda stood behind him, off to the side, looking out to the paddocks which were eventually consumed by the night. She still clung to her shoes and every now and then she sniffed.

"I'm sorry," Dan said softly.

The door opened with the sliding of bolts and clicking of locks. Dan stepped back, the porch light suddenly all around them.

She was surprised to see him of course. It was 2am and his face was bruised and bloody, his clothes drenched with rain. A normal mother would have pulled him inside, full of questions and touching. But Theresa wasn't a normal anything.

Instead, she stayed hidden behind the security door, slightly back as if he would lunge at her or try to force himself inside. They both remembered years ago when he thundered his way out, while she grabbed at him to stay.

Things had changed since then.

"Mum, I need to stay for a while."

Her eyes showed the whites. Her fingers, blue and creased with age, wrapped around the edge of the frame, but she made no effort to open the security door. There was no sign of the Theresa from earlier in the week, no sign that she saw him as anything other than a threat.

Dan wanted her to remember. He felt exhausted, felt desperate for her to shake off her cyclic manic-depression, to wake up from her medicated torpor.

"I really need some help," he said and sniffed. "Please?"

He could feel himself losing control, the weight of the night crushing his throat so he couldn't talk anymore. And the tears were coming too, even though he'd promised himself never to come back, never to ask for help from her again.

Dan suddenly slammed his hands against the wire mesh of the door, shocking his mother back inside in a flurry of locks and muttered prayers. He whipped around and walked back to the path, his face down, not daring to look at Miranda. She followed him around the edge of the house through clumps of weeds and lavender and other plants that were wet and heavy.

He came to a window and reached up, feeling the edges. He pulled out a strip of metal, shining in the moonlight, and slotted it into the edge of the window. He moved quickly, with practiced ease. The metal lifted the latch on the inside and he pushed the window up, breathing out finally, a mist forming in the night.

"Was that your mom?" Miranda asked.

Dan nodded, wiping his face with his sleeve, wet against wet.

"Let's get inside," he said, and waved her over closer. "Put your foot up here. Watch the edges."

She stepped up into Dan's linked hands and reached her fingers over the window edge. He lifted her up a bit and she scrambled inside, feeling her way into the dark room, first onto a desk by the window and then carefully to the floor. Dan followed after her, scraping his already damaged hand as he scuttled inside.

Shaking the hand, he muttered under his breath and walked to the other side of the room, flicking on the light switch. He stood by the door, relaxing a little as the light showed up the bedroom which hadn't changed. Behind the door he could hear the sounds of his mother as she moved like a ghost around the house, but out of the rain and surrounded so suddenly by the reminders of his childhood, he switched off caring about his mother.

Miranda dropped her shoes on the desk and pulled at her wet hair, straightening it while she looked around the room. They both glanced at the posters, the scattered action figures, frozen in a battle that would never be completed. There was a layer of dust everywhere and Dan wondered if anyone had been in the room since he had left.

"Yours?" Miranda asked, as she picked up the guitar leaning against the end of his bed. She sat down and studied the strings, tightening one, then another, her face full of concentration. Her fingers moved like they owned the instrument, and in a way Dan's never had.

She smiled then, and put the guitar down on the bed.

"You're not as cynical as you pretend to be, Dan," she said, and stood up, looking around some more. "I like your room."

"Thanks," Dan said.

"Can I borrow your shirt?"

She picked up a shirt from the back of his chair and pulled at her wet top. Dan looked down at his own clothes and smiled. He had left home at fourteen but he figured his old clothes would fit her.

"Help yourself," he said, and then stepped back to the window, kicking off his wet shoes and pulling at his socks. "I'll just … uh … check the window while you get changed."

She laughed, and Dan smiled, despite feeling like an

idiot. He pressed his forehead to the cold window pane and looked outside. Out of the corner of his eye he watched Miranda's reflection in the window. He knew he should turn away or close his eyes, but he didn't. And watching her change made him feel a little at peace.

"Come here."

Dan turned around and looked at her sitting on the bed. She wore a white t-shirt and track pants and sat cross-legged, eyes down, tuning the guitar.

When he sat down on the edge, she passed it to him.

"What?"

"Play me something," she said.

Dan shook his head and passed it back, but she folded her arms and refused to take it. He felt awkward holding it out to her, and the way she smelled, the way she looked at him, the way everything seemed to shout at him to seize the opportunity, made Dan move next to her, like he was being reeled in. He pulled his legs up and sat across from her, like two school children, Indian style. His mind tried to lock on to a song, one he wouldn't mess up.

"I can't."

He shifted the guitar to the side and looked at his hands. The bandage he'd managed to wrap around his right hand was wet and dirty. The tips of the hand were still red. No matter how much he wanted to pretend they were sharing a moment, Dan knew it was just a dream. Reality was a psychotic grandfather and a showdown in the morning.

"I don't remember anything," he said.

And he wished it was true.

The guitar moved back to Miranda and he realized he was holding his breath.

Miranda's voice was light as she sang softly. It floated in the space between them. Just a word, followed by another. But so much more.

The chords melted with her voice as the words of Janis Joplin materialized. She kept her eyes down, singing to the strings, and although her voice remained low the power behind them was undeniable. Dan reached out and touched her knee as she shifted into the chorus. Her head lifted eventually, their eyes met, and she stopped singing, although her fingers continued the music.

"That's cool," he said. She gave him a mocking smile and wound up the song, wiggling a little as she moved to put the guitar away, dislodging Dan's hand.

"Cool?"

"No, I meant that was... you know, beautiful."

"But you hate my music."

"Yeah, well, maybe I was a bit..."

"Maybe you don't know what you like," she finished for him. "One day I'm going to sing something of my own, you know. Right now I've got everything, you've said it yourself. But the songs aren't mine."

"You should sing like that, like you just did."

"Maybe you should sing," she countered. "I know you used to."

"I can't."

"You won't."

He knew she was right. She knew she was right.

"So my mum is kind of insane," Dan said, smiling to distract.

Miranda shrugged.

"What about your mum? Does she put heaps of

pressure on you, lives her life through you? I bet you've got some stories to tell."

"No," she said simply, her gaze still locked on Dan's, daring him to answer her.

"Oh, right," Dan said, unsure of how to untangle himself. "It's getting late."

She shrugged again.

"What?"

"Who are you supposed to be?" she asked.

"You've asked me that before. Hell, you've seen me in action, seen my psycho family, what more can there be?"

"When are you going to do something for yourself?"

He wasn't sure if she was being serious. She wasn't smiling, but she worked in show business, knew how to act and play the audience.

"Serious, you want me to be selfish?" Dan laughed. "All my life people've said I'm selfish. Are you kidding? I always do things for myself."

He went to stand up but she reached out and took his wrist.

"What do you want right now?" she asked.

The lights flickered and Dan felt a tremor through the electrical network as lightning struck a router box a few miles away. Thunder rolled across the bay.

"I'm not going to kiss you, if that's what you mean," Dan said, laughing in the lightly strobing light. She didn't blink. She watched him, took him in, and he wanted to stop everything, right there.

"Oh thank God," she said finally, releasing him. She rapped him on the shoulder with her fist as the lights steadied. He winced in mock pain.

They sat silently on the bed, just breathing.

Dan found himself pushing his mind outward, searching the grid absently, dulling his other senses, trying to distance himself.

"You can though," she said, refusing to let Dan wander off. "If you want."

She didn't look like the pop princess. There was no glamor, just honesty. Dan rubbed his shoulder. Torn.

"Ah, you're Miranda Brody," he said finally, and he felt a little removed, like he'd suddenly gotten older. "Even I know you're way, way out of my league."

She looked hurt, her jaw moved a little, but she kept her eyes on him.

"I'm just a girl."

"You're not just a girl," Dan said slowly. "And I'm not just a boy."

He looked away and stood up.

Miranda scooted up the bed and turned her back to him as she lay down. She put her head on the pillow and closed her eyes. Dan stood with his hands across his chest, trying to work out what he was supposed to do.

"You'll be here, won't you?" she asked. "All night?"

"Yeah," he said softly.

"Don't let the bad guys get us, Dan."

He breathed out. She seemed so far away from him now. He stepped to the door, turned off the lights.

"I won't."

Of course he couldn't sleep.

The electricity was shooting around his body, intertwined with his nervous system, making him twitch if he stayed still for too long, and generally keeping him on edge. Since cracking the restraining cuff he had been holding on to as much energy as he could siphon, just in case he needed to let loose at whoever would come after them next. But the energy was rogue, too erratic and pulled from too many sources, not all of them of equal quality or power. He felt like he had gorged himself on junk food: seedy, full but not satisfied.

And there was only one way to purge his system and start afresh.

Outside his bedroom window, Dan could hear the distant roll of the ocean. It was dark out there, and cold and a storm was coming. He should stay there, inside, but he knew he wouldn't.

Miranda slept. She had her knees drawn up slightly and hugged his pillow to her chest. Dan caught himself watching the way her lips were parted, the way her shoulders lifted and dropped with a steady rhythm. She was alive and that was good. She needed him and that was good too.

With a sigh he turned to the door and tested the handle. It was locked. Whatever happened on the other side, Miranda would be safe. He remembered the nights of his past in that room, a small sanctuary tacked on to a mad house. His mother lost it finally, terribly, after he was arrested. For his whole life she was on a precipice, teetering between a normal life and the absurd. Blue skin wouldn't have helped, of course, and being a single mother complicated things further. She hid herself away and reluctantly pushed him out to school when it was time. He knew it was only because the police had come around and told her that she couldn't keep him at home forever. They were nice about it, but the uniforms and the flash of official badges had sent her into a spin.

But that was the past.

It was time for Dan to let all of that fall aside. The present was more important. He checked the door again and grabbed a beach towel which hung on the back of the door. A wetsuit would have been better, but even if his steamer was still in the wardrobe it would have been too small.

"I'll be back," he whispered to Miranda as he lifted the window. The breeze pushed inside and brought with it the smell of salt and ocean.

The water was freezing, like it always was along the southwest coast of Victoria. Locals laughed at the tourists who stood along the bluff, shivering in their beanies and fleece. They laughed and then swept into the dark water like seals, wetsuits or rash vests depending on how much they had to prove. Even with a full steamer, the water was usually too cold for most.

Dan sat on his board beyond the break, alone in his boxer shorts; bare legs either side of the board. He watched the silver line of the beach, waves crashing in white bursts, while the currents gently tugged at his legs, pulling him out further. It wasn't much of a current but a part of him wanted to lie back and let the ocean drag him away from the land, away from Miranda and the mess of his life.

He rubbed his wrist where the restraining band had

been. There was a tingling sensation there still, but otherwise he was unfettered, his body free to draw upon the electricity around him. And that was the reason he had taken up his board and stalked down to the beach. Well, it had been one of the reasons. Miranda's words, her presence, the crazy possibility of actually kissing her had also driven him out into the night. But the main reason, he kept telling himself, was to shake off any lasting effects of his grandfather's dampening field, to hit the reset button so he wouldn't be ambushed again.

He slipped off the board, sinking silently beneath the surface, dropping away from the stars and from the sky.

Ever since he was thirteen, Dan had used the ocean to cleanse his system and even though it was painful and probably dangerous, he always returned to it. When his body slipped under the breakers, kicking forward into the sea, it discharged its reserves of electricity in bursts of iridescent fireworks. Underwater the discharges were incredible and Dan sometimes sat on the ocean floor and watched his body force out the electricity. It hurt, but with his body enveloped in water everything seemed muted – cut off from everything.

He sank now, his hands gently pushing his way into the darkness. And then the bright bubbles began to burst out from his skin, blistering and bursting all along his arms and then his chest and neck. Dan blew out some of the air from his lungs and it came out in bubbles, entwined with blue electricity. He blew again and watched the energy twirling like half-formed smoke rings.

Looking beyond the lights, he began to see images from the past. It had happened before, in the sea or in dreams. The visions always started with swirling shadows, but most of the time they coalesced into faces. Sometimes they were his own face, as a child, perhaps, or more recent; but often they were of his father. Nico.

Dan only had a handful of memories. The photographs were destroyed before he'd grown old enough to understand he even had a father, and neither his mother or grandfather mentioned him in any real way. They spat upon his name, cursed his stupidity. Dan grew up embarrassed by the man he never really knew.

For a short time, Nico returned. Dan remembered him as a startled man, eyes almost too wide for his face, perpetually surprised by the world around him. He drank. A lot. And he couldn't seem to find the words for his estranged wife who had grown frail and shattered while he was in prison. Without words, they turned their backs on each other. Theresa holed herself up in her room while he was in the house, so eventually he found reasons to leave.

And there was no time for Dan. His father would find excuses to leave whenever his son appeared, hurriedly climbing into the attic at the back of the house like a possum. Dan's grandfather soothed him with attention and after his powers manifested, Dan found himself easily distracted with new ways of imposing his will on the world around him. Nico would hide away, and so would Theresa; but Dan and his grandfather would take over the living room and use it as a base for exploring the wider world through electrical wiring and, later, through television.

The sea pressed against his chest and Dan knew it was time to kick back to the surface. He lifted upward, slowly, turning in the water like a seal, the lingering trail of energy spiraling behind him.

When his head burst from the surface he shook himself clear and looked to the dawning sun coming up from the east. He treaded water and noticed his board rising over the waves closer to shore. And there on the beach were two figures, standing where he'd dropped his clothes and shoes.

He could tell one was Miranda.

He dipped his head under the water and glided towards the breaking waves. The other was his mother. He surfaced and then dived again, coasting along with the waves, anticipating the bodysurfing to come.

Theresa was waiting.

When he stumbled through the choppy waves at the beach, Dan found himself without a plan. There was a genuine sense that things would change, somehow, but the expunging of energy hadn't brought with it a revelation on how to face down and destroy his grandfather.

He stopped at the thought, the water still running upward passed his ankles before pulling back to the ocean again.

He hadn't thought of destroying the Mad Russian. He couldn't do it. Not back at the bridge and not in the future. He knew there had to be a different way.

Miranda's arms were wrapped around her body but she was looking at him, and he could tell she wanted to come down and meet him. Her life was in danger. She was a pawn and the longer they played the game, the more likely she'd become a victim.

He half-raised his arm and walked out, his toes feeling the hardness of the sand make way as he moved up the beach. He stopped at the pile of clothes he'd dropped and scooped up his shirt, wiping his face in it.

"Hello," Theresa said, eyes averted.

He smiled. The wind picked up and blew his hair forward.

Theresa looked old. Her arms were wrapped tightly around her body, too, the elbows jutting against the white t-shirt which served as a nightie. Her legs were bowed and blue, her bare feet calloused but now comforted by the sand. Seeing her there, out in the open, her hair whipping about, Dan felt like shouting. He had no idea what he would shout, but he just felt the need to exhale loudly, to get rid of something. His mother hadn't been to the beach, as far as he knew, for nearly ten years. But here she was.

With Miranda.

"You said you'd watch me," Miranda said softly. It wasn't a reprimand. She pushed back the hair which escaped from her pony tail and sank her hands into his jeans. They looked good on her.

"I had to … the waves were calling," he said, hooking his thumb back towards the water. Miranda smiled and looked down at the white sand, leaving Dan to look at his mother. "What are you doing here?"

Theresa was watching him, her eyebrows turned up in confusion like they always were. Her thin lips were guarded but she was looking at him, really looking at him.

"Aren't you cold?" he asked, stepping towards her, shaking sand off his towel and opening it for her. She stepped back a little, her arms still wrapped tightly around her frail body, but Dan slung the towel around her shoulders and settled it there. They were close now, his chin level with the top of her head. As he pulled the towel around her he caught the smell of his mother's hair. And then he felt her arms shifting beneath. He stepped back but her arms shrugged their way out and her hands reached out to take his hand between them.

"Mum."

Theresa lifted his hand and placed it against her cheek. He could feel the coolness of her skin, windblown as she stood on the beach. He could feel the scratchy dryness too, something which had plagued her for years.

"We've made breakfast," Miranda said. "Back at the house."

Dan turned into the offshore breeze and saw Miranda smiling at him, like she'd just orchestrated some kind of miracle. He couldn't stop smiling back even though he didn't want to concede anything to her just yet, and he felt his eyes strain against the wind and tears.

"Come on," she said.

Back at house the three of them ate in silence. Theresa kept her eyes down and ate like a bird, bony fingers playing with toast, tearing it apart slowly, methodically. She'd drop a crumb into her mouth as she listened to Dan talk about the ocean and answer Miranda's questions.

"You'll have to come back another day," Theresa said softly, and she stopped moving her hands, as if surprised to hear her own voice.

"That'd be great," Miranda said, and reached under the table to take Dan's hand in hers. He nodded, eyes on

Miranda's, his fingers entwined with hers. She said it would be great, he thought, over and over in his head.

Theresa smiled a little and then stood, supporting herself on her chair.

"I shall go and …" her voice trailed off and she shuffled out of the kitchen.

When she was gone, Miranda dropped Dan's hand and lifted her handbag onto the table. Her eyes were bright, filled with something Dan thought might have been excitement or fear. He'd seen both so often in the past day.

"I got a call," she said, and pulled out a phone.

"Okay," Dan said. He looked at the phone, but he was more worried about Miranda pulling her hand away from his.

"It's not my phone," she said. "It was in my bag."

"I don't get it."

"It rang twice. I ignored it the first time. I was kind of wondering where you were, so when it rang again I picked it up. Thought you might have left it for me to make sure I wasn't worried when you left."

Dan shrugged and felt his cheeks burn.

"It was your friend," she said.

"Who?" Dan wondered if he had any friends left. "You mean Halo?" he asked.

"The same."

Dan picked up the phone. He could sense the power in it but it was just a normal, throw-away phone. He focused and the phone turned on. The call history had already registered in his mind but he scrolled through the recent calls list anyway.

"He wants you to call him," Miranda said.

"He's an idiot."

"I don't think so."

Dan looked at her suddenly, the memories of his jealousy uneasily fresh in his mind. She took the phone back from him, and as her fingers touched his he forgot it.

"What did he say, what else?"

"Nothing," she said. Her fingers pressed at the keys and with each impression Dan received the number. "Just to call him."

"So you're calling him? Are you nuts?"

"Probably," she smiled. "But you're stubborn and we don't have time. He got you your mojo back and he didn't have to. We don't have back-up, not anymore."

"I'm sorry about Sully," Dan said.

She passed him the phone.

"Hey Dan," the voice of Halo came through clearly. "Enjoy the surf?"

Dan stood up and cupped the phone to his other ear, his eyes out to the front yard, bordered with gums and hidden from the road. The highway was beyond and the ocean beyond that.

"What do you want?" Dan asked.

"You need to finish this. There're a lot of us who need closure, Dan, not least of all, you and the lovely Miss Brody."

"I thought you and the Russian were doing well enough," Dan said.

"I was doing fine when he was dead, actually. The old guard are past their relevance and you know it. They're still dangerous; your grandfather probably more than the others."

"Is he there with you?" Dan pushed his senses outward even as his eyes scanned the trees again. He picked up the other outlying houses in the area and a few cars on the highway.

"He's flipped again. Thing is, he doesn't want you back anymore, Dan. He wants to consume you, make you part of him, rub you out entirely."

Halo laughed again.

"I don't think it's funny," Dan said.

"No kidding, but he's losing it here. If he can't get you face to face he's going to rip Melbourne apart."

"He won't get far," Dan said. "The Knights will be back soon and the army would've been mobilized after last night. Like you said, he's an old man now."

"But crazy-old. He's not going to let this go, Dan. You have to come back. You have to face him and stop it from spreading."

"Why don't you do it?" More laughter. "It's not funny, Halo. Why the hell don't you do something about it?"

"Because I'm not in your league. None of us are, you idiot. What do you want me to do? Read his mind? It's pretty clear he's wigged out. You don't need to be psychic. I've given you the break you need, the chance to go head to head and beat the old man. But it's your choice."

"That's not a choice. You want me to come back and die so he'll not blow up Melbourne?"

"You're not going to die."

There was silence.

Dan put his hand and the phone down against the bench. He could hear Miranda behind him: her body was crackling with electrical impulses. He closed his eyes and for a flash he could sense everything around him: the walls, the electronics, Miranda, his mother sitting alone on the veranda. Humans were made up of electrical impulses and he could see Miranda so clearly, so intricately.

"I have to go," he said, bringing the phone back to his jaw.

"I know," Halo said. "I guess you've traced the call by now."

CHAPTER 28

BREE

B REE STOOD ON the edge of the cliff, looking down at the beach. She wore a hooded jumper and running gear, but she knew she wouldn't complete her circuit. Halo slid a phone into his jeans and joined her at the cliff edge. His self-satisfied grin reminded her of the younger Halo. He kicked a clump of clay over the edge, but didn't even bother to watch it tumbling down.

It had been his idea to get the Small Gods back together. After years of growing, each in their own way, Halo suddenly decided they needed to be reunited, that the world needed some kind of apology from them for the crimes they almost committed. Bree thought it was a ruse for some new Halo-scheme. She knew he was embedded in a handful of crime families, playing them off against each other by systematically uncovering their secrets and then selling them to the person most likely to cause trouble. He had undermined the criminal network in Melbourne, even Madame Pearl, the untouchable one.

But Bree agreed to listen, at least. She had managed to keep away from crime, even as she deliberately avoided heroism and altruistic endeavors. Keeping below the proverbial radar was her goal, and it worked for her. Dan became an indentured servant of the government, while Halo and Lily became pawns of bigger bosses. Only Bree was her own person, and she wouldn't be giving that up any time soon – especially for Halo.

Bree could tell the others made decisions based on family pressure. Lily had no chance of escaping her grandmother's influence, while Dan was left in a vacuum with no one to care for him. One was drawn deeper into the criminal world while the other floated around, aimless. Halo, on the other hand, had outgrown his family. He was forged by a desire to be the best, to outstrip everyone and everything around him.

Her own family was simply a veneer. When she was fifteen she realized her adoptive parents were employees of the Mad Russian. She had faded away from them, turned to dust and never returned. It was her way: to disappear when things became too demanding. Halo pointed it out to her frequently.

Still, there was a part of her that wanted to erase the sins of her childhood. The Mad Russian had done horrible things in their name, had brought upon great destruction and death while they stood in the public's eye, even if it was just for a few days.

He would have to face justice.

Death.

Bree knew it was the only way, and so did Halo. Interestingly enough, it was Dan who seemed the most reluctant, even though he suffered the greatest. Bree assumed it had something to do with guilt and family.

They tended to go hand in hand.

"Is Dan coming back?" she asked.

"Of course he is," Halo said.

"What happens if this doesn't work out?"

"Nothing, really," he said. "At least, nothing for the two of us."

She smiled sadly and turned away from the cliff, walking towards the car park. Halo trailed behind her.

"You go on being his hound, and I'll just flit away," she said. "You haven't changed, Sohail."

"We never do," he said.

At his car, Halo handed her an envelope. She hesitated, watching his eyes rather than his hand. She had no more secrets to hide from his penetrating stare, but she hoped to catch a glimpse of his true motive. He winked at her and flicked the envelope.

"Memory stick inside. Details about Grandfather Time and the hostage. We need to get him back into the game or Dan's not going to last long."

She nodded and tore open the envelope. Sure enough a small memory stick lay at the bottom. She tapped it on her hand and it slid out.

"You do your bit and I'll do mine," Halo said, smooth voice close to her ear as she examined the USB. "We need to get Dan all juiced up and angry, just like the old man planned. We push him, pull him, move him into place where he can go all-nuclear like his dad and take out the Russian."

"You make it sound like a game," Bree said as she slipped the device into her pocket. She didn't like the way

Halo used everyone around him, but she wasn't surprised. "Don't you care about Dan at all? He was like your brother."

"Dan's a good kid, no problem. But he's wasting his life and I'm not going to lose five years' work just to give the kid a second chance at what he's already blown. The Russian has to go, and Dan's the easiest way to get rid of him."

"You make it sound so easy," Bree said. "And it's never that easy."

"The girl's the key. Dan really loves her, stupid kid, and that makes it easy."

"You've told the Russian that Dan is coming, haven't you?"

Halo smiled and pulled on his shades. He jutted his chin towards the ocean and Bree followed his gaze, taking in the sweeping and diving gulls. She felt a pang of regret, like her choices were slipping away. She hadn't felt that way for years.

"You can't see the storm," Halo said. "It looks blue and forever out there, but you can feel it. You can't stop it, so I figure why not get it over with?"

"And what if this works, then?" she asked.

Halo shrugged.

"Seriously, what happens if the Mad Russian is stopped? What happens if Dan actually steps up and does something for once?"

"We cheer, I guess," Halo said, smiling. "Maybe throw him a parade. It doesn't matter, Bree, baby. You and I both know there're already other people shuffling to get into position. The Russian should have stayed dead and gone. Pearl had the place running smoothly enough. Now he's back, things are confused."

"Not you, though."

"I have a feeling about this," he said. "Everything that happened before, it was meant to be. The old man was right about us, about us being the future. Thing is, he wanted us to be his version of the future, but I don't think we're those kind of people."

"No. But if this ends with the Russian out of the picture, we'll need to work out exactly what kind of people we are."

Halo leaned forward and kissed her cheek. His lips brushed against her skin so quickly that he was back watching her before she could react.

"Good luck," he said, and then opened the door.

She stepped back, hands in her hoody.

When his car moved out into the street and towards the city she relaxed a little. A part of her wanted to run, to push herself around the coastal track and forget, even briefly, about what would happen that night. But her fingers closed around the memory stick and she knew she had to leave immediately. There was no time.

She smiled at the reference.

Bree remembered Grandfather Time from an evening long ago. She had been with Lily and Luke Ma, at some gathering of criminals. The tall, dark-suited man with the top hat had simply appeared amidst the Chinese business-men and corrupt local councilors. Bree remembered seeing his eyes looking right at her from across the room. She saw his pupils, was transfixed by them. She had known in that instant, that one day they would face each other, and that it would be the death of one of them.

Bree took a breath and shook off her memories. Halo knew about the premonition and probably every other secret she had. All a person had to do was look in the man's eyes and nothing could be hidden. She had learned that a long time ago, but she knew Halo well enough to know that he would never betray her.

Her eyes closed and she felt her feet begin to swirl, faster and faster, transforming into a dust devil until her body had vanished. She allowed herself to dive down towards the ocean so she could skim across the surface, but before she had fully enjoyed the sun through her granulated body it was time to leave, and so she turned herself back towards the loft.

With the ability to reduce herself to dust particles, and even smaller if she concentrated, Bree was able to get into any place, no matter how secure. And while she usually relied on her ability to get *out* of situations, there were times when she was called on to break *in*.

Grandfather Time was an enigma. She had only met him once, but hadn't spoken with him. He was English, she knew, but of an indeterminate age owing to his own strange abilities – the talent to step through time at his own pace.

The house he was using while he was in Australia was in the eastern suburbs of Melbourne. It was large and sur-rounded by high walls and a secure gate, although Bree sim-ply flew above the barriers and then down one of the many chimneys, into a drawing room. She could tell immediately that the house didn't belong to him. The interiors were modern, and Grandfather Time was almost chronically tied to the past.

Bree swept through the house, moving in a swirling pattern from one floor to the next. She eventually found a room with the definite touch of the master of time. Clocks lined the walls and covered the surface of desks, shelves and cabinets. The ticking sound seemed to push against Bree's incorporeal body, so when she pulled herself back into solid form it was a relief from the pressure.

She reached out and picked up a medium-sized clock made from a rose wood, with a clear globe over the clock face. She put it down and looked at the others, shifting some around to get better views at the ones behind. Many of the clocks contained people, or specters of people. She wasn't surprised. She had heard the stories. Her fingers closed around a tarnished clock and shook it lightly but the image of a red haired woman didn't move. Bree felt some recognition there, in the woman's green eyes and pale skin, tugging at her memory. She shook the clock again and then replaced it on the shelf, turning her attention to the other timepieces. Dozens of faces stared out at her and she felt uneasy.

They didn't move, though. Their faces were slightly elongated, like they'd been caught in some kind of warp, which she supposed they had. She didn't read science fiction, didn't have the patience for make belief, but she knew Grandfather Time had captured these people, and captured them for some deliberate reason. There were always reasons.

An ornate clock with a long-stemmed lily engraved along its edge drew her attention. She ran her thumb along the edges, even as she recognized the man trapped inside. He had a small black beard and a strong face, although his eyes were closed, like he was simply waiting.

"Well, your waiting is over, Suleyman," she said, and

cracked the clock face against the edge of the shelf it had been standing on. The wood splintered and gears sprung out along with a purple mist which quickly formed a larger cloud in the room. Bree stood back as the cloud dissipated, leaving a hefty, slightly beaten man in its place.

He took a deep breath through his nose. His eyes remained closed.

"Mister Suleyman," she said. "I'm not the enemy."

He smiled, eyes still closed.

"Would an enemy announce herself, do you think?" he asked, breathing out, rather loudly. Bree placed the shattered clock on the shelf. "Still," Sully continued, opening his eyes and looking at his new surroundings. "I do not suppose you are the enemy. I recall the one in question wearing an impressive top hat."

"That was Grandfather Time," Bree said.

"That name would be apt," Sully nodded.

"I'm here to get your help," she said. "Miranda Brody needs your help, actually."

"Of course," Sully said. "And she will always receive it. What is your name, though? Perhaps you would enlighten me while I take a breath or perhaps two."

Bree wasn't used to being questioned. Her clients were generally in such a hurry that her reluctance to communicate was gratefully accepted. Still, Sully's eyes held her in place and she felt compelled to speak.

"I'm Sebriya," she said.

"Berber?"

She nodded.

"Hmm," he nodded. "You are a gifted one, like Dan. Perhaps you even know him."

"We're friends," she said, although the word sounded unusual, even to her own ear. "The thing is, are you as gifted as they say?"

"I am magnificent," he said, bowing slightly.

"You better be," Bree said.

He smiled again, flexing his arms as he moved towards the desk. His large hands picked up a clock Bree hadn't checked yet and he lifted it to the light above. She noticed it held a swirling slate-grey cloud inside the globe. It looked like a storm in a snow-dome. She moved beside him and was amazed to see moving pictures in amidst the clouds.

The Mad Russian was pounding his fists, revealed in the vision as if from above. He was in a study, surrounded by bookshelves. She hadn't seen the place before, but she knew the old man.

"This would be a spy glass," Sully said.

"Grandfather Time is spying on the Russian," Bree said.

"The vipers always watch their backs."

Sully grunted and placed the globe back on the desk, pressing with his thumbs on both sides which magnified the image, projecting it against the wall behind the desk's chair.

"How'd you do that?"

"I have been in the business," he explained.

"What business?"

Sully shrugged and stroked his bearded chin, his eyes intent on the image. Bree followed his gaze and saw the Russian yelling. She'd heard the rants before, although never directly as the target. When he lost his temper, the earth moved. She could see the room he was sitting in tremble. A woman stumbled into view, falling forward from where she had been hidden and nearly hitting her head on the desk.

The Russian stood from his chair and yelled at her as she picked herself up.

"My kingdom for a volume control," Sully murmured.

"Do you know her?" Bree asked.

"I thought perhaps I did."

The woman was thin and young. Her blonde hair was short and she looked like she'd been caught in the headlights of a truck. Another person appeared, his hands on the girl's back, pulling her back from the desk.

It was Halo.

Suddenly the girl shook herself free of him and lunged at the Russian, her finger pointing at him with a silent accusation. Halo grabbed her arm and pulled her back a second time. The Russian's eyes glowed white.

"And now we go," Sully said.

Bree didn't understand. The globe mesmerized her, but Sully gently turned her around and she saw the shadows in the corner of the room begin to shift. It was the hallmark of Grandfather Time.

"I do not look forward to a rematch," Sully said. "Although honor dictates I do not back down from this."

"Huh," Bree said, but didn't waste time. She touched Sully's arm and they both began to disintegrate, even as Grandfather Time materialized.

Like trains passing in a station, Bree mused, catching his timeless eyes before she vanished completely.

CHAPTER 29
MIRANDA

THE STADIUM CAR park was full, and stragglers moved towards the gates under the protection of umbrellas and glow bands as the rain pelted down around them. It was well-lit but no one noticed Miranda Brody arrive on the back of a stolen Kawasaki Ninja, and that was a relief, because she knew they wouldn't have been able to get anywhere near the entrance with a riot of fans clamoring around her. Dan slowed the bike and kicked the stand back as it stopped at the curb.

Miranda had been at the stadium only a few days before, but since then she had been shot at by snipers, nearly blown up by a roadside bomb and then abducted by a supervillain.

They were late.

So many of her fans were already inside.

She let her hands drop from around Dan's waist as she sat up and slid off the bike, landing on the soaked road but with her helmet still on. Dan switched off the engine and got to his own feet, looking through his visor into hers.

She heard herself breathing again, the breath fogging up the inside of the helmet. The drone of the engine was gone too. It was just the two of them and a car park. Miranda had been holding him close during the ride, her body pressed against his, and she missed the feeling so much.

A couple of technicians emptied out of the doors just ahead of them and the noise distracted Dan long enough for Miranda to take off her helmet. When he looked back at her things had moved forward, the pieces of the plan falling into place.

She had to go inside, even if a monster waited in there for her. She had to go and stand between the Mad Russian and her thousands of fans.

Dan looked at her and took off his own helmet slowly.

His hair was curling slightly, and damp. A wisp of it stuck to his cheek and she pulled off her gloves and wiped it away, giving him a smile. He shook his head.

"Don't worry about me," she said.

Dan let his helmet drop to the road.

"You should put on a hat or something," he said.

Back at the beach house they had watched news reports. Miranda was the lead story. Her people were panicking, media outlets across the world were trying to predict the outcome of what looked like some bizarre kidnapping. And Dan's face was being shown too. There had been an interview with Alsana and she was not impressed. She had called him dangerous and looking right into the camera she told the world of his history with violence. Miranda turned the television off.

"I'm coming with you," she said.

Dan shook his head.

"I'm serious, Dan. Those kids need me. They're in that stadium because of me and I'm not leaving them there for your grandfather's sick plans."

"You can't help them," Dan said.

"You're wrong," she said. She sat next to him on the sofa and took his hands which were shaking. He thought she was going to die. She could see it in his face and in his body. "I'm going with you," she continued. "You might think I'm a passing blip, that my music will be gone this time next year. It's probably true, but right now, out there… those kids worship me. They sing the songs and they wear the clothes and they're waiting to see me on stage."

"You'll get hurt," he said softly.

"I can't abandon them. I owe it to them, and you know that's true. You're going because you think you need to atone for your grandfather. I'm going because I know I owe it to the fans. They're there because of me, no accident. I am responsible for them."

"He's a killer, Miranda," Dan said. "He won't hesitate, not a second time."

"I can't abandon them. I can't sit here while they risk their lives because of me."

She leaned across and kissed his hair, holding her lips against his head for a few seconds, smelling him so close.

The Human Tour was at its final concert. Halo had told Miranda about the Mad Russian's plans to blow up the stadium, to obliterate her fans if he couldn't burn her. Eventually she had convinced Dan to let her come, to let her draw the attention of everyone while he found a way through the madman's armor. In the end, he didn't have a choice, anyway. She could get her own way back to the city.

She could hear music from the support band inside the stadium. Dan looked like he didn't know where to go. He was stuck there in the rain.

"Come here," Miranda said and tugged at his jacket. She unzipped him and peeled the jacket off, laying it over the bike's seat. She slipped out of her own jacket and realized she was still wearing one of his old t-shirts. It brought a smile to his lips.

"You look good," he said. "Really good."

And then he reached forward and kissed her. His lips were soft and a bit cold, but she pressed back against him and she forgot everything. He reached his hands out and held her hips against his. But then she pulled back and caught the smell of his wet hair as she opened her eyes.

"It's time," she said.

As soon as she slipped into the doors she was discovered. A woman wearing a microphone headset took her arm and marched her down the corridors without a word. Two more officials joined them, chattering away to unseen people.

Todd Christie appeared around a corner, fury etched across his face. He looked at her with wide eyes, borderline crazy as he took in her wet hair, her clothes and shoes. Then he looked at his watch. She could see the veins in his neck.

"I'm not late am I?" she asked, shaking free from the woman. "The band sounds great from out there."

Christie clenched his jaw again, biting back words.

Miranda moved past him towards the dressing room, but he grabbed her arm and pulled her back, shoving her against the wall. His beady eyes pinned her there with memories of Chinatown and the Mad Russian.

He swore at her.

And she closed her eyes against it; against the smell of his breath and the heat of his face so close to hers.

"Get your hands off me," she said slowly.

She opened her eyes and stared directly at him. He hesitated but then the grip relaxed and he started breathing heavily through his nose.

"You work for me," she said in a low voice. "Don't forget that, Todd. If I want to see the city where I'm performing, then that's exactly what I'll do. If I'm late, you wait. If I'm unhappy, you make me happy."

She waited for a response.

"Do I make myself clear?" she asked.

"Clear, Miss Brody," he said, running his hand over his forehead.

"Good. Now, I need you to organize an orderly evacuation."

"What?" Christie's eyes bulged again and he bared his teeth, spittle flecking outward. He punched the wall and turned around in a rage. The other assistants moved back while Miranda remained calm.

"We need the people out into that parkland," she said. "That's not negotiable."

"That's insane!" he yelled. "Your little star is fading

269

Brody. Your time is over, tonight. Mess it up and you go down with pain, your whole family will be bankrupted, you'll be ruined."

"I don't think…"

"You don't, do you?" he hissed. "Get up on stage and sing your little heart out. Save what little you have left."

He punched the wall again and stormed away, leaving the assistants to guide Miranda to the stage door. A girl started working on her hair as they moved, while another slid a black and diamond t-shirt over her head. She looked back but Christie was gone. Ahead of her was the thumping of bass and the distant sounds of a boy band. She didn't know their names, hadn't met them yet, but they were out there on stage.

In the line of fire.

She shook off the assistants and walked forward.

She was supposed to arrive via the roof elevator but there was no time. The band had stopped. The main entrance was in front of her. Miranda adjusted the headset microphone and looked to the girls around her. None of them looked familiar.

"Let's do this," she said softly.

The doors opened and a roar lifted across the stadium. Lights strobed and then found Miranda walking out onto the main stage. They concentrated on her in a bright white spotlight, shunting everything else into darkness. Flashes from cameras and phones punctuated the crowd. She could hear her name, over and over. Miranda held up her hands and the noise lifted even more, sweeping around the stadium.

"Hello Melbourne!" she called and laughed at the further roars and whistles. "It's so good to be here!"

The lights came on across the crowd, sweeping around the screaming fans and their signs. Parents smiled along with their children, costumed fans flaunted their freak chic. Miranda moved to the edge of the stage. Security gates kept the fans from actually getting close enough to touch but she reached out to them anyway.

"I'm sorry for being so late," she said to the crowd. "But you've got such a lovely city here."

Behind her came the freaks. She saw Kyla leading a group of three girls, all dressed up in bird feathers. The girl's skin was so pink under the lights, the swirls of blue ink moved across her skin and were magnified on the giant screens flanking the stage.

Miranda turned back to the crowd. Thousands of people had come to see her final show. She let herself think of Dan and hoped he was somewhere close. She needed him.

"Can I tell you a secret? Just between you and me?"

The crowd screamed back at her.

Kyla and another girl came to stand next to her. The band started up softly, leading her into the first set. Miranda was running out of time. She cupped her hand to her mouth and smiled.

"You see, Melbourne, there's this boy..."

More screams. The intensity built and twisted.

She held her hands out and waved the sound back, smiling across at Kyla. She saw the green lit exit signs at the edge of the stage, and then turned to spot them throughout the stadium.

"There's this boy..." she said again. "But I want to take you someplace special and talk a little more. Do you want to come along, Melbourne?"

Stage hands at the edge of the platform looked confused. She imagined Christie fuming in the darkness.

The lights flickered.

"I need you to be extra sneaky, okay? We're going to be a little bit naughty. I hope the mums and dads out there don't mind, but I want to take you all on a journey. Do you want to come with me?"

The crowd surged, faces glistening with excitement. The security guards looked a little anxious but didn't look up at her, their eyes on the crowd.

"Let's start with all you lovely freaks in bays 10 through to sixteen. I want you to move out through the gates. Come on now, let's be sneaky, no rushing."

It took some time, but then the people directly opposite her started to move. Fans in other areas shifted too and several exits opened.

"Now all you lovelies over there in bays five to ten, you can start moving. We're all going to meet outside. I've got a surprise for you, a piece of me you can keep forever."

The lights flickered again and she caught sight of Christie in the wings.

"Come on girls, come on boys, we need to get this party started. Everyone else, you can start moving too."

There were ripples at the gates. People were stumbling. Security was there, assisting but unsure of how to deal with such a mass exodus.

"You think this stage is something?" she called.

Miranda looked over at the runway leading to the elevator. She moved backward, arms up and smiling at the crowds.

"The real magic is out there. We've decked the whole

park in magic freak chic, just a little intimate thing for you and me, for my final show."

The crowds moved again. She could see empty seats but there were still too many people inside. The lights went out for a few seconds and screams spread through the air. Her microphone dropped out.

"Get out of here," she whispered to Kyla. "Get outside."

"What's going on?"

"You're in danger here," she said. "Get the dancers out of the building, please."

Kyla nodded, the blue ink on her face flaring quickly before it pulled back under the pink and disappeared. She touched Miranda's hand lightly and then moved back towards the other dancers.

Miranda retreated to the runway as the lights returned. White balls of light flickered up and down the path to the elevator. She kicked open the box with her foot and saw the ray-guns. Her chest felt tight as she bent down and took one out, slipping it into the waist band of Dan's jeans.

"You see, there's this boy," she said again, the microphone only transmitting some of her words. "And he's out there somewhere, trying his best to be a better person. He's out there for you and he's out there for me."

Kyla disappeared off stage, along with the band and dancers. Miranda was left alone in the flickering lights.

"And he's a freak."

The lights cut out again. There was a scream from her left and then more around the arena. The microphone crackled and she pulled it from her head, dropping it to the floor.

"But he's my freak and I'm not going to let him down."

CHAPTER 30

DAN

SHE STEPPED AWAY from him, walking backwards with her eyes still on his. He could sense the explosives behind her, threaded through the stadium like a brightly strung web. They weren't hidden from him. That wasn't their purpose.

Miranda waved at him as she reached the door. And then she turned around, her hair spreading a little as she moved and stepped through. It only took a moment before the doors closed again and she was gone.

"We have to do this," she had said back at the beach. "You do your thing and I'll do mine."

Dan jogged to the doors and slipped in, but Miranda was already gone. He could still feel her lips against his, and as his eyes adjusted to the darkness inside the access corridor he realized how much he had been thinking about that kiss. It'd been coming for a long time.

He breathed out and focused on the network of explosives. He pressed his fingers against a wall and felt the electricity pulsing there. A door unlocked ahead of him, the electronic mechanism no match for him tonight. With a last glance down the corridor, Dan moved into the maintenance room. He let the door click behind him and took in the monitors lining one of the walls. He saw a band on stage and cameras cycled through a loop of security footage from all the exits. He saw Halo on a screen, looking defiantly up to the camera, tapping his phone which shined in the light of the service corridor.

Dan shook his head but already his mind had burst outward, into the stadium, to lock down that phone. He located the camera and pin-pointed Halo's location. Level 2. Dan knew the way.

It was quiet. The well-lit corridor had several doors leading off on each side but he needed access to the higher levels. Halo's phone signal called to him from above. He closed his eyes quickly and scanned the area, pushing his mind outward and when he came across surveillance or locks, Dan over-rode them and closed off their circuits. He switched off the explosives as he moved as well, sucking the energy dry and leaving them disengaged husks. Security could cut them out of the walls later, when it was safe.

It was all too easy.

The lights remained on in the corridors, but as he moved further into the bowels of the stadium the cameras began to go down, flicking out one by one. The Mad Russian was in the building. Dan moved to the end of the corridor and found the stairs. Beside them were elevators, big service ones which ferried goods up and down the center. He thought about using them but decided against testing his luck so early in the night. He pushed open the door to the stairs and jogged up to the next level.

As he stepped out into more corridors, two people walked past him, talking fast into their headsets. Dan smiled at Miranda's name and ducked his head as they passed. Halo's phone signal led him away from the main corridor and into more dimly-lit spaces where cages held oversized props and promotional material. The air was cooler here too. He saw a Christmas tree slumped up against the wire mesh.

With the air conditioner chugging away above him, Dan relaxed a little and looked around, his fingers pressing the edge of the tree against the wire. Christmas seemed so far away. He let the plastic pine needles go and stepped further into the semi-darkness. Besides the noise and the physical vibrations from the machine above, the corridor was abandoned and his steps echoed. The wire fences enclosed storage cubicles, protecting brown paper-wrapped merchandise, signs and display cabinets from concerts gone by. It gave the corridor an appearance of order by hiding the clutter behind wire and padlocks.

The passage led from the service elevator along eight cubicles on either side, right to the back where a compactor sat silently behind double doors. It was funny, he'd made deliveries to this place during the daylight hours, smuggling hot food to the staff who craved something fattening but couldn't be bothered walking across to the food vendors. It looked the same: low light, slight echo of the rumbling air conditioner. Normally there would be a handful of workers congregated around the compactor room, stealing a cigarette break, away from the prominent smoke detectors, waiting for their chicken combos and wraps. They would be leaning against walls, nodding in agreement over poor wages, tyrannical supervisors or the football.

But tonight the place was empty.

He walked slowly, a strange feeling of being disconnected coming over him. Out in the fluorescent world of the stadium, Miranda would be commanding the attention of her loyal fans. All eyes on her. Even the predators. She knew the dangers. At least, Dan hoped she knew. It had been her choice, her gift to him, a last minute distraction to draw the world to her and let him slip into the stadium and through unmarked doors into the world beyond.

But it was a different, cut-off world. He wasn't being chased, threatened, beaten up and left for dead. He was hidden and it felt safe, like he could just stop and let the world pass him by. It was familiar. It was the *other* option, the safer route. He knew he could return to his old life, he'd just need to stay in one spot, not challenge his grandfather. Let Miranda die.

He hadn't even stopped walking, his fingers trailing along the wire mesh of the cages. The idea faded, not even fully formed. When he got to the corner with the compactor and the stairwell, there was no indecision. He didn't want the shadow half-life anymore, living from day to day, hour to hour, with nothing to look forward to. He'd seen his mother fade into a vague blue smudge of a person.

Was she back now, he wondered. It was too early to tell.

He knew he would protect her, though. The Mad Russian had messed with all their lives, and now he wanted Dan to be stellar, to grow into the family name, to eclipse his unpromising father who had blown himself up, and perhaps even to replace the Mad Russian himself one day.

He slid the door open and looked into the compactor room. On the edge of the gaping hole which led down to the box crushing machine in the basement, Dan saw a phone with its power on.

"Crap," he said, pushing out with his senses, searching for Halo.

And then he was kicked in the small of his back, and stumbled forward. Halo landed on the ground as Dan crashed into the compactor room, his hands up to stop his head from hitting the metal. In a flash, he spun around and looked out the door, eyes blazing with blue energy.

Halo stepped to the right just as the electricity blasted outward and past him. Dan pulled himself up and tore energy out from the surrounding electric grid in violent bursts. The dim lights were extinguished and the air conditioner cranked to a halt, their power source lancing out and into Dan. He clenched his fists and moved out of the room, a blue glow emanated from his body.

Halo punched low, crouching as Dan came out of the door, but it missed and Dan's palms flared with a sudden light. Even blinded, Halo moved like a ninja, leaping up to the mesh roof, grabbing a hold and leaping to the top of one of the cages.

"Where is he?" Dan called out. He traced the line of metal, seeing the criss-crossing mesh with his special senses, all the way to Halo who crouched above. It wouldn't take long to stun him.

"Take it easy," Halo said. "You've got all night, Danny."

Dan reached out and clamped his fingers around the

mesh. He flexed and electricity burst outward, travelling like lightning through the wires. But the energy was blocked and re-routed, shooting through a second, hidden network and back into Dan, knocking him back with a burst. He fell to the ground, his hands glowing brightly again.

"You think I'm an idiot?" Halo called out. "I brought you here."

Dan could sense the subtle circuit-breakers attached to the mesh. It had been hidden from him but now that he had activated them they were revealed. He didn't recognize whose work it was. Surely not Halo.

Halo leapt down, landing in front of Dan who sat on the floor, his legs splayed to each side, still looking surprised at his glowing hands. Halo's foot shot out at head level, but Dan deflected it with his charged forearm. Sparks flew and Halo spun again, switching his feet, moving like a street fighter. The second kick connected with Dan's chest, shoving him against the opposite fence.

"Don't be shy," Halo said and fell back to a defensive stance.

Dan pulled himself up using the wire mesh. He was still fully charged but the kick had winded him.

"Where is he?" Dan asked again.

"Your conversation is a bit boring."

"I'm not here to talk."

"Good to hear," Halo said and punched outward, but pulled up deliberately short. "What's your plan?"

"I'm going to kick your ass."

Halo smiled, his face bathed in the blue glow. Dan felt a rising anger, a hatred for the way Halo could still smile so easily.

"You've got your juice back," Halo said. "Don't waste it on me."

Dan clapped his hands together in front of him, releasing a thunderclap which blew Halo backward down towards the service elevator. Crackling energy wrapped around him as he stumbled, kicking his legs out and falling.

Dan followed him, coming to a stop next to Halo's twitching boots.

"It's a decoy," Halo said, surprisingly calm. His eyes looked to the roof, but then crossed to meet Dan's eyes. "You're being played. Again."

Images from the hotel explosion replayed across his eyes. The shooter collapsed once the trap had been set, and now Halo had set him up again. Dan pushed his senses outward, taking in the surveillance camera network which was still down. Most of the explosives had been deactivated but he could sense more of them on the other side of the stadium.

"Where is he?" Dan mumbled, searching still.

"Don't follow him, Dan. You don't have to be the one trick pony."

Dan stepped over Halo's body as he twisted on the ground and raised himself up on his elbows. Halo struggled again, his legs numb from the shock. Dan punched the elevator button. Then he looked back at Halo.

"I'm not anything like him."

"Probably not," Halo said.

"Why are you here?"

Halo shrugged.

"I mean it," Dan shouted. "He treats us like puppets. Why are you still with him?"

"Because I can't cut the strings, Dan. Only you can do that." Dan thumped the wall and sparks flew out. He hit it again. "Look for the separate line," Halo said. "The old man's set up a single camera loop down there. Especially for you."

Dan narrowed his eyes but he was already searching below. Most of the cameras were down, the locks deactivated; but then he stumbled across a transmitting signal. He concentrated further and broke into the visual feed.

"Sorry, man," Halo said.

Dan's eyes widened as his began to assemble the fragmented images from below. A camera system had captured a woman, dressed in a silver outfit. It was Miranda. Her dark hair fell across her face as she clutched the microphone stand and Dan could see she was trembling. It was a stage, and posters of Miranda rippled in a manufactured wind behind her as she stood in front of the microphone.

Her lips moved. He could see that. They moved quickly like they were reciting a prayer or going over lines before the performance.

Her hands shifted on the microphone, fingers lifting and moving to take hold of it again. She didn't look up at the camera.

She breathed out.

Dan held his breath.

And then electricity shot towards her from all sides, white light shooting into her chest and blasting out the back. She stood, clutching the microphone, refusing to let it go. Her mouth opened and more light spilled outward, directly towards the camera that Dan had hijacked.

Everything was consumed with the blinding white light.

The elevator door opened and he stumbled into it,

pushing madly for the floor below, using his hands and his mind. The doors closed again and Halo was gone.

Time seemed to stop.

The image of Miranda burned into his mind. He shut his eyes and it was there. He opened them and she was still there. He pushed his way into the corridors again as the doors opened and stumbled towards the camera's fading signal. It drew him in like a line. He knew it was a trap, that his grandfather would be waiting.

But he didn't care.

He had lost everything.

He came to a stop at the stage door. The signal was clear but he couldn't do it, the door stopped him. He pressed his face against it and felt the coolness. He realized he was crying.

He could smell burning.

"Miranda..." he whispered.

He didn't expect to gag, had told himself that it wasn't any worse than other times, but when Dan pushed through the doors onto the stage he had to step back again quickly. The stench was like a solid force, pressing against the door and the walls, shifting itself through the molecules, wafting like a wave.

It was like burning meat.

He slid down the door with his arms crossed over his face, the sleeves of his shirt blocking the smell. In the second he had opened the door Dan had seen her body, on its back with legs bent at the knees, melting into the canvas floor. The jagged struts of bone and the withered torso were unmistakable.

He tightened his arms and heard his heartbeat thumping in his ears.

A sob escape from his throat.

The electrical pulses around the stage were chaotic, having been re-channeled into the microphone. He could trace the networks and see how they had been re-routed. It was deliberate, delicate even, but even now the resolute hum of the independent camera played in his mind and he knew it was safely transmitting moving pictures out of the stadium. He didn't know where. He didn't know why. The scene would be flashing across the internet even as he sat on the floor choking back the bile.

"It's not Miranda," Halo said, from behind the door.

Dan rubbed his arm across his eyes and scuttled forward, daring to lift his eyes back to the girl. The first thing he saw was the charred wig. He clutched it and threaded his fingers through it.

The room wasn't a stadium.

It was too small.

Halo slipped in around the half-open doors, keeping his back to the wall.

"It's not Miranda," Halo said.

Dan looked back at the girl. She was ruined. But he saw the slender neck now, closer than before, and the hint of blonde hair. It was Evie. He choked back another sob and shut his eyes feeling all his strength seep out of him.

"It's not the end of the world," Halo said softly. "Not yet, anyway."

"Fuck!" Dan said, spinning his head to stare at Halo. "Shut up."

He felt the spit and sparks of blue lightning fly through

the air and rubbed hard at his face again to regain something of himself. He tasted salt.

"He wants you to break," Halo said again, ignoring Dan's warning. "It's not Miranda."

But it was Evie and that was Dan's fault. He knew it was his fault, and he knew he'd never make up for it, not even if he got to leave this place and return to his rat hole of a life. Halo crouched down and put a hand on Dan's shoulder. Dan went to shake it off, but Halo held firm.

"I know it's hard, mate," he said, close to Dan's ear. "But you'll find out there's usually more Evies out there. You're missing the end game."

Dan felt himself shout but he couldn't hear it over the explosion of energy which burst from his body. The cracking sound of the blast echoed through the studio even as the lights exploded and the last camera was obliterated.

CHAPTER 31

THE MAD RUSSIAN

ABOVE HIM, THE storm crashed together in bursts of lightning. He floated a little above a stage in the center of the stadium, directly under an ornate glass dome which had replaced the normal roof. All around him, the humans watched in terror. They were too frightened to run, petrified at the sight of the Mad Russian. He had his hands to the side, his bearded face looking up to the night sky through the dome.

In times past he had appeared in crowded places like this with one thing on his mind: murder. Berlin in the 1990s, Vienna and Minneapolis before that. He had crushed the life out of them, leveled large tracts of their human world and etched his power in the minds of what few survivors remained.

"Behold your last night," he said in a voice which cracked a little. His powers amplified the words and the crack seemed to career into madness, echoing as it was directed through the complex. "No one can save you."

He was welcomed with screams and he bowed as if receiving applause.

Bodies were already littering the walkways, attempts at heroism met with casual cruelty. Security had retreated after the Russian had impaled more than a dozen of them with iron ripped from the walls. Their speared bodies served as boundaries for his final performance of the night, stabbed into the floor at each of the exits.

The celebrity girl stood in the middle of the stage, flanked by fairy lights leading to an elevator. He had commandeered the light and sound systems, leaving the previous operators dead or dying in their little control rooms.

He turned his attention to her, his eyes moving from the sky above to her slim figure. She was pathetic. Her hair was flat against her head, drenched from the rain outside. She wore a shimmering black t-shirt and jeans, an everyday girl. He wondered briefly how she had captured the hearts and minds of the people.

Posters of her were spread like giant sentinels throughout the complex. As people regained their ability to move and scamper to safety, Miranda Brody stood her ground. She looked up at him, defiant.

In the old country, he had known another girl with those daring eyes. As her town burned and her family and friends screamed themselves into hysteria, she had stood against him.

"Sima," he whispered and glided towards Miranda, lowering himself to float just above the stage. He spoke in Russian. "*Kak dyela*? It has been so long."

Sima had been his enemy and his love, switching from one to the other as easily as she changed bodies. Her dead eyes were the only constant. He reached his hands out and took hers, looking into the face which she now wore.

"This is for you," he said softly. "Our great work, coming here now."

The girl shook her head and struggled against him. He let her hands drop as it dawned on him that this was not Sima.

"You're a monster," Miranda said, stepping back, reaching behind her.

"Ah," he said, forcing the sadness away and replacing it with the moment. "You are the Miranda Brody. Do you see these men and children and women? They worship you like the television, like the god."

He shook his head.

"But you are not the god," he continued.

"And neither are you," she shot back at him and drew a gun, leveling it at his head.

She closed her eyes as she pulled the trigger and a blast of light exploded from its end. The Russian withdrew into the air, his eyes burning and his hands pressed against the skin.

The light of the flare gun pulled into him, slipped in through the sockets, absorbed into the raging sun that lived inside his body. He opened his eyes, blinked, and steadied his body as it hovered above her.

"Ah…" he said.

He looked down at her from his height, hovering over the ground, and he took a hold of her with his mind, pulling at the invisible threads which formed her body and her clothes. She lifted into the air, although she struggled, and soon her eyes were level with his. He compressed his hold on her and she stopped moving, her body rigid as he sent electricity through her.

"You should be happy," he said as she screamed. "These people, they worship the dead celebrity persons, more than they do the living."

There was a disturbance in the air, a familiar one which made the Mad Russian halt his torture of Miranda. He turned to look around the stadium seating. People huddled in groups, holding each other as they trembled, as if there was safety in numbers. His eyes fell upon them, but he was looking for a familiar form, his former star pupil.

He smiled as he saw the girl in the crowd. She was on the second level, directly opposite with a clear view of him.

"Come, come," he beckoned to the girl who secretly formed in their midst, most likely out of thin air. He had always loved her.

Bree wore a black hijab and cloak which covered her body to her toes. Under the cloak was a scarlet shirt and black pants. Her hair was hidden, but she looked very much like her mother.

"I've brought you something," she said loudly through the veil. "Although I don't think you'll like it."

"I am not liking very much of this city," the Russian said. "Perhaps your gift will change this."

"Probably not, Sir."

She bowed, and then the air around the stage began to coalesce, spinning itself into a sandstorm which then became more solid, taking the form of a large bearded man. It was the man who had battled Luke Ma and Grandfather Time. He wore white trousers and a white turban with a ruby in the center. His chest was bare and rippled with strength.

"Salam," he said and then thundered his two fists into

the ground, sending a shockwave towards the Mad Russian. The force passed by underneath his floating feet, but then Suleyman leapt forward himself and crashed headlong into the floating man. They fell to the ground and landed on the jagged mess of concrete and seating. Shards pressed up into the Russian's protective field, and together with Sully's bulk, it managed to disrupt his concentration.

Miranda fell to the ground and shuffled to the side, her hands rubbing her arms, trying to rid herself of the numbness she felt. She crouched against the runway and tried to control her breathing, tried to convince her body that she wasn't dying. On the ground in front of the stage, Sully slammed Galkin into the ground, wedging him between the broken security gates and the concrete slab of the floor. The big man lifted his fists slowly into the air and then slammed them repeatedly into the Russian's face, each pound like a jack hammer. Galkin's vision was shattered and blood flew into the air. He gasped for breath as his body was pummeled. Sand began to fly around the two men and then into the Russian's nose and mouth, choking him further.

He couldn't see Bree, but he knew she was there. Despite his body failing, his mind was still sharp, fuelled as it was by anger and sudden fury.

Overhead the thunderclouds roared. Rain pelted the roof, glass crashed in the distance. And the Russian's body surged as well, his very core rising up against the assault. His fingers gripped Suleyman's arms and electricity surged through them. Flashes of light erupted within the larger man's body, his skeleton illuminated in the fury, the blistering skin popping up and down his arms.

The Mad Russian grinned.

And then he threw Suleyman clear, blasting him through a concrete column in a torrent of lethal blasts. Even as his adversary disappeared in the collapsing rubble, the Mad Russian rose back to the stage, tendrils of energy sparking off his body. He turned to where Bree now stood, lines of sand and rock orbiting her in shifting arcs. She had moved closer, standing at his level, the shifting rock and concrete under her complete control.

"You disappoint," he said, spitting blood to the ground. His body had already healed itself. He spat again, forcing out the last vestiges of blood which lingered after the wounds covered over. "You all of you disappoint."

The sand and rock weaved through the air around Bree, transforming into four barbed lines, like scorpion tails, all primed to strike. She held herself well, as poised as ever, but the Russian had taught her that trick. They wavered in the air.

"You should have stayed dead," Bree said, and he felt his chest constrict with emotion, with betrayal. His hand was raised, ready to tear her apart, but he hesitated. She had been the loyal one, the one who listened to what he said and never disobeyed. The boys had been immature and selfish, and Lily was always too quiet and inhibited; but Bree had been intelligent and worthy.

"You hurt an old man," he said, his hand raised still.

"That's the idea," she said, and moved swiftly, ducking low and then rolling across the floor into a crouch, even as the scorpion stings flew towards him from four directions. He waved his hand and destroyed two before they even got close, but the other two hit his protective field, shattering against it. He steadied himself but the fields remained firm.

He moved his hand in a cutting motion and an arc of electricity ripped out towards Bree, but she was expecting it, and rolled to safety. He fired again, using both hands to channel twin arcs of lightning into the ground. The blast spread through the floor, forcing her to shift into her sand form and vanish from view. He pushed out with his senses and tracked the millions of specks that made up the girl, and as she formed herself again behind him, he was fully prepared.

Bree struck out with a rock-covered fist but the Russian merely held up his hand and reinforced the barrier between them. She punched again and he felt a tremor through the field, impressed at her strength. She had always been resourceful, eager to experiment with her powers.

"Don't look so smug," Bree said after smashing into the barrier again. Her black robes had transformed into stone as well. "You never were a very good teacher."

"This lesson does not please me, Sebriya," he said softly.

He closed his right fist and felt Bree's body tighten in his invisible hold. She tried to slip through into her sand form, but he held her steady.

"No, it does not please me."

Her eyes widened as she pushed against his invisible grip. The veins in her neck rose to the surface as rocklike indentations. He could feel the pressure building within her, but all the strength in the earth couldn't oppose the forces he now wielded.

He met her eyes, stepped closer to her so she could see the pain she had brought him. And then he flicked his fist open, exploding Bree's stone form into thousands of pieces. They ricocheted against his protective field and as her body scattered to the stage around him, Galkin found that he was laughing.

It was mad, uncontrollable laughter, and it echoed through the plaza.

He could not stop. He did not want to stop. He no longer cared, and if this would truly be his last night, then he intended to consume the world even as his own body consumed him.

CHAPTER 32

DAN

DAN FOLLOWED THE high pitched laughter. It had echoed through his entire life, drawing him into places he never wanted to go, heralding things that were never good. As he pushed the access door wide with a blast of lightning and stepped out into the artificial light of the main stadium Dan nearly choked. He saw a body hanging from a jagged metal spike, slumped and broken and bloody. He could see other examples of his grandfather's insanity, and the crippled, fearful people trembling in the wreckage.

The laughter ricocheted off the walls again as thunder rolled overhead.

Dan was still glowing a little. His bare skin pulsed with blue streaks of lightning and he felt like he was seeing the world twice: once with his normal sight and the second time with his enhanced sense of the hidden world around him. Down on the stage was the whitest concentration of energy he had ever witnessed, hotter and whiter even than his father just before his final explosion.

He began to walk down the causeway. To his right were three teenage girls, all of them huddled behind the seating which looked like it had been struck by lightning, the burn marks clearly evident. The girls hid their faces and shuddered but Dan recognized at least one of them from the hotel where he delivered pizza, the night he had met Miranda for the first time. He opened his mouth to speak to her, but then he saw the glow from his skin, and heard the crackle of energy when he walked.

She wouldn't find comfort in anything he could say.

She would see a monster.

She would scream and scream and scream.

He moved on, taking notice of where the people were hiding, how many there were, and whether they were injured or simply frightened into shock and despair. Even though he saw death and destruction, it looked like the Mad Russian had so far restrained himself.

Dan could see the old man now. He was floating above the main stage flanked in red velvet curtains. Tendrils of electricity flared out from his body, whipping around the air and back into him – like a human lightning storm. His neck was arched weirdly back, his face looking up to the broken dome above, his laughter mirrored in the flashes of lightning which could easily be seen from where he stood.

Dan couldn't see Miranda, though, but as he scanned with all the powers at his disposal, he noticed a shift in the debris near the stage. Pillars had snapped and twisted, glass and plastic were strewn across the ground; but the pile of heavy rubbish moved and fell away to reveal the battered form of Sully. Miranda's bodyguard was scratched and bleeding, his turban lost someplace which had allowed his waist-length black hair to tumble out.

Sully staggered out of his burial place and called out

to the Mad Russian. Dan moved quicker, closing the distance, feeling the powers concentrating around his grandfather, ready to strike. Sully stood defiantly in front, his fists clenched and to the sides as if daring the man to strike him down a second time. Or was it to be a third time? Dan had no idea how furious the battle had already been. He reached the stage and found his aura had begun to reach out toward that of his grandfather, lightning calling to lightning.

The Mad Russian swung both his arms around and pointed his hands, palms up, at Sully. The laughter followed and behind it was an incredible surge of electricity. It leapt outward but Dan reached his mind to intercept, his own command disrupting the charge, and sending it upward into the ceiling. Tiles and wiring rained down on Sully but he was standing.

The Russian spun to face Dan, insanity etched across his grin and reflected in the white glow of his eyes. He raised his hand at Dan and released a second wave of energy. Dan didn't move but caught the wave and brought it safely into his body, spreading it across his skin and then deeper into where he could concentrate and store it.

Sully leapt at the Russian's back and his huge arms wrapped around the protective field, squeezing hard, making it look like the old man was trapped inside an hourglass. He squeezed his grip further and the field began to crack, sparks fizzing into the air. Sully brought his legs up in powerful kicks sending out more sparks and spreading the fractures.

Dan pulled at the field with his own mind too, weakening it enough for Sully to break through. The large man's arms collapsed down hard, beating the Russian back to the ground where they fell together in a lump.

Sully maneuvered himself to strike down at the Russian, fists slamming into the prone man's back and head. It was a blur, but Dan could already feel his grandfather's malevolent energy rising again like some kind of demented phoenix.

Dan whipped out with a burst of energy and knocked Sully away from his grandfather just as the Mad Russian's body convulsed and released an explosion of heat and light and fire. Sully tumbled off the stage to safety while Dan ducked to the ground and deflected what didn't pass over his head.

There was a crashing sound as more of the glass from the dome overhead shattered and fell to the floor. Dan covered his eyes even though he knew that his body in its current glowing, overcharged state, was not going to be harmed by shards of glass. When he looked up again he saw that Sully had clambered back to the stage and lifted the Russian up over his head.

Dan leapt to the stage, propelled by the energy in his body. He landed like a cat, impressed with his own enhanced agility, and then began to pull at the Russian's power again. Sully slammed the man into the stage and wisps of energy shot through the air and entered Dan's body.

Sully shot him a smile.

Dan couldn't help but return it.

"Is this a good Friday night out with you, Daniel?" he asked.

"It beats watching the telly," Dan said.

Sully laughed and drew himself up to tower over Dan and the crumpled figure of the Mad Russian. There were sounds of people moving around in the darkness, of technicians and fans finding the courage to get a better look now that things appeared to be going the way of the good guys. Dan could feel it too.

"That it does," Sully said. Dan had lost track of the conversation and had to think about what the man was talking about. He smiled and then concentrated back on his grandfather. There was still so much energy there, a reservoir which reached out for him while at the same time repelling him like opposing magnetic fields.

The Russian sat up, his hands pressed down to the broken stage, his back hunched a little. But the protective field had returned, brighter than before. Sully reached out to get a grip but was sent backward with a shock. Dan tried to weave his mind through the field but he was stopped.

The old man stood.

He looked directly at Dan, the white eyes still burning in their sockets. Sully tried to hammer the field but the Russian simply waved his hand and the big man was pushed away.

There were no words.

Dan felt his core shift. The place where he stored his energy was being tugged out, strip-mined by his grandfather. It felt like he'd lost his breath and Dan nearly passed out as electricity shot out of his body: from his eyes and nose, his mouth, his chest, out of every pore of his body.

It was ripped hard, yanked with a raw violence Dan hadn't experienced in years. He staggered forward and came to rest against the field.

Their eyes were on the same level. Dan couldn't move.

The laughter returned but Dan couldn't see the man's

mouth moving at all. It echoed around him, through his ears which were throbbing with the escaping energy, but also somewhere deeper, like within his mind itself.

Sully staggered forward but the Russian swatted him away again, sending him straight up into the air, through the remains of the dome and into the stormy night beyond. Catapulted into the night. Flicked away like an annoying insect.

Dan's whole body was numb.

He had never seen his grandfather in such a state – burning with such power, such ultimate inexhaustible power. His whole life, Dan had been told that he and his generation would be the new gods; but it was clear now they would never match the power of the Mad Russian.

Lightning exploded across the sky above them and condensed into a column of churning energy which crashed down from the heavens. Its blinding light hit first, followed quickly by a thunderous pulse of heat which flew outward, knocking everyone backward with its force.

Dan and his grandfather were consumed by the column of light, but they remained standing, clutching at each other with their hands while their bodies wrestled with the whipping energies around them, absorbing them into their bodies. Dan felt his reserves of power bulge with the extreme energy, his connection with the world smashed to a new evolutionary level. He could touch it in ways he'd never imagined, but the new awareness was short lived. His grandfather leeched it from him, tearing it from his body as easily as before. But the light didn't fade. It continued to slam into the ground from above, tendrils of wilder energy flicking outward and striking at the seating and what remained of the stage. It charged them, fed them, whispered alien words into their ears.

Dan felt his mind stretched in all directions, his body burning with the currents of power. He blinked and the world shifted into impulses and radiation, strobing colors that made the everyday appear monstrous.

He was going crazy.

The power rushed into him and then out again, making him nauseous and weak, but he couldn't let go of his grandfather. The Mad Russian held him firm, using Dan's body as a conduit to take in as much of the alien, god-like power as he could.

Dan didn't know if his eyes were open or closed. Images shot across his mind: his childhood, his mother, the park he had lost a kite… and then he began to hear his grandfather's words and thoughts. It was as if they were merging.

Hatred morphed into anxiety and then leapt to ramblings of other worlds, secret places, sanctuaries. He saw the old days, the epic battles over Europe, the cloak and dagger world of spies and mad men. He saw the birth of a child which spiraled out to multiple births, multiple children.

Dan tried to hold on to his own mind.

He thought of Miranda.

Their kiss.

And it anchored him.

His mind held to the last image from his grandfather: another world, untouched. A world with children, important children. Dan didn't recognize the places or the children's faces, but he knew that it was where his grandfather had been for the last five years.

A woman stood on a cliff with her long red hair

whipping behind her in the wind. She was replaced by a golden door, twinkling with gemstones.

The door opened.

And the landscape shifted and he was looking directly into the pits of his grandfather's burning eyes.

"I bring you back to me," he called. And Dan felt himself slipping. His own arms seemed to be melting into his grandfather's, their chests reached out for each other as if the Mad Russian was trying to consume him. "I bring you back to me!"

The power balance was impossible to shift. Dan knew he couldn't beat his grandfather through force, so he scrambled for alternatives, reaching back with his mind for the fragments of his grandfather's memories. They returned immediately and Dan felt himself link with them, able to pull up the ones he knew and amplify them, focus on the details or shift their focus.

His physical body was being absorbed, but his mind was still mostly his own.

The image of childbirth came to him. He shifted it to the side and brought up a sunny day with a younger Galkin and a beautiful woman. He shifted that memory as well and waded through more from the days of the Cold War, of garish costumes and grand battles. A flash of Castus made Dan flinch, but he shifted the memory of the Celestial Knight away too.

He recognized his father, laughing as a child and then growing rapidly darker as he transformed into an adolescent, his skin black and smoking. His mother was there too, and family members who spiraled back through time.

His grandfather walked down a hillside graveyard, a

single blue rose in his hand. Behind him the sky was rolling with dark clouds, lightning flashing just out of sight. Dan pushed past the scene, digging through the oldest memories with fairytale monsters, chicken-legged houses, hairless ogres.

Memories flittered around his mind, and in between the shuffling he saw what lay beyond. It was only a glimpse, at first, and then it was gone; but Dan persisted. He shoved memories aside until he exposed the sensitive networks beyond. Memory, fine motor controls, the delicate areas of the brain which were all fuelled by electricity. Millions of impulses flew within the brain's network: firing neurons, tempering synapses, maintaining control of the body.

Dan saw it unfold before him like a road map.

He could feel his powers draining. His body was numb and he could smell the distant burning of his own hair and flesh.

He concentrated on the thin lines of electrical light. He overtook them and wrapped his mind around them, pulling them to a standstill. Then he moved to another laneway and broke it, snapped it with a thought. The lights shot around the tracks like fireflies and he chased them.

Another light stopped.

Then another.

The grandfather struggled as more of his mind was isolated and shut down. Dan felt it in his own body too and with his eyes which were sore but forced wide by the transfer of power. The balls of fire in his grandfather's dark eyes were gone. Dan saw the deadness in there, the dull grey. He felt the man's breath against his face but it was the eyes that held him, the clutching mortality that stared back at him. Somewhere beyond those eyes was a broken mind.

And then everything stopped and fell away.

The present had vanished and Dan was on someplace else, a moment between time.

He was twelve again.

His grandfather was leaning on a stick, a little out of breath, but smiling like he was enjoying the greatest moment of his life. Dan had been learning to dance, like the ones from his grandfather's homeland. He had called it the *kazatsky*, and Dan had been trying to learn the squatting dance but his legs couldn't keep time with the music.

"You are good boy," the grandfather said. "Make me proud."

"I couldn't get the steps right," Dan apologized.

The old man coughed a little and looked weaker than he had in a long time.

"No, you did well. My legs, they move quicker than yours only because they know the patterns. You will learn and you will get faster."

Dan wanted to reach out and reassure the man, but he didn't want to get him angry. Signs of compassion were for weaker people, not for Galkins.

"Are you going to die?" Dan asked.

He didn't mean to ask it. It was just a dance.

"Perhaps," he said. "But we all must die, at one time. Even the gods themselves must one day make way for the newer ones."

The grandfather chuckled.

"If we did not die, this place would be very full of old men like me."

"That's not a bad thing, is it?" Dan asked.

"I think, perhaps, it is a bad thing, Danya."

Dan reached out and held his grandfather's hands. He gripped them tightly and was surprised to see a small smile cross the old man's creased face. His grandfather squeezed his hands back and then pulled him down into a hug.

It was not a real memory.

It never happened.

Dan gulped for air. And felt a flash of heat.

CHAPTER 33

MIRANDA

I T WAS LIKE a dance the way Dan and his grandfather spun slowly within the too-bright pillar of light. Miranda could see their silhouettes but she couldn't tell who was who. They shifted, blurred. She crouched low and shielded her eyes. The deafening roar of the energy was accompanied by whipping tendrils of electricity which reached out and struck the elevator behind her. Her cheeks were wet with tears but she couldn't leave Dan to die alone.

And she knew that it was bad, really bad. Dan was never going to be a match for the maniac who had terrorized the world for decades. He was just a boy.

The thought made her sob. It wasn't true. No matter how he acted, no matter how often he tried to hide from the world, Miranda knew he was more than that. He wasn't just a boy.

And she wasn't really just a girl either.

She stood and looked around for something to help break the storm, for anything to disrupt the wild electricity and heat whipping around the plaza. The ray-gun was charred and broken, but there were more in the box. She cupped her forearm over her eyes to keep them open, and stumbled through the debris as she searched for the box.

Behind her a few survivors moved towards the exit doors, helping each other, calling out to those who were still hidden. She couldn't see Kyla or the other dancers and hoped they were safe back behind the stage.

Suddenly another explosion blew outward from above, ballooning over them, fragments falling to the ground. Miranda dropped to a crouch again and looked up, her eyes burned by the intensity, but not before she witnessed the fall of fire.

It was so close to her, the churning orange and red flames, rolling in on itself, reaching out with hungry fingers. A boy falling backward, downward. The heat flushed her face, dried her tears. The boy's arms were at his sides, falling gracefully, peacefully. He was so close, the flames reaching out to her like her name on his dying lips. She didn't know what she was seeing or remembering.

When her eyes cleared enough she looked to the broken stage. She could see the bottom of Dan's shoe closest to her and beyond that the two bodies lay crumpled together, entwined and on fire. Dan's head rested on his grandfather's chest. They looked like they were asleep. Miranda pulled herself up over the broken wood, scraping her knee but ignoring it. She tore at the red velvet lining the front of the elevator and pulled it free, ripping a long strip to beat back the flames.

Standing above, she looked down at Dan and saw the boy form Jakarta again. She crashed to his side, pulled him off his grandfather and thumped the curtain on his back, hammering it down with her hands and then her whole body, to extinguish the flames.

She kept hitting him, chasing away the flames.

And then she felt his arm move around her and pull her close. She collapsed into him, their faces together, cheek to cheek. His skin was so hot, her tears ran uncontrollably. She kissed his ear.

"Oh god…" she whispered, still lying on top of him.

The storm had broken. Only light rain fell down from the broken roof to land around them. The people in the seating kept their distance, although a large crowd of them had gathered by a far exit, banging loudly against the barricaded doors. Closer to her, dark scorch marks radiated from Dan and the Mad Russian. She ran her fingers over the charcoaled surface, smooth but crumbling. The black starburst reflected the reckless power they had unleashed.

Dan shifted under her weight and Miranda pulled back a little, bringing him up with her so he was sitting. She kissed him, her hands hesitating over his arms which had horrible burns running up and down them.

"Does it hurt?" she asked. His fingers were a mess of blisters.

He shook his head. She reached out and touched his hair which was singed and missing in places. The smell of burning was everywhere. She held him to her again, his face pressed against her t-shirt. She looked around again.

There was no one to help.

Her eyes fell on the Russian and fear gripped her again, like coming face to face with a nightmare. But he wasn't moving. His mouth lolled open but his eyes were closed, his face scarred with a bright burn. The red mark crossed his face like an elemental slap. He might have been dead, she thought.

Minutes passed with her cradling Dan on the scorched stage. She couldn't leave him but she couldn't carry him either. Eventually the exits were forced open and the police moved cautiously inside. They moved in like a line of beetles, full riot gear and drawn black pistols. The survivors fled to the safety of the car park and the audible shouts of relief from outside, but Miranda stayed with Dan.

The police reached her first but they didn't ask questions. She watched them surround the Mad Russian and hastily set up some kind of electronic collar and manacles combination. She closed her eyes and rested her head on Dan's hair, breathing him in, closing out the rest of the scene.

Her own people swept in soon after. She heard her name first, but then felt their touch. A paramedic lifted her away from Dan. Todd Christie was there with his slicked back hair and his beady eyes. He wore a police-issue vest and looked down at her with open-faced elation. Bodyguards, the tour manager, other faceless essentials flanked him.

"You look a million dollars," Christie said.

"I'm fine," she said softly to the ambulance woman, ignoring her tour manager, but letting them move her off the stage. Two ambulances had been brought in somehow, their back doors thrown open.

"We'll see," the woman said with a nice smile. They examined her, noting the scratches and bruises. As they bandaged her leg Christie moved in again.

"We've got media out there Miranda, darling. Let the girls have a look at you."

Two stylists moved forward, reaching for her hair, stepping over the paramedics. Christie stood back and watched her. The paramedics moved on to other survivors.

Miranda nodded to everyone, letting them do what they had to. She watched as the medics treated Dan. He was awake and looked silently across to her as they bandaged his head and arms, gently wrapping gauze over his blistered body. She wanted to be with him, to hold him again even if it meant they had to face the evils of the world every single day. But she knew it couldn't happen that easily. Her people fussed around her, teasing at her hair, applying product, shaping her back into the Miranda Brody the world had grown to love.

Time wouldn't stop. Not even for her.

"Honey, you're crying," a stylist said, chewing sympathetically on minty gum. Miranda sniffed and wiped her nose, nodding her head and smiling to put the girl at ease.

"Been a big night," she said, sniffing again.

A trolley was assembled beside Dan and the paramedics prepped him to leave. Miranda covered her mouth with her hand, her throat tightening against what she knew would have to happen next. He held out his arm to her, tubing restricting his movements. She stepped away from the stylist and ran to him, pleading with herself not to cry. At his side she looked down and brushed a strand of his hair from his forehead. Dan smiled self-consciously up at her.

"Hey," she said, taking his hand. She gave the men holding the trolley a quick look and they waited. "You rest, okay?"

"Don't go," he said, so softly that she felt like he was still slipping away from her. He let his hand fall from hers.

"I'll be here," she promised, knowing it was a lie. She bent down and kissed his forehead once and then a second time, tears unleashed and a tremble in her voice. "I love you."

When she pulled up his eyes were closed. The trolley was pushed away and Miranda stood watching it.

Outside the stadium, rows of lights were erected behind even more reporters and cameramen. Beyond them were crowds of people but she couldn't see their faces or decide whether they were here for her or for the tragedy which had taken place. She saw flashes from cameras and glimpses of posters and costume, and she knew there were people out there who cared about her. Todd Christie swore under his breath and gave her a firm push. She stepped into the light and the media shuffled in their seats.

"Miss Brody!" called a woman from the front, a signal to the others that questions would be taken. Hands shot up everywhere. More flashes exploded. Miranda managed a slight smile and sat down on a canvas director's chair which had been set up along with a table and promotional posters. As she sat down, her newly cleaned and styled hair swept across her vision. She ran her hands back through it and focused on the crowd. The woman who had called her name first was still mouthing words.

"Yes?" Miranda asked, pointing at the reporter, trying to catch the woman's question. The other voices fell to the side.

"What happened in there, Miranda?"

"That's a hard question to answer," Miranda said leaning forward, reading the woman's name on her press pass. "I think the police will know more than me. It'll be pieced together eventually."

"But you were there," the reporter pushed.

"I was stuck under a broken prop for most of it, actually," Miranda said. "This wasn't part of the show."

There was a burst of more questions but Miranda held up her hand and they died away again.

"This isn't entertainment," she said softly. "It's not part of the Tour, but tonight a lot of people died. My fans, my little freaks… and the brave people who tried to help when it seemed the whole world was falling apart."

She looked directly into the banks of cameras.

"I want to thank everyone for what they did in there. I want to thank my crew, the security team especially, and the moms and dads with their terrified little kids. I want you all to know that I thank you. That I know how much this has cost each and every one of you, but that I love you."

"How many people got killed in there?" called someone from the back. Miranda winced at the way it was thrown at her.

"Too many."

"Is it true that you were kidnapped, Miranda?"

"No," Miranda said simply.

"You've been reported missing," the reporter continued. She looked at her iPad and then back to Miranda. "Your management suggested you might be under threat."

Miranda looked across at Christie and wondered what he had been doing while she had been running for her life. He had his phone to his ear, nodding enthusiastically.

A woman by his side was taking notes on her blackberry. Miranda Brody's entourage had reassembled in spectacular fashion: elegant, sophisticated and unencumbered by conscience or trauma.

"Pretty sure she was under threat," another reporter called out and many of them laughed.

Miranda turned back to the reporters. They were so far removed, so caught up in a whole other world.

"I think what happened tonight wasn't about me," she said softly.

"Will you be cancelling the Human Tour?"

"This was the final concert. I'm back in the States tomorrow. I'll keep you in my heart, I promise, but – yes, the Tour is finished."

There was a murmur of voices and somewhere beyond the crowd of journalists someone cried out. Miranda held up her hands.

"Is this the end of Miranda Brody?" a reporter called out from the back.

Miranda shrugged.

"I'm still here," she said. "And that's thanks to a boy in there."

She looked directly at the cameras again, composed herself with the breathing exercises she had learned. She would be gone by the morning, but Dan would remain.

"There's a boy," she said. "His name is Dan Galkin, and he saved my life."

Once she was in the air, Miranda allowed herself to sink

back, to let out the breath she'd been holding as her people organized a hasty exit from Australia. Thurston Klein had already taken the reins back from Christie and lined up a string of television appearances across several key chat shows in the States. He was destined for disappointment, though. Miranda had already made her decision to quit. The only place she was going was Riverside, back to her family, back to the life she should have held on to. The hum of the plane's engines calmed her. The dimmed cabin was a relief after the hordes of cameras she'd walked through to get there.

She looked out the small window and saw the Melbourne lights twinkling below her. Her phone vibrated and she picked it up, biting her lip as she realized it was Sully. He had wandered back into the car park after her media conference. She'd never seen him so banged-up but he was alive and she threw herself into his arms and let him take her away. But that was hours ago, she knew. Her thumb pressed the connection.

"Sully?" she asked.

"The very same," his voice came through, throaty and healthy. "Daniel is recovering well. I have had him released into our care and away from the other people."

Miranda knew Alsana Owens had already started to move in to take advantage. It gave her some pleasure to know the woman would have to get through Sully before she'd be able to get a piece of Dan.

"Is he..?" She didn't know how to ask.

"He is sleeping," Sully said.

"But did you tell him about me? Please say you didn't tell him, Sully."

"I did not, as requested," he said.

"Thank you."

"Your wishes are my commands, Miranda. As always. I shall see to our friend and then return to California. I presume you will return to your father's house?"

Riverside. Even thinking about the city made her tear up. She could smell the horses, the oil on her father's work clothes, the Californian breeze, the comfort of family.

She nodded.

"Yes, thank you."

"You have thanked me already. But until that time we meet at your father's house, I shall bid you a restful night, child."

And she tried to rest. She closed her eyes, she breathed deeply. But she couldn't shake the final images of Dan, scarred and helpless. He was so young, so different to anyone she'd known before. He'd have to grow up now, but on his own terms. She would only complicate things.

Her world was a mess, and it would only get worse now that she had decided to step down from the limelight, no matter what it cost her. She would wait for the furor to die down and then she would start again.

She'd pick up the guitar. She'd find the words, her own words.

And Dan would be struggling too, faced with choices. He would wake up in a new world where he had a chance at everything.

Except her.

EPILOGUE
DAN

Five weeks later

DAN LOOKED AT the girl across from him. She had wandered into the office on the corner of William and Collins Street just after they'd opened. She didn't have an appointment. No one had an appointment.

"You want to volunteer for the up-cycled program?" Dan asked, incredulous. He had been given the job of looking after the small portfolio of uberhumans after Alsana Owens had been reassigned to a Canberra office. At first, he resisted, but somehow he found himself behind the desk and wearing a white shirt and tie. The only reminder of Alsana Owens was her desk fan. The government people had thrown it out but Dan rescued it as it was being carted away. He didn't miss her regular insults, degrading assessments or out and out rudeness, but Dan didn't want to wash her completely away. He felt out of his depth already, so having a reminder of what he'd replaced felt a little reassuring. He figured he couldn't possibly be as bad as Alsana Owens. "You know it's not really a thing you volunteer for, right?"

"Yeah," the girl said. Her dark brown eyes were holding back tears, he could tell, and she clutched a backpack in her lap. She was a runaway. "I need help with this stuff. I can't do it by myself anymore."

"Stuff?"

"I'm like you. I saw you on the TV and I did some research back home. You're the only one who can…"

Dan held up his hand.

"Don't say it," he said. "This is for kids who've broken the law… uh, what's your name?"

"Jess. I'm really serous about this."

"Right," Dan said, shrugging. "We don't really do good kids. We don't really do serious kids either."

"Do you want me to break something, then?" Jess asked and picked up the desk fan. Dan reached for it, standing up and reaching out, but Jess pulled it back towards her.

"What? No. It's just that, I don't think we can help you," he said, reaching again.

"Why?" Her eyes were so wide. Tears pushed their way out and Dan sat back down in his chair, the surrender spinning it slightly as he settled. Jess held the fan to her chest.

"We just deal with the bad kids," Dan said.

"I don't think you're bad, Mister Galkin. What you did with Miranda and your grandfather, well, that was kind of … awesome."

Dan looked to the door. It was closed, but he could see the silhouettes of Sal and Wicks in the front office through the frosted glass. They were having an animated discussion. He could hear the slamming of cabinets. They worked for him, in an indirect way. He looked back at Jess.

"Don't call me Mister Galkin, okay?" he said, drumming his fingers on the desk. "I'm Dan."

Jess stretched out her hand, her pack slipping to the floor as she reached right across the wide desk. She still held the fan.

"I'm Jess. I can break things with my mind."

"Welcome to the program," Dan said. "Can I get the fan back now?"

After lunch Dan met with the police liaison who had another two candidates for the program. Detective Schwarz had managed to get himself assigned to the job as a consultant, but it was the dark haired Jo Ryan who was the official liaison. Dan brought his staff with him: Wicks and Sally. He still found it difficult to belief he had made management level, with staff of his own. The guys at Birdie's would have been impressed, if they remembered him at all.

"That'll be three, then," Ryan said. She had the files opened on a tablet and Dan had his own in front of him.

"Four, actually," he said, eyes to the screen. "Just had a volunteer this morning." He looked up at the police woman and smiled. "She can do weird stuff with her mind."

"I don't think you're allowed to actually recruit them yourself, Dan," Ryan said slowly.

"See, that's probably where Alsana got it wrong," Dan said. "We're dealing with kids here. It's not just the files and the court orders. They're kids, like with problems and stuff."

"Says the seventeen year old," Wicks added, raising his eyebrows.

"Like I said, they're kids and we can help them. Now. Not when it's too late. We don't have to wait till they step over the line," Dan said. "Let's do some of that pre-emptive stuff."

"They do it in Sydney," Sally said, sharing a glance with Dan. "They've been doing it there for years."

"I can't authorize it," Ryan said, but there was hesitancy in her voice. "It makes sense, it does. I just have to…"

"It's taken care of," Dan said. "Executive decision."

"Power's gone to his head already," Wicks said.

"Your guys tapped me on the shoulder to do this," Dan said to her. "And I will. None of them has to do what I did, not if I can help it."

He had floated in the air, a god. Five years before.

While his friends slipped away through the cracks of a broken city square, Dan had lifted into the skies and defied the power of the Celestial Knights. He had resisted them, punished them.

But the power faded.

And he was twelve years old and alone.

Stumbling to the ground, surrounded by blackened concrete and smoldering roads. He fell to his knees, bare hands against the heated surface.

And he was lost.

He couldn't hear the electronic world, couldn't feel the hum around him, nor the bathing light of the city's power.

His father was dead. Reduced to atoms.

His grandfather was gone too. Broken promises cutting him like glass.

It was just Dan.

And the police.

And the sirens.

"I'm calling it," Dan said, standing up from the meeting table. "Meeting's over."

Dan picked up the tablet and slid it into his satchel. Wicks stood by the door and opened it when Dan reached for the handle. The man gave him a grin and they quickly shook hands before Dan left via the stairs, jogging down the final steps and out into Collins Street. He paused as the people moved around him on their way to other places, oblivious to him or who he was in the past. Dan slipped on his shades against the early afternoon sun and breathed in the city.

It'd been five weeks since he defeated his grandfather. Five weeks since Miranda had flown away. Looking up and down the street, he noticed the cranes at work. Melbourne hadn't fully recovered yet, and he figured he still had time to feel a little broken too.

And yet, the sun was bright and warm against his skin.

Dan smiled and jacked in his earphones.

The world hadn't ended.

Alsana was gone. He had her office to prove it.

He was free to do what he wanted. Mostly.

As he walked back to his new apartment, a silly Miranda Brody tune started up in his head. Her voice carried him back to the beach even as his legs carried him towards Spencer Street where he shared a place with Tabitha from Birdie's. It had made some sense. He didn't have anywhere to live anymore and her place had been reduced to fire, concrete and slag.

Tabitha was on holiday in Europe though, relaxing her way through the insurance money she'd scored from Marco. She promised to return but Dan wasn't in any hurry to share the new space.

He reached his door and fumbled with his keys. Leaning to pick them up he banged his head against the door and dropped his phone, the plugs coming loose as it hit the hard floor and cracked the screen. Music crooned out of the broken phone, and he knelt to pick it up.

"Are you listening to my music now?"

He looked up and saw a girl in jeans and a Union Jack t-shirt. She'd been waiting for him. Miranda Brody stood with her arms crossed, a smile on her face. Dan picked up the phone and pressed the music off. He stood up slowly.

"This is awkward," Miranda said, and she looked back to the elevator. "Maybe I should have called first."

"I tried to come after you," he said.

She looked back at him quickly, her teeth shining. She'd scored a tan back in California, her olive skin even darker.

"I did, I really did, but they wouldn't let me. Said I was a dangerous weapon."

"Flattery," she said and leaned forward, a hand on his hip while the other touched his jawline. She kissed him and he kissed her back, the taste of cherries bursting from her lips. He held her close, kissing her again, and she pushed him against the door. Miranda pulled back a little, her hands still on his hips.

"I can't get a passport," Dan said, eyes closed. She kissed them and he pulled her into a hug, standing there with the sound of trains rushing below.

"I'm here," Miranda said, finally. "I had to do some things back home, but I'm here now."

She pulled away again, and looked at him. She touched his short hair with the back of her hand and then pulled at his tie. Dan felt his skin flush and tugged the tie loose, unbuttoning the top of his shirt.

"It's the new you," she said.

"It's just a shirt."

"Can I come in?"

Dan retrieved the key and stumbled inside. Miranda followed but he couldn't tell if she was impressed with the interior. It was a two bedroom apartment without any remarkable views of the city. The train lines were close – you could feel their passing – but you could also see the sky and Dan knew the place was his.

"Have you seen him?" Miranda asked, looking at the lounge, slowly walking around with her fingers touching everything. Dan pulled out some water from the fridge.

"Who?"

"Your grandfather."

Dan clinked glasses together from the cupboard and poured the water. He felt a little overwhelmed by the conversation already, and his hands shook as they poured. He'd been shown photos of the old man: grey and absent from his own body. He was hooked up to a machine that kept him alive but only just.

"They've got him someplace. They won't let me see him." Dan tapped his temple and smiled. "Dangerous weapon in here, y'know?"

Miranda took one of the glasses.

"They cancelled my contract," she said.

"Oh crap." Dan tossed his tie away.

"No, it's good. I've been writing. My own stuff, like you told me."

Dan didn't remember telling her that, but he felt good that she was there – with him. She moved to the other rooms, looking inside and making little sounds of approval. Dan sat at the kitchen bench, watching her.

"Are you here for good?" he asked, and she stopped at his bedroom door. "I mean, you're not going to leave again, right?"

She smiled at him.

"Is this your room?"

Dan woke at 3am. Even with his eyes closed, he could sense it from the oven-clock in the kitchen, from the phones tossed to the floor. The whole electronic world was calling softly to him that morning was still a far away place.

His eyes opened suddenly: wide and happy. There was a sense of having just lost a moment of time, a second perhaps; like they'd just paused in their conversation, just taking a breath between acts.

He could feel her beside him. Miranda. In his bed.

Dan looked up at the ceiling and saw the motionless fan. He felt the smile on his face, the almost audible hum that charged through his body, eclipsing anything he might have generated himself.

And the hum was happiness.

He could feel her skin now, his fingers exploring without upsetting the covers. Warm skin, and close and charged. Biting his lower lip, Dan turned his head so he could see her beside him. She was a tumble of dark hair and smooth olive skin. He wanted to kiss her again, to hold her. He ran his fingers down her shoulder and along her arm. She moved a little and he sat up slowly, moving the pillows behind his back so he could look at her bare shoulders.

"'s cold," she mumbled.

Miranda slid her hand back towards him and took a hold of his fingers. He moved closer, kissing down on that beautiful shoulder, lingering there. She pulled his hand across her skin into an embrace and he slid next to her, his lips touching her ear. They fit so well together.

"Miranda Brody," he whispered and she screwed up her nose. "Miranda Brody," he teased again. "*The* Miranda Brody. Oh my God…"

"Shut up," she said softly.

Dan pressed himself against her and kissed her neck, his hand moving down her body. She pushed back against him, reaching back to grab his hair. She turned her head and brought his mouth to hers.

He smiled into it.

She still tasted like cherries.

EPILOGUE
HALO

Rainmaker Four Holding Facility, South Australia

IT HAD TAKEN only a few weeks to locate, and another week to gain entry to the government holding facility where the authorities had dumped the Mad Russian. It was called Rainmaker Four, an unmarked secure facility to the west of Cooper Pedy, buried away in the dry and forlorn wasteland of the South Australian outback.

Halo already had the contacts within the Uberhuman Affairs Offices in Melbourne and Sydney, so it didn't take long for him to uncover Rainmaker Four. He drove three days to get to Cooper Pedy and then spent the night at a hotel, drinking with the locals as he slowly wove his magic among them.

It only took a single look from Halo, a connection of eyes no matter how fleeting or guarded, and he could step right into another man's mind. He pushed through recent memories, carved up insecurities and passions, until he caught a psychic whisper of the Rainmaker facility. The man was a cleaner. A further push into the man's mind and Halo uncovered the names of other cleaners, the supervisor, the passcodes and the schedules. He bought the man a drink.

Later that night he dumped the man's body in the back of his hire car. Time was running out. Halo had to find the old man before the Celestial Knights returned and took him out of reach forever.

Inside the facility, Halo stuck to the cleaning routine. He pushed the mop along the floors, cleaned the washrooms and helped take out the garbage. The other workers called him Lockheardt and forgot the differences they saw in front of their eyes. They'd worked together for months. Lockheardt wasn't an overweight forty-six year old joker from Perth. He was a skinny Pak kid. Always had been.

After a couple of days Halo located the room where the old man was being held. He used his coercive powers to shift Lockheardt's name onto the duty roster, convinced security that it had always been that way. The room itself wasn't anything special. There was a simple security check on the door, but Lockheardt's pass was configured to get through, as long as he was scheduled for the shift.

The Mad Russian looked like a regular old man. His skin was pale, stretched tight over bones, and his hair and beard had been shaved back to a short fuzz. The eyes were taped shut with skin-tone adhesive and a pair of tubes disappeared up the man's nostrils. Along his wrists were more tubes, jacked into different points and leading back to monitoring devices.

There was a dull hum in the room.

The monitors all seemed passive. Heart rates and brain activity moved steadily across the screens, although they were very close to the baseline. Halo figured that meant the old man was alive, but only barely.

Halo closed the door behind him and moved to the end of the hospital bed, his eyes scanning the electronic tablet attached to the steel frame. It was password encrypted. He was tempted to go back and hunt down a medical staffer, to rip the password out of their skulls, but in the end it really didn't matter what the medical reports said. Halo was interested in the old man himself, the body and the mind.

He reached out and touched the man's eyes, pressing down on the tape which held them closed. There was a satisfying lack of resistance there as he pressed. The old man had no strength in him. Halo pulled the edge of the tape and lifted it away. He would only need a single eye, a single entry point.

The eye was completely white. It surprised him and he let the lid drop for a moment before pulling it down a second time. Halo reminded himself that the Mad Russian was now just a husk. Nothing to fear.

It took a bit of manipulation to get the iris into place but as soon as he did, Halo found himself pushing inside the man's mostly-vacant mind. There was an immediate sense of stepping into an abandoned building, but one so vast that it must have once held a museum or expansive gallery. Halo had never dared look into the old man's mind before. The consequences would have been brutal and irreversible.

But the old man was helpless now.

Halo started with sequences of numbers, of hidden

accounts and passcodes. He always started with the numbers. Emotions were more difficult to handle, especially in cases where the subject was a raging psychopath like the Russian. It came easily, the flow of numbers and the links to banks and institutions. Halo had long ago trained himself to compartmentalize his own mind, to shift new data into 'boxes' which he could unpack at a later, safer, time.

There was a clicking sound from the door. He had expected it, knowing he only had a short window of opportunity with the old man, but it still irritated him. He pulled out of the Russian's mind, replaced the tape and stepped back, his hands already moving to the mop and bucket. When the door opened he was pushing the mop along the wall opposite, his headphones plugged in and a look of general disengagement firmly on his face.

The nurse moved to the end of the bed and checked the tablet. He looked at his watch and moved past Halo to a small locked cupboard. Halo smiled at the man and then pushed his mop and bucket out into the corridor.

Outside he moved up the corridor to the next room which was empty but still required cleaning. As the door closed behind him he returned to the old man's memories, the after taste of the invasion laying in his own head. There was something wrong, something lodged inside.

He shook his head. A rogue memory had been brought out along with the financial data and it was dominating his own thoughts. He couldn't shake it, it was so brilliant.

It was all blue skies and bright sun.

A recent memory, it had the distinct feeling of being a turning point in the Mad Russian's life. Halo stumbled over these events all the time, but he usually shook them off after regaining his own mind. Each person was built upon the foundations of key memories, the clarity and hyper-realism of them sometimes surprised him.

Blue skies.

But not the skies of this world.

There was something missing: an invisible hole, bound up with the Russian's overwhelming sense of failure, his drive to return.

He pushed back the headphones and concentrated on the memory, clearing away his own identity and extraneous thoughts, leaving nothing but the snapshot of skies. It was a real memory. The Mad Russian wasn't as mad as everyone believed, at least not all the time. It had the energy and pseudo-corporeal feel of a foundation, and as he reconstructed the images around other memories and experiences he had pillaged Halo soon discovered it was from the old man's missing years.

The pieces fell into place, lining up in a way that Halo knew could make him a lot of money. Everyone wanted to know where the Mad Russian had disappeared to, and, more importantly, why he had returned.

Now Halo had the answer.

For the whole five years the man had been desperately fighting to return, his rage a firestorm within mind and body. But beyond the rage and the mad intellect, the Mad Russian was powerless. In the other world he had no mastery over the elements; it had stripped him back to a pathetic, rambling old man.

It was like their world, but different.

"The bastard," Halo murmured. "A world without ubers."

The second time Halo visited the Mad Russian was also the last time. The night before he had broken dreams of his childhood: of giant, crashing waves and monsters hurling boulders. The invasion of his homeland was the stuff of legend, the one time when the full potential of uberhuman armies became a reality. India marched into Pakistan and Sri Lanka, their demi-gods laying waste to any defenses and proclaiming a new India in their wake.

The world did nothing.

He felt his mother's dying thoughts again.

Love you, love you.

And he woke slowly, half-child, half-adult. The room he rented in the dusty township was small and damp but in the darkness of early morning he could smell the explosions, the plaster dust and the terror. He closed his eyes and imagined the shifting forms of Rakshasa and the twins, Saraswati and Fusion. He heard the roar of Bagha and his father yelling at him to get into the car.

He lay in his bed for an hour, replaying his own memories, pushing his consciousness back to the last days he had with his mother back in Bahawalpur. He remembered walking with her through the markets, grudgingly carrying her basket. He remembered the swish of her dress, but he couldn't remember her face.

Back at the facility, Halo checked in to the staff room and talked briefly with his co-workers, but in his mind he was counting down the minutes until he would walk out and never return. He checked the time, but he was early. The passcodes wouldn't allow him access until he was officially on duty. The others noticed his nervousness. They laughed at him. He laughed as well.

When the time did arrive he faked a stretch and moved with the others into the elevator. He balled his fingers into fists inside the pockets of his overalls.

When the doors opened, Halo let the others leave first, satisfied with the way they moved into formation, slipping out of conversations and into work-mode. He missed Melbourne. Beyond the elevator Halo saw the strangers and paused. Their presence complicated matters and he couldn't hide the sudden flush of anger which spread across his face. The other workers gave the Celestial Knights semi-interested glances as they approached, but kept moving. It wasn't that unusual to see the heroes at the Rainmaker; the organizations were connected, feeding each other information, providing resources and back-up when required.

Parhelion stood with three doctors and listened to a report. The current leader of the Knights wore a white lab coat over his light blue power suit, but his face was unmasked and he seemed like any other visiting official. He was a medical doctor himself, among other things, and Botswana's most famous uberhuman. The other man was Castus, a more brutal and abrupt man. Where Parhelion conversed with the facility's staff, Castus stood apart. Heat pushed outward from his massive body and butted against the underground facility's air conditioning.

Halo kept his eyes down as he passed, although he couldn't mask the smirk that slid across his face. The anger had dropped away. Castus bore paper-thin white scars across his face. They made him look inhuman and fierce. That was us, Halo thought. Dan had blasted the hero with the power of Melbourne all those years ago, and it still left its mark. That meant something.

"We will move him to Sanctuary One," Parhelion said. "No need to endanger the people here."

Halo knew they were talking about the Mad Russian and he walked away a little quicker, his headphones clasped over his ears although no music was playing. He tapped his card against the access panel and pushed into the room. The old man looked even smaller than he had the day before.

"This is our goodbye, teacher," Halo said, coming to sit next to the man. He reached out and pulled off the tape covering the left eye. "This might hurt."

Normally Halo took his time with the deep mining of memories. He enjoyed the feeling of stepping through people's most secret and hidden thoughts. However, as he slid back into the man's mind he felt a rush of hatred. It rose up in him, overwhelmed him suddenly. For years, the Russian had promised Halo so much and then on the ultimate day of fulfilling those promises, he had vanished. He had abandoned everyone.

Halo stabbed at the man's mind.

He scraped the memories raw, rip-harvesting them as he pushed through the lingering decrepit, crumbling walls of defense. He smashed the memories of Dan, of happiness and the quiet, introspective moments. There would be no peace in the old man's mind.

Taking a breath, he paused from the destruction and turned his attention to the memories of the other world.

No uberhumans.

He glimpsed children in that other place, and they seemed familiar. Important. Faces streamed past like a collection or an exhibition. Halo shoved them aside and devoured everything the old man had. Thousands of hours, minutes and seconds, rushed through the connection and into Halo's mental boxes.

No uberhumans.

No war.

He blinked himself back into his own body and rubbed his eyes which were only half back in the real world. He could tell one of his ears was dripping blood and suddenly felt the need to vomit. Cluttering to the floor he found the bucket and retched.

The door opened and the group of doctors entered, equally surprised and appalled seeing Halo on the floor. He felt Castus in the room, too. There was a clear increase in the room's temperature. He felt trapped but weak. There was no way he could walk out of the room.

"Are you alright, son?" a doctor asked.

Halo vomited again.

And then Parhelion was kneeling beside him, a reassuring hand on Halo's back.

"Just breathe," the man said. "Everything will be alright, once your stomach settles."

Halo nodded and wiped his sleeve across his mouth. He turned to look at the superhero and was taken in by the man's impressive white smile.

"Thanks," he mumbled and coughed a little. "I think I ..."

"No need for talking right now," Parhelion said. He turned back to the others and spoke, but Halo tuned out, his head still spinning.

A nurse and an orderly helped him to his feet, their

hands lifting him from under his arms. They moved him outside and as he stumbled away from the Celestial Knights and from the comatose Mad Russian, he regained a little of his strength. He saw the elevator doors ahead of him, the exit, and he could imagine the staff room above and the car park beyond that.

The nurse made a joke. Halo smiled and managed to pull away from their support. They let him stagger by himself, but stayed close. He knew them and felt comforted by the concern in their faces. These were real people. Small, unpowered, unimportant, real people. He had seen that concern, that love, before. It reminded him of the dream, of his mother.

And he wanted that back.

More than anything.

ACKNOWLEDGEMENTS

Thank you for reading the novel. Choosing to pick up this book, to jump in to the story of uberhumans and popstars, is the greatest outcome for me.

However, *The Miranda Contract* would never have seen the light of day without the support, feedback and friendship of my writing group. Originally brought together by the grandfather of Australian science fiction, Paul Collins, our little group has gone on to become a beautiful monster of imagination in its own right. Thanks to Linda Bibby, Hayley Barry-Smith, Mark Glazebrook, Fleur Guenther, Michael Greene, Kathryn Hall, Leanda and LynC. I hope you enjoy the story and take pride in knowing you helped shape it into what you now hold in your hands.

There were eight beta readers for this novel, and their feedback and enthusiasm for the 'whole story' was invaluable and kept me going when it would have been easier to give up. Matt Langdon and Megan Langdon provided streams of positive advice, bringing in their experience of heroes and bookshops. Megan, especially, brought objective eyes to the novel having never read the genre before. Thanks for reading out of your comfort zone. Brian Healy brought his vast knowledge of novels and comics (not to mention his professional knowledge of music), and Leah Sung brought a set of librarian's eyes to the book. Sallie Muirden, a noted author and writing teacher in her own right, continued to provide support and encouragement, and Jodie Webster from Allen & Unwin also provided a professional perspective on the novel's strengths and weaknesses. Hayley Barry-Smith and Kathryn Hall spent the most time with Dan and Miranda, coaxing them into existence over the course of years. I like to think of them as Dan's 'stand-in' mums.

The idea of writing a superhero novel comes from my (many) years of reading X-Men comics as a teenager, but also from the Uberworld community of writers and gamers. While there have been dozens of Uberworlders, I'd like to send special thanks to Chris De Young, Mark Floyd, Christopher Lockheardt, Neil Ma, Andy Matthews, China Pittenger, Rob Rogers, Noah Thorp, Ben Trafford, KL Wilson and Darren Woods. Of those talented writers, I need to especially thank Noah Thorp for his character, Suleyman the Great. I hope I did him, and his backstory, justice as Sully.

As a high school teacher I come across avid readers every day and I would like to thank my colleagues and students: past, present and future. I draw inspiration from you even when you don't realize it. Joe Logan needs a special thanks for the unlikely key word, 'up-cycled', which formed the basis for Dan's rehabilitation program. It's amazing what comes up on long road trips.

And finally, thanks to my family, because all writers test

the patience of loved ones. Jack, Eliza and Luca. You don't realize how amazing you are.

February 2014

Ben Langdon was born in Geelong, Victoria, and is a graduate of Deakin University and the University of Ballarat. He is the editor of *This Mutant Life*, a Neo-Pulp anthology.

This is his first novel.

benlangdon.net
benlangdon@kalamitypress.com
Twitter @LangdonBen